## THE BATTLE RAGED AROUND BILI

as he withdrew his nicked, dull blade—now cloudy with sticky, red blood—from just below the breastplate of a gasping, wide-eyed pikeman. Suddenly, the back of Bili's helmet was struck so hard that the force of the buffet all but drove him to his knees. Staggering slightly, he turned to face a swordsman in three-quarter armor of an alien pattern.

The Skohshun was swinging his sword with both hands and his greater than average strength was evident in the crushing, numbing force of his blows. Bili caught and deflected two swordswipes on the face of his buckler and tried to deflect another down the flat of his blade while fetching his opponent a shrewd buffet in the exposed armpit with the steelshod edge of the buckler. But Bili's much abused blade shattered, leaving him totally weaponless before his enemy's sharp and deadly blade . . .

## Great Science Fiction by Robert Adams from SIGNET

# CHAMPION OF THE LAST BATTLE

## A HORSECLANS NOVEL

by
**Robert Adams**

A SIGNET BOOK

**NEW AMERICAN LIBRARY**

TIMES MIRROR

SIGNET TRADEMARK REG. U.S. PAT OFF AND FOREIGN COUNTRIES
REGISTERED TRADEMARK—MARCA REGISTRADA
HECHO EN CHICAGO, U.S.A.

SIGNET, SIGNET CLASSICS, MENTOR, PLUME, MERIDIAN AND NAL BOOKS
are published by The New American Library, Inc.,
1633 Broadway, New York, New York 10019

FIRST PRINTING, MAY, 1983

1 2 3 4 5 6 7 8 9

PRINTED IN THE UNITED STATES OF AMERICA

# Dedications

For Morgan Llywelyn, a lady whose vast literary talent is matched only by her dark, Celtic beauty;
For John Steakley, Brian Burley, Kim Mohan, Dell Harris and David Cherry;
For all of the fine folk who made the '83 Mystery Con so enjoyable for me;
To Motor-mouth #1, #2 and #3 (they know who they are and why I call them that);
For Doug & Sandy Wilkey, Texas HORSECLAN-NERS;
For Eric Lindsay, Australian HORSECLANNER;
For Fritz Goetz, Bill Müller, John La Bianca, Gerard Thomas and all of my other friends of The German-American Society of Central Florida, Inc.

# INTRODUCTION

Today is June 22, 1982, an auspicious day for me as well as for the hordes of Horseclans fans, both those of the various Horseclans Societies and those as yet unorganized. Twelve years ago on this day, I finished the book that I later titled *The Coming of the Horseclans;* eight years ago on this day, I commenced work on the book, first of the Bili the Axe Cycle, that was later retitled *Revenge of the Horseclans* (very much against my will, incidentally; I had wanted to call it *Bili the Axe!*). For those reasons, I thought this to be an especially good day to write the introduction to the last book in the Bili the Axe Cycle, this one, *Champion of the Last Battle*.

Ever since the publication of *The Death of a Legend*, last year, I have been getting fan mail critical of my killing off of the character Bili Morguhn; but as I said apropos another matter in my introduction to *The Coming of the Horseclans*, I make no apology, for Bili's demise is necessary if the series is to progress . . . but do not think you have seen the very last of him in this book, for there are more schemes bubbling about in my brain than are dreamed of by even my literary agents.

By the time this book is released, Fantasy Games Unlimited should have two or three Horseclans games on the market and the first Horseclans convention should be imminent.

May Sacred Sun shine always upon you all.

Robert Adams
Seminole County, Florida

# PROLOGUE

When once his assistants had, under his supervision, administered the drugs and departed the chamber, the old, wizened Zahrtohgahn physician stood beside the massive bed for long and long, just observing the old, dying man who lay thereon. Master Ahkmehd was, himself, but a bare score of years the junior of his patient and had been his personal physician for nearly twoscore years, his friend and trusted confidant for almost as long.

Unconsciously, the stooped practitioner wrinkled his nose at the stench of corrupting flesh from his patient's inflamed arm, that arm which he had not been allowed to amputate properly after a wounded bear had so torn and mauled it that it would never have been of real use again even had infection not set into it.

"Ah, Bili, my dear, old lord," he sighed at last in his own guttural language. "Yes, you surely were a stark warrior and were well named Bili the Axe by friend and foe alike. But you were so much more, as well; you brought true and abiding peace to a much-troubled land in the near fifty years you ruled it.

"Assuredly, Ahláh granted you a long life and you used it well. So well did you use that life you shortly will depart that I cannot but regret that you die an infidel, for if any man ever deserved the Paradise of the Prophet, it is you, Lord Bili of Morguhn. Ahláh keep you, my good, old friend. Never will there be another like unto you."

To the dying old man upon the bed, the words made no sense—for all that he spoke Zahrtohgahn fluently—they were but a muted drone to senses dulled by drugs, hypnotism and fast-approaching death. During the week or so since the pain of the suppurating flesh had become of such intensity that Zahrtohgahn wiles and drugs had been necessary, his consciousness had spent precious little time in this present world of his—that of a suffering, slowly dying, aged man.

Rather had he retreated into his own mind, into his memories, to live again the tumultuous, exciting days of his life of nearly fourscore years before—days of war and love, of hard, rough living, of crashing battles, of priceless moments of passion shared with the long-dead woman he had never ceased to love and to mourn through all the decades that had followed.

2

Now, once more, he left the aged, almost-dead husk to again inhabit that young, powerful, towering body of the young *Thoheeks* Bili, Morguhn of Morguhn, the Bili of some seventy-eight years agone.

# CHAPTER I

A bit before sunrise, young *Thoheeks* Bili of Morguhn was wakened by one of his menservants. When he had made brief use of the chamberpot and downed a small draft of honey wine and water, he was dressed by the first servant and two others, then armed. Once fully attired and in a splendid set of half-armor, with sword slung on baldric, dirk and daggers belted at his thick waist and a crested helm under his left arm, he departed the sprawling suite through doors opened by servants or armed guards and descended the palace stairs to the main hall and the waiting knot of officers and noblemen.

Like him, all belowstairs were half-armored, and, although they had been taking their ease on the various benches and chairs before tables now bare of anything save cups, ewers and small braziers for the heating of mulling irons, they one and all came to their feet upon his entrance.

Waving them back to their places, the tall young warrior paced the length of the hall to take his usual place at the high table, where he was quickly served a tankard of spiced cider to which he added a dollop of apple brandy.

When he had downed half the contents of the tankard, he said, "Good morning . . . I hope. Before anyone asks, no, my Lady Rahksahnah has not yet dropped her foal, thank you.

"Now, let's get this business of reports out of our way, then we'll walk the usual circuit, attend to any necessary things in the city, and by that time perhaps the day's meal will be ready for the eating. Eh? Who's first, this day?"

One by one, those who had been duty officers for the preceding day and night rendered routine reports. Little had occurred in that period, it seemed. The Skohshun army still squatted in their camps on the plain below the city, but seemed to be licking their wounds from the latest attempt to storm the almost impregnable city some month or more agone and had demonstrated only their normal, now familiar routines of camp life.

There had been some deaths in the city, of aged, ill or wounded, but this was to be expected. Captain Kahndoot's war-mare had dropped a fine, sturdy bay colt, and the big, stocky Moon Maiden could only beam her pride. A smile never seemed to leave her plain, broad-cheeked face.

Junior Captain Frehd Brakit reported that for all that the siege was now entering its third month, there was no dearth of food anywhere in city or citadel for man or horse. The compulsive squirreling away of stores by King Mahrtuhn I and all his successors was now paying off. The heavy rain of the day before had not been needed, not with the city's steady supply of clear, cold water from the spring-fed lake within the bowels of the mountain upon which New Kuhmbuhluhnburk had been built.

Bili grinned wolfishly. "I'd not care to be living in the Skohshun camps, this morning. The way that rain came down, they're certain to be a slippery, sticky, stinking quagmire from end to end, right now."

The next officer to step forward was Sir Yoo Folsom. The bandy-legged, blond, late-thirtyish knight had been the first of the northern nobles to greet Bili and his squadron after the abominable march up from Sandee's Cot, early last spring. Sir Yoo was also one of the few survivors of the late king's bodyguard, and he now acted as a vice-commander of the lower city.

"For all the actual plentitude of vittles, here in the city and citadel, m'lord duke, I'd liefer be eating and drinking the produce of me own lands, *on* me own lands. A scurvy pox on t'damned Skohshun bastards!"

Bili smiled warmly. "Would that we both were there for the eating of another of your fine, fat steers, Sir Yoo. But alas, I suppose our enemies are doing that."

The knight rumbled a laugh. "Ohohoho, not my stock, by Steel! Whatall couldn't be harvested was burned, most of whatall could be, along with most of the larder and cellar and smoke-house was either wagoned up here or buried safe for after them Skohshuns is gone or dead. The cows and such was all drove up into the south moutains, and all my neighbors did the same, too.

"But I did leave barrels of fine beer fer the Skohshuns. Hid it was, but not hid too well, and flavored with a herb what grows wild in some places." A sudden attack of laughter bubbled up, but he managed to finally quell it and went on.

"Privy-root, that herb's called round here, and fer good reason, too. Any damn Skohshun bastard as drank as much as a pint measure of thet nice, cool beer is gonna think afore too long thet a torch dance is going on in his guts, and he won't do no fighting for at least a week, he'll be too busy squatting, he will." Once more the laughter gained control of Sir Yoo, and this time Bili and the rest joined with him.

The field campaign against the northern invaders, the Skohshuns, had been an almost unmitigated disaster for the army of the King of New Kuhmbuhluhn, fatal to the royal personage and for far too many of his faithful supporters as well. And worst of all, to Bili Morguhn's mind, was that all or most of it was completely unnecessary; there had been no real need to march out and meet the enemy at his full strength and on ground of his choosing. Bili had himself counseled that such be avoided at all costs, that these Skohshuns be forced to first blunt their teeth on, and bleed a bit before, the walls of this very city. But the late king had for some reason felt himself honor-bound to go to his death and lead many a follower with him.

From the very outset, King Mahrtuhn's organization—or, rather, studied lack of same—of the progress of armed men toward certain battle had offended all the lessons, precepts and training of Bili and had set his teeth edge to edge. For all his relative youth, the young *thoheeks* had seen and had taken part in such marches done properly, had experienced the sudden, terrifying shock of an ambuscade, and was all too aware that King Mahrtuhn was at the very least courting fatal consequences, proceeding as recklessly as he was. Not one, single flank rider preceded the column or paralleled the route of march. The so-called van was far too close to the head of the main column, and there was no rearguard, save a gaggle of stragglers.

Moreover, the monarch had deliberately left every one of the Kleesahks—those huge, hybrid, part-human creatures whose preternatural senses might have partially at least replaced the missing security forces on the march—to be part of the garrison of New Kuhmbuhluhnburk, remarking that since the enemy Skohshuns lacked Kleesahk allies, he felt that it would be less than honorable to set out with a detachment of them.

In the light of so royal a degree of utter stupidity—which was how Bili saw it, then and ever after—he had sent the prairiecat Whitetip out on the night before the column left the fortified city. The big feline had first performed a reconnaissance of the proposed route-of-march for a bit over a day's ride from New Kuhmbuhluhnburk, telepathically beamed his discoveries back to Bili, then found a safe, dry, comfortable place to lie up until the march actually began.

Soon after the tail end of the column had quitted the lower approaches to New Kuhmbuhluhnburk, a young New Kuhmbuhluhn knight had ridden back down the files to the head of Bili's squadron of lowlanders. Following an old-fashioned, intricately formal salute, the youth had stiltedly conveyed his message: The esteemed and courageous Duke Bili of Morguhn was summoned to ride at the side of King Mahrtuhn for the nonce. Leaving his force under the capable command of Freefighter Captain Fil Tyluh, Bili had urged his big black stallion in the wake of the returning galloper.

Like Bili, King Mahrtuhn was an axeman, using that weapon by preference in battle, rather than the more usual sword or saber or lance; his was only slightly less massive than Bili's own double-bitted axe, being single-bitted, but with the usual finial spike and another, cursive one behind the blade. Both axemen carried their fearsome weapons cased between pommel and knee on the off side of their horse housings and so within easy reach in an emergency.

Although nearly fifty years Bili's senior, the only hints of advanced years about King Mahrtuhn were his white hair and wrinkle-furrowed face. He rode tall and erect in his saddle, his broad-hipped and -shouldered, thick-waisted body all big bones and rolling muscles. At his left side rode a younger, carbon copy of him, his chosen heir, Prince Mahrtuhn Gilbuht of New Kumbuhluhn.

Both royal personages smiled cheery greeting to Bili and opened the space betwixt their warhorses that he might ride between and so converse easily with either or both.

But King Mahrtuhn's warm smile metamorphosed into a frown as he said, "Cousin, we are informed that you have developed and schooled your squadron in a maneuver designed to gap the Skohshun's pike hedge. We hope that your means are honorable. We cannot and will not countenance the use of bows or darts or slings or such other cowardly, dishonorable methods aimed at the murders of brave fighting men. You have heard our views on that distasteful subject."

"No, your majesty," Bili replied, "this tactic makes no slightest use of missile weapons. Of horses either, for that matter, save only to bear us up to the points of the pikes. Then will we all go in afoot, in half-armor."

The younger prince—younger than the king, but still a good ten years Bili's senior—raised a dark-red eyebrow. "It sounds a bit like suicide, to me, Duke Bili. If mounted men in full armor can't hack a way through that hedge, what possible chance has a contingent of warriors in half-armor and on foot? Many a trick that looks good on a sand board or the practice field proves worse than useless when push comes to shove with steel points. How can you be certain that his majesty is not just allowing you to fritter away the strength of your squadron?"

Bili nodded. "I appreciate your sincere concern for my command, lord prince, but this will not be the first use of this tactic on a hard-fought field. It was first developed by one of my maternal ancestors, a certain Duke of Zuhnburk, and with it he defeated numerically superior forces on more than one occasion. Others in the Middle Kingdoms have, over the years, emulated him with equal success. I have drilled my folk hard and well, and I expect equal success against these Skohshuns."

King Mahrtuhn bobbed his head, his plumes nodding. "We were assured by our nephew, Prince Byruhn, that your new mode of fighting was honorable and, if performed bravely, had a good chance of succeeding to its purpose, but we wished to hear the same from your lips, cousin."

"Uncle Byruhn," said the younger Mahrtuhn with a grin, "while he is purely honorable, has been known to stretch the truth a bit when certain of his personal stratagems were involved . . . and to wax most wroth upon being put to questions a second time. And he is angry enough, just now, because his majesty and I decided to leave the bowmen and the slingers upon whom Byruhn dotes back in New Kuhmbuhluhnburk."

Bili silently reflected that in Prince Byruhn's place he, too, would be angry. The mountainous man had fairly quivered with rage as he had detailed the monumental folly of his father and nephew to Bili on the evening before.

"My royal sire is not a stupid man, Cousin Bili, nor is my nephew, so I can but assume that they both have taken temporary leave of their senses. I was at that meeting whereat the heralds of the Skohshuns were heard, and if the chief herald had been a wizard, then surely his spells would have affected me, as well, not just the king and young Mahrtuhn. And their strategy, if such ill-conceived plans can be truly called such, smacks unmistakably of either witchcraft or insanity.

"Hark you, because these trespassing foreigners own no bowmen or slingers in their own host, the king has come to feel that it would be an act of dishonor to include such in our own array, for all that it was those same missilemen who enabled me and what was by then left of our last year's army to win back to the safety of these stout walls after the autumn disaster; had they not nibbled and pecked at the Skohshun pursuit, none of us would be here today to fight again.

"Moreover, his majesty is of the opinion that use of our traditional allies, the Kleesahks, would also be unfair and therefore dishonorable. I've never before heard such gross foolishness from my father, Cousin Bili, and I'd suspect encroaching senility, save that my nephew is of exactly the same idiotic bent in this matter."

"Could it not be, Lord Byruhn," suggested Bili, "that the prince your nephew's voiced opinion is but a reflection of that of the king your father? You know as do I that the old often influence the young both for good and for ill."

The prince gusted a sigh, his big hands absently clenching and releasing only to reclench the chiseled-silver goblet which was still half full of wine. "Yes, I, too, had thought of that, of course, cousin; but such is not the case, here. My nephew and my father have always been like to but one mind in two bodies— one younger, one older—almost from the birth of the young prince. That is one of the reasons that I declined to become heir upon the demise of my elder brother, the present heir's sire, years agone.

"As you are by now surely aware, my royal sire and I differ in many a way, both in thought and in actions. The royal councilors of that time recognized and feared the possible strife and discontent that might be caused should the kingship pass from my father to me, and with the good of our kingdom in mind, I could not but agree with them.

"It is not mere flattery that he is called King Mahrtuhn the Good, you know; my royal father is a good king, a very good king to his people . . . up until now, at least, when he seems firm bent on dragging a number of the best men in all the kingdom down to bloody death with him.

"I now deeply regret that I did what I did to bring you and your force up here to quite probably die with us in this . . . this royal madness, young cousin. You and yours had served us well in the Ganik Campaign. You deserved more of a recompense than I saw you served. But what has been done has truly been done and cannot now be undone. However, you and your squadron just might represent the only chance that some few of us might survive the battle toward which we must ride out on the morrow, you and this new tactic in which you have drilled your squadron. Do you truly think it will work, will break the pike hedge enough for horsemen to hack a way through?"

Bili's thick shoulders rose and fell in a shrug. "Who can say for sure what way a yet-to-be-fought battle will go, Lord Byruhn? I only know that the squadron performs the drills well, that if done properly the exercise has never failed to break a pike formation, and that I am certain that my squadron will perform well . . . dead certain, your grace. I have wagered my life upon it. But our own fighting will have been for naught unless heavy horse quickly follows us and consolidates our gains. Can we be certain that the king, your father, will hold his charge for the length of time our work will require for accomplishment?''

Byruhn frowned. "To be frank, no, not if he comes to feel his pride has been pricked. But I hereby assure you that I will hold my battle, the left battle, until the time is ripe to follow up your squadron, no matter what my royal father and my nephew do with their own two battles.''

And despite the occasions on which Prince Byruhn had misled him and misused his squadron to the advantage of New Kuhmbuhluhn, still Bili felt that he could believe the present assurances of the hulking, hairy nobleman. "And I had better be right, in this instance,'' thought the young *thoheeks*, "else damned precious few of us will live to hack a way out of the Skohshun pike hedge.''

After the departure of the prince, Bili mused silently as he went about the chamber snuffing the candles, prior to taking up the last and repairing to the bedchamber.

"Even if he is true to his word, though, it still will be a chancy thing. After their losses last year, all three battles combined number less than twelve hundreds of horsemen, with the left battle—Prince Byruhn's own—the lightest, three hundred . . . maybe, three hundred and fifty men. There's no doubt that we can gap the hedge, me and mine, but no gap lasts long, not in a disciplined hedge of pikes, and from all that I've heard of these Skohshuns, their precision and discipline would put the best professional Freefighter infantry to shame.

"Now if the king and all three battles were to charge together, drive a wedge of steel into that gap before the pikes could close up again, King Mahrtuhn might very well win that field. But with only Byruhn's battle to back us . . .?'' The young man sighed and shook his shaven head. "The very best we can anticipate is stinging the foe sorely, then getting the most of us out alive. And once we—my squadron and I—are out of that hedge, we are through with King Mahrtuhn, Prince Byruhn and their damned misfought little war. If these New Kuhmbuhluhners persist in disregarding good advice and planning suicidal campaigns to no purpose, they cannot expect hired swords to proceed with them to a certain death.''

Fanned by cooling breezes from the north and west, the royal army of New Kuhmbuhluhn moved at a steady pace through most of that first day, covering in excess of thirty miles, despite several longish—and, to Bili's mind, utterly unnecessary—halts for "conferences'' amongst the king, his captains and senior noblemen. That night's camp was made upon the banks of a swift-flowing stream, just off the corduroy road that paralleled its south bank as far as a ford that lay a couple of miles to the west. There was at least an hour of daylight remaining when the column halted, so Bili was at a loss to explain to himself, much less to his seasoned squadron, why the king failed to press on and make camp where his army might guard that vital stream crossing throughout the night. But the young warrior knew by then the futility of pointing out tactical advantages to the headstrong, stubbornly honor-bound hereditary ruler of the New Kuhm-buhluhners.

But when it became obvious that King Mahrtuhn didn't intend even to ditch the perimeter of the camp or to post more than a cursory guard throughout the hours of darkness, Bili could no longer restrain himself, and sought out the king in his pavilion.

King Mahrtuhn, whose breath was thick with the heady fumes of the powerful New Kuhmbuhluhn apple brandy, heard his young captain out. But when once Bili had said his piece, the white-haired monarch shook his head and spoke in tones of mild reproof.

"Oh, young, young cousin, you are so suspicious-natured, so very untrusting, and you slander our valiant foemen, the Skohshuns. Those who command the Skohshun pikemen are noble gentlemen all, and of ancient lineage; such men would not stoop to the attack of respected foemen whilst they slept. No, they desire an open, stand-up, breast-to-breast fight every bit as much as do we.

"You have spent the sum of your young life at war with men lacking any save the barest trace of honor, this much is abundantly clear from your actions and attitudes, but our brave Skohshuns are not of that ill-found stripe, we assure you. Our own son, Prince Byruhn, and others of our vassals have warred with these Skohshuns, and we ourselves have entertained their heralds, so we know whereof we speak on these matters."

The craggy features of the monarch had been firm while he spoke, but now he smiled warmly. "But now, sit you down with us, young cousin, sit you down, we say. Fill you that goblet from the ewer of punch and hack off a bit of the ox, then tell us more of this new-model tactic of yours to break the pike hedge, eh?"

In Bili's absence, Rahksahnah sat on a low camp stool in the small pavilion they two shared. By the dim, flaring light of a lamp, she was patiently rehoning the edge of her Moon

Maiden saber with stone and oil, her sinewy, weather-browned hands moving with the sureness of long practice at their task. She had let down her long hair, and the gleaming, ebon cascade reflected almost as much of the lamplight as did the length of oiled steel she held.

Then, silent as death itself, from the darkness of the smaller, outer chamber of the canvas pavilion, stepped a huge feline. The beast was of a golden chestnut hue, with the ghosts of slightly darker rosettes faintly visible here and there about the body. And that body bulked big-boned and powerful, with smoothly rippling muscles, and large paws housing a full complement of eighteen sharp retractable claws. But his most easily seen armament consisted of his huge white cuspids—long, thick, sharp-pointed fangs the needle tips of which were nearly an inch below his lower jaw when it was shut.

His overall size—he stood almost ten hands at the withers—those fearsome fangs and one other facet of his outward appearance set him and his ilk apart from all other felines of this land; that other facet sparkled in the depths of his wide-set amber eyes, and it was intelligence. True intelligence, not the mere cunning of some beast of prey. And there was yet another, though invisible, quality that he owned: telepathy.

The cat advanced a few feet into the inner chamber, in the direction of the busy woman, then sank onto his thick haunches, bringing his long, furry, white-tipped tail to lap over his forepaws. So seated, his big head was almost on a level with hers.

"Mate of my cat brother, Chief Bili," he silently beamed to her familiar mind, "if only you two legs would breed for claws and teeth of a respectable size, you would not need these sabers and axes and whatnot that must so often be re-edged."

Without looking up, she answered him just as soundlessly. "If properly wielded, axe or saber or sword can shear through or penetrate armors of metal, against which your claws and your fangs are useless, Chief Whitetip. Have you now any more opinions to state? Have you eaten this day, or would you care for some cheese?"

The cat gaped his jaws sufficiently to allow a vast expanse of red-pink tongue to emerge and glide raspingly over his thin lips and their furry peripheries. Closing his eyes to mere slits, he sighed audibly in a surfeit of happy gustatory memory. "Thank you, but no, mate-of-my-brother. I found a tasty young goat wandering on the other side of the stream. He was juicy and tender and just the right size for a fine meal."

As her hands moved the saber to concentrate the strokes of the stone on another section of the blade, Rahksahnah asked, "And what of these folk we go to fight, these Skohshuns—what saw you of them? How near are they to this place?"

The big cat slid forward onto his belly and rested his chin upon his forepaws. "A short march the other side of this stream is a low ridge, and beyond it is a small valley that angles toward the north; this valley is flanked by other ridges and in its center runs a smaller stream that joins this larger one a mile or so to the eastward. The road of treetrunks goes over the nearer ridge and through that valley, along the east bank of the smaller stream. The Skohshuns are camped on and about the two flanking ridges, and I think they mean to block that little valley with their army, when next Sacred Sun shines."

It stood to reason, thought Rahksahnah. The Skohshuns had been able to field very little heavy-armed cavalry to start with, and last autumn's battles had almost extirpated those few. That meant that the Skohshun pike hedge would have little if any horse to guard against a flank attack, so throwing the pike line across a narrow vale and anchoring the vulnerable flanks on ground too rough or precipitous or wooded to allow for passage of mounted men was a sensible idea.

"How many watchers have they on the ridge closest to the larger stream?" she beamed to the cat. "And are there any troops making ready to block the ford in the morning?"

"No," the cat replied, "none of these twolegs-with-the-overlong-spears are any closer to this place than the north side of the first ridge . . . at least, they were not when I left to come here."

"Just so," Rahksahnah nodded, while silently beaming her thoughts to the feline. "They could easily have moved to new and more threatening positions whilst you were not there to observe them. So go back across the stream and watch for any change in their ranks, any movements out of their camps. But don't come back here to let us know; farspeak us the message."

"I cannot farspeak your mind, mate-of-my-brother," said Whitetip. "Yours is simply one of those twoleg minds that I cannot range."

"No, I know you can't," she replied. "But you can farspeak Bili or Captain Fil Tyluh or Lieutenant Kahndoot, and all of them are here in camp. But you must go back, for this mad king has not and will not send out twoleg scouts or even post a decent camp guard for the night, so the squadron must have the benefit of your observation of the enemy to be certain that we are not surprised by a sudden attack by dark or dawn.''

Not bothering to shield a mind seething with most unflattering opinions regarding King Mahrtuhn's probable antecedents, personal traits, usual practices and present lack of foresight, the huge feline flowed effortlessly back onto his big feet and stalked out of the pavilion, his white-tipped tail swishing his displeasure. Not only must he swim back over that icy-cold stream, but the scent of the night air presaged at least a splattering of rain before the dawn, and he had anticipated sleeping it out in the dry comfort of a tent, not under the dripping leaves of some misbegotten tree.

But he was a cat of Clan Morguhn by free choice, not by a mere accident of birth, and Bili of Morguhn was his chief as well as his cat brother. The black-haired mate of his chosen chief and brother spoke for the Morguhn in his absence; this, Whitetip knew, and so—knowing well the duties and obligations of an obedient clans cat, for he was, himself, a sept chief—the prairiecat obeyed.

Upon Bili's return from the royal pavilion, Rahksahnah recounted the information brought by the cat, whereupon the young commander mindcalled his principal lieutenants, those of them as were mindspeakers. He sent his two guards in search of the others.

First to arrive was Lieutenant Kahndoot of the Moon Maidens. Though but of average height, the woman was chunky and powerful and the only other person in the squadron, male or female, who had proved able to handle Bili's big axe as well as did he . . . or almost as well. Alone of the contingent of surviving Moon Maidens who had followed their hereditary leader— the *brahbehrnuh,* now called Rahksahnah by all—into this savage, often hostile land, Kahndoot had not yet done the announced will of the Silver Lady, the Moon Goddess, and taken a man as mate and battle companion, for all that she had given up the ways of the irrevocably lost Hold of the Maidens of the Moon and no longer had a woman as lover and battle mate, either. When anyone presumed to ask her, she would simply smile and shrug and state that she had not as yet found a male who suited her and was uncommitted to another Maiden.

Hard upon Kahndoot's heels came Captain Fil Tyluh and Lieutenant Frehd Brakit, both Freefighter officers, both younger sons of Middle Kingdoms nobility and, perforce, making their way in the world by hiring out their swords and fighting skills to those in need of a few bravos or a temporary army.

Bili's maternal heritage was of a Middle Kingdoms noble house, and he had, moreover, fostered and had his arms training and experienced his first few years of warfare at the violent court of the Iron King of Harzburk, so he frequently understood Freefighters better than he did his part-Ehleen paternal relatives, and he always had felt more at home with the burker mercenary soldiers than with either Horseclans Kindred or Ehleen aristocracy.

The last three subordinate officers to arrive crowded in at the same time. One was a distant cousin of Bili's in the paternal line. Like Bili, he was of mixed blood—part Horseclans Kindred, part Ehleen, although he and most of his peers considered themselves to be Kindred, nothing else, nothing less—and like Bili, he was holder of a hereditary title in the Confederation, whence most of them had originally come. He was *Vahrohneeskos*—he was called "baronet" by the Freefighters—Gneedos Kahmruhn of Skaht.

Vahk Soormehlyuhn and Vahrtahn Panosyuhn bore a clear racial similarity to each other and a less striking one to Rahksahnah and Kahndoot. The two were Ahrmehnee warriors, and they shared command of the contingent of their tribesmen who made up a part of Bili's squadron.

Bili nodded curt greetings and said, "Don't bother to get comfortable, any of you; this won't take long. Then you must all go back and spread the word, but quietly, amongst those you directly command, bidding them do the same amongst their own subordinates. I want no big, loud-spoken, easily overheard meetings, you see. What I have had done for me—for us, rather—would be considered strictly dishonorable by the sovran we now serve.

"Whitetip, the prairiecat, left New Kuhmbuhluhnburk well before our own departure and has been scouting out our line-of-march, with orders to mindspeak me from afar only in the event of his discovery of an ambush site, ready-manned and awaiting our column.

"When it became clear that King Mahrtuhn intended to halt and camp here for the night, I farspoke Whitetip and sent him on across the stream to try to find trace of the Skohshuns and possibly determine their distance from us. That he did, and more. He brought the report to Rahksahnah whilst I was still at the royal pavilion, this night.

"By Whitetip's witness, these Skohshuns are about as demented or, at the least, as strategically unschooled as the royal personage we now serve. They have gone into camp a good hour or more of marching time from yonder ford, and although they too have thrown out a few pickets, they are clearly not preparing emplacements for engines with which to harass those making use of the ford, have not even occupied the crest of the ridge that lies between the ford and their camp and, indeed, have a campsite every bit as ill defended as is this one."

Vahk Soormehlyuhn, the bald, gray-bearded elder of the two Ahrmehnee, asked, "How many of them are there, Dook Bili?"

The broad, thick shoulders of the young *thoheeks* rose then fell in a shrug. "Intelligent as are the prairiecats, Lieutenant Vahk, numbers larger than a bare score or so have ever been beyond their calculation abilities. But he did say that their camp covered two hillocks on either side of a vale through which the road runs and in which he thinks they mean to take their stand on the morrow and so force a battle. Lacking cavalry as they do, that would be the sensible thing—to run their flanks up the slopes on either side. That's what I'd do in their circumstances, anyway. Either that or form my pikes up into a porcupine . . . but of course the ever-present danger to the porcupine formation is that it is damned hard to maintain that formation should it be necessary to move forward, backward or sideways for any reason, most especially over the type of terrain we'll be fighting on.

"There is one thing that might be to our advantage or just as easily to our bloody disadvantage, considering that battles seldom go as you plan them. Whitetip noted that a stream, a smaller tributary of this one beside which we are camped, flows southward smack down the middle of that vale, with the road paralleling it.

"Now, *if* it flows sufficiently shallow, *if* the bottom be firm and even and *if* these Skohshuns are proved not astute enough to have blocked the way with felled trees or boulders or suchlike, it just might be the key to more easily breaching their hedge. Those poor pikemen would have more than enough to do merely keeping their balance on cold-numbed feet and slippery rocks, while handling twoscore or more pounds of hardwood and steel against the big targets presented by horsemen, but if they are suddenly assaulted by fleet, nimble, hard-to-close-with opponents engaging in a new and unorthodox maneuver . . .?

"Of course, my folk, this is but idle and probably hopeless speculation, for no seasoned commander who is not either addled or senile is going to put good men in so exposed—obviously exposed—a position without giving them the cover of an abattis. Therefore, I think we had best anticipate attacking on the levelest stretch of ground we can espy, which will likely mean up the road to their lines. And because the road clearly offers an ideal avenue for a cavalry charge, no doubt the hedge will be thickest thereabouts, too.

"So look you for a brisk engagement, a hard fight and a good possibility of heavy losses despite our training, our heavier armor and the body shields."

Captain Fil Tyluh spoke as Bili paused to take a draft from a jack of ale.

"I have no doubt that we can break the hedge, Duke Bili, for a brief time, anyway—it's all been done many times ere this, up north, in the Middle Kingdoms. But there are just too few of us, even before battle casualties, to improve upon the breach or even to hold our initial gains. Can we be sure, certain sure, that this King Mahrtuhn will charge with his three battles to consolidate that for which we will have fought so hard?"

Bili shook his shaven head brusquely. "In one word, Fil, _no;_ no, we cannot. As ever—at least since we have known him— King Mahrtuhn will ride when and where his honor drives him . . . and his heir will be beside him.

"However, I have the sworn word of Prince Byruhn that he will definitely bring his own battle to support us whenever we have clearly weakened or breached the pike hedge."

Tyluh slammed fist to callused palm. "But, Duke Bili, that's not enough! His grace, Prince Byruhn, commands the smallest, most ill-armed and -mounted battle of the three, dammit. Even adding our numbers—or what numbers we might by then have still on their feet—to his, there still will be insufficient strength to roll up the exposed flanks fast enough so they can't reclose, likely trapping us all behind their line in the process, to be slain at their leisure."

Bili clenched his two big hands together, snapping the knuckles with loud cracks which punctuated his words. "Yes, Fil, I know; I, too, have thought it through, and all that you say is only too true. That's precisely why I've come to at least one decision.

"That decision is this, and all of you hear me well: We will do what we have said we would do. That is, we will perform our function or all die in the attempt. But when once that section of the hedge is broken and in temporary confusion, our horse holders are to bring all of the mounts as near as possible and we will withdraw, remount and retire; that's _if_ none of the battles come to reinforce us.

"However, in the event that Prince Byruhn brings his battle

alone, we still will withdraw, but we will allow his attack to screen our withdrawal. The only circumstance in which we will not withdraw will be if all three battles come to consolidate the victory, in which case we will remount, but then return to the fight a-horse.

"Do all of you fully comprehend all that I've just said? If so, I'll now take on questions or objections."

# CHAPTER II

Atop the crest of the ridge nearest to the larger stream, in the driest spot he had found—beneath a rock overhang and but bare yards from a Skohshun watchpost—the prairiecat Whitetip observed the enemy camp occupying the tops of the two hills on the other side of the vale. His keen hearing, however, did the yeoman share of his "observation," for his was not the long-distance vision of a hound, though he could see better in dim light than hound or horse or man.

He could, for instance, see the forms of the large body of men working in and about the small, swift stream at a point just past the narrowest part of the smaller vale that separated the hills and entered the larger vale at a right angle. He could not see well enough, however, to be certain just what the men were doing. His ears told him of vast splashings in the water, groans and gasps of effort, cursing and occasional shouts in tones of command.

The camps themselves seemed quiet, with most of the host sunk in sleep, after having fed heavily on roasted meat and grain porridge. Now and then, here and there, a horse stamped or whickered, oxen lowed or small rocks shifted under the feet of pacing sentries. With a single exception, all that was visible of the hilltop camps through the dark and the misty rain was the dim and flaring glows of the torches that marked out the camp perimeters.

The exception was at the center of the westernmost camp to Whitetip's left. There, the environs of several large tents blazed inside and out with the light of torches and lamps and battle lanterns. The figures of men, tiny with the distance, scuttled hither and yon like beetles over a fresh cowpat. Whitetip could dimly discern the rattling and clinkings of their weapons and armor and spurs, the creaking of their leather goods as they moved; but the distance was just too great to strain out speech from all the other noises.

"The only known way to completely waterproof boots is to first grease all the seams, then coat them with hot tar . . . and we have no tar, either hot or cold. That little brook runs cold as ice, brigadier, and if my pikemen have to stand in that running water for longer than a few minutes, every one of them will not only be in agony, but useless for any quick movements in any direction."

The aged officer looked up from where he sat before the large map his staff had prepared for this meeting, smoothed his flaring mustaches with the back of his thumb in an unconscious gesture and asked in a mild tone which was belied by the glare fixed on the speaker from beneath his shaggy brows, "Yes, colonel, we all know well that mountain brook water tends to run cold, that infantry boots tend to leak unless tarred and that living flesh and bone immersed in cold water tend to become numb. But what, pray tell, would you suggest? That we leave a gap in our pike hedge, mayhap?

"Your regiment still was holding the point of embarkation on the north bank when last we fought these Kuhmbuhluhners, colonel, but surely you are aware of how very close they came to breaching our hedge last autumn. They are the most dangerous foe we have come across in many a long decade, and God is to be thanked that there are so few of them. But, few as there now are, were we to give those feisty bastards such an opening, I doubt me not they'd be rolling up one or the other of our wings from inside out in a trice, and more than your pikemen's feet would become cold and stay that way with bellies full of steel and all their blood run out."

The old man paused, and, prominent Adam's apple working, he downed a good half of his pint jack of beer. Sir Djaimz, the senior colonel, chose this moment to say a few words, hoping to soothe some of the sting of his superior's bitterly sarcastic comments.

"Colonel Potter, we all of us recognize and appreciate your insistent solicitude for the welfare of your pikemen. It is an attitude that all of your peers and subordinates would do well to emulate. But Brigadier Sir Ahrthur has given the matter his usual well-thought-out planning and rigorous attention to details. He and the earl and I have discussed this projected action at great length, and the course he has recently outlined to you all is the sum of our mutual thoughts. However, as no man or group of men can ever hope to be all-knowing, we still remain open to suggestions . . .?"

The officer so addressed drew his big-boned, beefy frame up to its full five-foot-six and said, a bit hesitantly, "Well . . . ahhh. Well, why not fill the streambed with stones and overlay them with planks or adzed-flat tree boles, eh? Not only would the ranks have a firm, relatively dry footing, but they'd be a bit above the horsemen."

"Which would also put them a bit above the flanking units," put in another of the assembled officers, "thereby making the hedge uneven and vulnerable at the two joints. Besides, what you suggest would serve to dam the brook and turn what little level ground exists into a quagmire of cold mud."

Colonel Potter shrugged. "What of it, sir? We could just form up a short distance north of that soft ground, then. It would certainly slow any cavalry charge at our front and might even necessitate that these Kuhmbuhluhners dismount and come at us afoot."

"You had better hope and earnestly pray, colonel, that such as that never happens," intoned the brigadier solemnly. "Get it through your head, man, these Kuhmbuhluhners are not the speedy lancers and lightly armed foot of the Ohyoh folk; rather do they war in full—or, at worst, three-quarter—plate armor. And on those thankfully rare—else none of us would be here today!—occasions when our formations have been broken in hand-to-hand combat, it was done by just such as these folk, *on foot.*"

"But . . . but, Sir Ahrthur," yelped one of the youngest of the assembly, "save for the cowardly attacks of bowmen or dartmen or slingers, our hedges are invulnerable in the defense and invincible on the attack. Everyone knows that."

The brigadier briefly showed worn teeth. "Whose puppy are you, youngster? Oh, one of Colonel Alpine's aides, eh? Well, spout that sort of propaganda to the other ranks as often as they'll stand still for it, but if you start believing it yourself, I doubt me you'll live long enough for your voice to finish changing.

"Invulnerable? Pah! Invincible? Twiddle! Were we either, why do you think we are not still living on our rich, hard-won lands up in the Ohyoh country, instead of hunkering on stony mountains and making ready to fight for such poor land, atop it all? Our entire racial history, ever since the Greeks drove our ancestors out of their rightful homes, has been a succession of fight-win-hold for a while, then fight-lose and move on to fight again.

"We have honed our skills over the generations, developed new ones in some cases, and that we average more wins than losses is the sole reason we still exist as a people. But never ever doubt for one minute that we are vulnerable, my boy, for we are, we are terribly vulnerable—lightly armored foot soldiers always are."

"This is probably no time to broach the matter," put in Colonel Bruce Farr, "but with all the armor we captured at the fortress-valley or have stripped off slain or wounded foemen in the last few campaigns, we could easily have put at least the first two or three ranks in half- or even three-quarter-armor, as we did the short-polemen and the horsemen. Instead, most of that fine armor lies baled up or locked in chests awaiting God knows what, while our pikemen still do their fighting in nothing more than breastplates, ring-sewn gauntlets, steel caps and boots fitted with horn splints for greaves.

"Now, I know, I know, I've heard it all before. It's a tradition that Skohshun pikemen need no walls about their towns or armor on their bodies, the pike hedge serving for both. But how many dead and maimed pikemen has this hoary, overhallowed tradition cost us over the years, brigadier?"

The old officer heaved himself to his feet with a crackling of joints and, as he strode stiff-leggedly toward the entry, said, "Would you care to answer the good colonel, Sir Djaimz? My bladder seems to shrink with increasing age."

The senior colonel nodded to his superior, then said, "Look you, Colonel Farr, one of the dearest values of Scotian pikemen is that, in formation mind you, they can move almost as fast as mounted heavy horse, but they would lose this definite advantage were we to weigh them all down with upward of fifty pounds of steel. Nor could our pikemen rapidly withdraw burdened with even half-armor. As all here know, they are neither trained for nor expected to engage in breast-to-breast encounters; that's what the horsemen and the short-pole-men are for. They are expected to be simply one more thorn in the hedge, doing what damage they do at a distance of no less than twelve feet from the foe, and if the hedge be sundered and cannot be speedily closed, they are expected to drop their pikes and withdraw as rapidly as possible, not try to take on armored and/or mounted foemen with a shortsword and a breastplate alone for weapon and protection. No new pike hedges can be fashioned of dead heroes.

"However, Colonel Farr, you may well be the voice of our future, do we stay hereabouts. The armaments and tactics I have just detailed were fashioned in and for the flatter, less forested terrain of those lands we just quitted. Maneuver on any broad scale is difficult if not impossible of successful accomplishment amid these thick-grown hills and stony mountains and narrow, twisting little vales. Does tomorrow's battle not win these lands for us, perhaps we will find it expedient to sacrifice unneeded speed for needed protection and put our pikemen in more steel."

Beyond the yellow-red glow of the bright-lit tents of the

noblemen and officers, lulled by the powerful soporifics of a long march, a heavy meal and extra beer rations, those of the Skohshun pikemen not guarding the perimeter or laboring in the vale slept deeply. Most of them were veterans, and battles and battle eves were nothing new to them—if they proved destined to die on the morrow, then die they would; if not, then life would go on.

The long pikes and the other polearms of each battalion stood stacked about the huge, thick pole of the unit device. The polished hardwood of the hafts reflected the wind-whipped light of the torches and watchfires, but most of the steel points were far above that guttering light so that only the occasional rising errant spark brought a glint in the bright white steel.

Grouped about each stack of polearms and pikes, in orderly lines, the pikemen rolled in their cloaks, their heads pillowed on their marching packs. Their breastplates, helmets, shortswords and dirks lay ready to hand for any sudden nocturnal alarum, though properly covered from the damp dews of the night. Every man's heavy boots stood in their assigned place, flanked by his horn-and-hide greaves.

Within five minutes or less, a regiment of sleeping Skohshun pikemen could be up and fully armed and in their ordered formation to repel attack. Within twenty minutes, all save the rearguards could have struck camp and been on the march. Inured almost from birth to fast, cross-country hiking, the Skohshun regiments could and often did cover better than twenty-four miles in a day's march.

Atop the ridge just south of those hilltop camps, a very damp and disgruntled prairiecat huddled as deeply as possible into the hollow beneath the rock overhang. The drizzle was finer than mist but persistent, and now and then a stronger gust of wind would bear it and its cold, wet discomfort in upon the big furry body.

Though Whitetip's amber eyes were closed, his every other sense was fully alert. Vainly, he tried to imagine himself where he should be this night, after having dutifully scouted all day and most of the night before that, too. He tried to will himself to well-deserved, well-earned comfort in a warm, dry tent, possibly with a couple or three nice saddle blankets on which to curl up. Once or twice, he could almost seem to feel the solid comfort of his reveries, but each time he was cruelly distracted. Once, a stronger gust of wet lashed in upon him. The second distraction came in the guise of an especially loud and protracted splashing down in the stream, followed immediately by the scream of a man in pain and an excited babble of shouts.

Chief Whitetip decided that this particular gaggle of twolegs were clearly far less rational than most others of their inherently irrational species. To willingly splash about and immerse their bodies in cold water on a hot, sunny day were a silly enough thing to do, but to do so of a distinctly chilly, almost moonless night . . . such clearly retarded twolegs should not be allowed out without a keeper.

Both Bili and Rahksahnah were young, neither yet twenty years of age. Moreover, they were deeply in love and mutually reveled in the intense joy that their two vibrant bodies were capable of bringing each other. So, despite the long, saddle-weary day's march, despite his hours in attendance upon King Mahrtuhn, despite the late-night conference with his officers, when at long last Bili and Rahksahnah sought their blankets, they made gentle, unhurried love, then fell soundly asleep still wrapped in each other's embrace, all of their youthful passion spent, for the nonce.

It was not yet dawn, however, when Rahksahnah awakened to the feel of life moving within her body. Bili had no idea of her condition, else he never would have allowed her to ride out on this present campaign. Only Rahksahnah and Pah-Elmuh, the Kleesahk, held the sure knowledge, and she had pledged him to silence. Her reasoning made sense—to her; she had strong pre-sentiments that she had not very long to live and she wished to spend every possible moment of what little life she had remaining by her Bili's side. That by riding out to war she was risking her life as well as those two new ones that the huge humanoid-physician had been able to recognize within her womb did not seem in any way contradictory to her.

Now, lying in the darkness of the tent, with the warmth of her man's body beside her and the dear, familiar smell of him all about her, she fleetingly wondered if ever another *brahbehrnuh* or any other Moon Maiden had ever cherished so strong and valiant, daring and loving a man.

"Probably not," she thought. "For in the Hold there had been no equality of the two sexes since . . . since the time of the *Brahbehrnuh* Nohdeva, anyway. Her it had been who had firmly established the new order of things in the Hold by killing or blinding the stronger, more stubborn men and first intimidating, then subjugating the weaker, so that the males of the race became little more than domestic beasts of burden, used periodically to propagate new generations of the Sacred Race.

"But now the Hold is gone, destroyed utterly, and all who dwelt therein—female and male alike—are dead, snuffed out like so many drowned torches. Only we few Moon Maidens are left of all our race, we and the children so recently sired of these Lowlander men. The Goddess, our Silver Lady, knew what was best for us when She bade us give over our lovers from the days of the Hold and choose as our new lovers and battle companions these fine, strong, brave men of an alien race. It has worked out well for us, as She surely knew it would, and precious few of my sisters would willingly return now to the ways and usages of the Hold.

"Only poor, crippled Meeree, once my own lover, and the bare handful of women she has gathered about her would try to go back to the old ways. But they are self-deluded; there will now never be another Hold of the Moon Maidens in these mountains or anywhere else. We few remaining can but mourn our dead mothers . . . and our fathers, too. But She has seen to it that our own lives will be cast from a far different mold."

Once again, she felt the new life inside her. Fiercely grasping the silver pendant that hung from the worn silver chain about her neck, she silently, fervently prayed.

"Oh my dear Lady, I have done all that You instructed me to do. I have seen to it that the most of Your Maidens obeyed Your Holy dictates, as well. The new ways were strange, exceeding strange, and for some of my poor sisters they brought pain and misery for a while, but now almost all are living new lives according to the new pattern.

"As for me, I have come to love this man, Bili, more than ever I have loved any living creature. I have borne him one child and now my body is filling with the growth of two more. I should be more than happy, Lady, save that I cannot escape the dire presentiment that my days of life and Bili are numbered and decreasing in quantity with the passing of each and every Moonrise.

"Pah-Elmuh was right, I should not risk these precious lives within me by riding out to war and close combat, but I feel that I *must* be by my Bili every possible moment that I can for as long as still I live. Oh, if only I knew the real truth of what is to be for me . . .?"

"*My child, My lover, My dear, devoted Rahksahnah.*" The never to be forgotten voice seemed to come from everywhere, from all about her and within her at the same time.

Rahksahnah opened her eyes to find the darkness gone, and

gone as well were the tent and the blankets. She now lay nude upon the soft, silver-hued sward which surrounded Her Abode. Where Bili had lain in slumber, the Lady now lay upon one hip and elbow, facing her, sympathy and concern in Her silver-gray eyes. Extending one hand, the Goddess laid a cool palm upon Rahksahnah's fevered forehead.

"*My own, not even I know all that is to be. The pattern is never so tightly woven that it cannot be slightly, infinitesimally altered. Yes, death hovers close to you, my dear, your presentiment is accurate. But I can discern no immediacy, nor is it a certainty that you will be the one taken when the time is fully ripe. The two children you now carry will be safely delivered of you and will lead long, full lives.*"

"And . . . and my Bili, Lady? He will live to rear our little ones, even though I do not?" queried Rahksahnah hesitantly.

"*Oh, my dear Rahsahnah, I am not omniscient. You ask more than even such as I know . . . for a certainty. The pattern of what is to be, what might be, what must be is fluid. Slight alterations can appear in bare moments, dependent upon so many variables—actions of humans, of other creatures, of the very fabric of your world itself, though most often of the actions and reactions of humans.*"

Rahksahnah sighed deeply. "My . . . my Lady can tell me nothing, then? Nothing of the fate of my dear Bili?"

The silvery being before her also sighed. "*So far as I can discern, love, Bili of Morguhn will come unharmed from this impending battle, as too will you, though many and many another now living will leave its husk upon that bloody field of battle. There will swiftly follow other dangers and another great, crashing battle which it appears that you both are destined to weather safely. Then, however, when it would seem that all danger be past and gone, will come suddenly and from an unexpected quarter the most deadly danger. It is possible that Bili of Morguhn will be there and then torn from his husk.*"

Rahksahnah's hard, callused hand grasped tightly at the cool, soft hand of the Lady, her hilt-toughened fingers sinking into that silvery flesh, heedlessly. "No, dear my Lady, no! It must not be! Far better me than him. Take me, if such must be, but . . . but, please, I implore you, let my Bili live on . . . with our children. Without him, Lady, I know that I would be of no use to them or to anyone else, anyway."

The Silver Lady sighed once more, sadly. "*That which I can do, I will do, my child. But think you well upon the matter; when that time comes, you will still have a choice, although there* exists always the possibility that both will leave the fleshly husk . . . or neither. As I have told you, nothing so far in advance is ever certain.

"But now, my love, I must leave you, for it is almost moonset, for you, and almost moonrise for others of whom you know not in far-distant places. But we two shall meet like this once more, possibly."

Gathering Rahksahnah's lean, hard young body in Her embrace, the Lady's silvery lips pressed upon the girl's dark-red ones and, when she again became aware of the scratchy blankets against her bare flesh, that lingering, tingling, kiss of the Moon Goddess, the Silver Lady of the Maidens, was still a palpable sensation there in the darkness of the tent she shared with her man, Bili of Morguhn.

It was almost the third hour after dawn, with the sun well up in the azure sky and beginning to radiate meaningful amounts of heat in promise of a hot, dry day. Only then did King Mahrtuhn of New Kuhmbuhluhn feel himself sufficiently arrayed and prepared and fortified to pace out of his pavilion and put foot to stirrup to swing astride his light-bay stallion. But his fighters had been ready for long hours, and within a few minutes after he had settled in his ornate saddle, he was leading his battle out of the camp and toward the ford at a fast walk.

Prince Mahrtuhn, the monarch's grandson and chosen heir, followed close upon the track of the first battle with his own, second battle. And his was followed by that of his hulking uncle, Prince Byruhn, of whose third battle Bili of Morguhn's condotta was a part.

Trailing a distance behind this third battle marched a few hundred infantrymen, their column led by the beplumed and partially armored royal footguards, armed with poleaxes and partizans. The marchers were only about half of the foot, the rest remaining as camp guards.

They would all have remained in camp had not Byruhn set his foot firmly down on the matter. "Father, you have had your way in every facet of this ill-starred enterprise, ere this; the only certain and painless way to break up that pike hedge enough for heavy horse to assault it successfully is to use archers and dartmen and slingers from a distance beyond the reach of those overlong pikes, yet you have left every missileman in the kingdom squatting useless behind the walls of New Kuhmbuhluhnburk."

"Win or lose, live or die," growled the king, "we mean to do so in honor, and there is no honor in allowing valiant foemen to be slain by peasants at such distance as they have no slightest chance to defend themselves. The Skohshuns' herald attests that they fight honorably, without missiles or such lowborn louts as use them, and the King of New Kuhmbuhluhn cannot do less.''

The tightness of the prince's voice, then, had told the tale of a temper rising fast but under tight rein. "It is too bad that I did not get the chance to beard that herald, Father, for I am of the opinion that a fine point could be raised in regard to the actual honor of using pikeshafts of such a length that men of normal armament cannot possibly get within a range to use their weapons. But that is neither the one nor the other, just now.

"What is pertinent here and now is that unsupported cavalry is at peril in this sort of undertaking—I know that all too well. If my royal sire will recall, I was so rash as to attack these same Skohshuns last autumn with only my van and my heavy horse, not waiting for the arrival of the rest of my army . . . and we all know the calamitous result of that, my folly.

"Even if our three battles are successful in hacking into and dispersing those pikes, we cannot consolidate a victory without infantry of our own. And should we suffer such a defeat as last year, then that same infantry will be needed to give us some cover during our withdrawal.''

The king had gnawed for a few moments on his lower lip, his blue-green eyes locked unwaveringly with the identical blue-green eyes of his huge, burly son. At last, however, he had shrugged and said, "Oh, all right, Byruhn, take the damned foot if you feel you must. Take my footguards and up to half of the levy. But, mind you, *you* are directly responsible for them, in march or battle. And see that they stay well behind—scant good it would do us to ride down a passel of our own foot and so lose impetus in a charge.''

"I am certain that our infantry would be equally regretful of any such happenstance, royal Father," Byruhn replied dryly. "I shall certainly see to it that the foot in no way hinder maneuverings of the mounted battles.''

"And see to it that your southron horsemen carry only one axe apiece into the fray," the king went on peevishly. "If a warrior chooses to throw his axe or his lance at a foeman, we see no harm to the practice—we've even done the like ourselves from time to time over the years. But when said warriors customarily bear a whole assortment of spare axes for the sole purpose of throwing them, then they become no better than a pack of honorless, peasant missilemen. We'll have no such low-bred louts forking horse behind our banners!''

*        *        *

As soon as the column was moving and in proper order, Prince Byruhn had summoned Bili up to ride with him. "Have you an experienced officer of foot, or two, in your condotta, Cousin Bili?"

Bili nodded. "Lieutenant of Freefighters Frehd Brakit, your grace. He was an infantry officer for some years. Then there's a Freefighter sergeant, one Ahskuh Behrdyn, who also soldiered with a light infantry condotta in the Middle Kingdoms, as I recall."

The prince nodded his big head. "Good. When we all halt while the first battle negotiates the ford, they are to take over command of the royal footguards and the rest, back there. I'll personally give them special orders at that time.

"I like none of this affair, young cousin, as well you know. I'm an old wolf and I can smell death and defeat in the very air. Do your own . . . ahhh . . . *special* senses tell you aught of what lies ahead?"

Bili knew that Byruhn referred to the prairiecat, Whitetip, for of all the royal host, only the prince and Bili's own folk were cognizant that the king's order that no scouts be placed ahead of the advance had been flouted in this regard.

Kneeing his stallion closer and lowering his voice, the young *thoheeks* replied, "There are a scattering of Skohshuns along the crest of that ridge yonder, your grace, but not enough to be dangerous to us; they keep sending back runners to the Skohshun camp, so apparently they are just what they seem to be—a screen to observe our advance, then fall back before us.

"They are the closest Skohshuns to us; there are none anywhere between the near side of yon ridge and this river. The main force of the Skohshuns is even now drawing up its formation across the vale through which runs the continuation of this road we now ride. Although they seem to have precious few horsemen, I doubt they could be easily flanked, not with their wings running up steep, brush-grown hills on either side. A feeder stream to this river bisects their line, with about two thirds of them to the west of it and the remaining third or so to the east of it."

"Ah, so?" remarked Prince Byruhn, one side of his single reddish eyebrow rising sharply. "How deep is this stream, and what is the bottom like downstream of the pike line?"

"I'd advise that your grace forget that line of attack," answered Bili. "These Skohshuns seem to be most astute at warfare. They've felled trees and constructed an abattis to block any approach up the streambed. Moreover, their lines of formation seem to run directly through the stream in as deep ranks as those on dry land.''

"Well, at least that much is a point to remember," the prince remarked a bit grumpily. "Those bastards belike have near-frozen feet already, if that stream runs as cold as do most hereabouts, and I doubt me they'd have gone to the trouble to throw out any abattises behind them. So, if we somehow manage to flank them or to hack through to their rear, those unlucky swine knee-deep in cold water will be slow to turn on numbed feet and therefore the logical ones to attack from the rear.

"Now, young cousin, you had best ride back to your force and notify those two Freefighters of their imminent takeover of command of the foot."

Bili smiled. "No need, your grace. Even while we two were in converse here did I mindspeak Frehd Brakit on the matter. By now, he has certainly notified Sergeant Behrdyn."

Prince Byruhn sighed. "It's right often I've wished that I were a mindspeaker, for yon's a damned convenient talent in war. Usually, of course, I have my Kleesahks to use their own mindspeak and communicate with others of their ilk; but what with my father leaving all of them in New Kuhmbuhluhnburk, for fear that their outré talents might give us an edge over the Skohshuns . . ." He sighed again and shook his head sadly. "If I could bring myself to truly believe such things, I'd swear that that thrice-damned Skohshun herald ensorceled my father and my nephew. Honor or no honor, it simply defies all reason to deliberately forgo the use of one's natural assets in battle, for battles are chancy enough exercises even when one is armed with every asset or weapon one can muster."

King Mahrtuhn was the first man across the narrow ford, which, though fast-currented, was shallow enough to provide quick, easy passage even to the trailing infantry. Once over, however, the monarch halted and waited until his battle was all on the north side of the river and once more in column behind him before pushing on toward the ridgeline. But he and they deliberately retarded their rate of march until Prince Mahrtuhn and the second battle were all across and advancing behind them. Then the king set his mount at the base of the ascent to the ridge crest.

As the column began the progress toward that crest, a single line of unmounted men were seen—black shapes against the blue sky—to arise from the places where they had been kneeling or crouching and, after a last, unhurried look at the oncoming horsemen, retire from view.

Whitetip, the prairiecat, beamed to Bili, "Those twolegs who spent the night up here on this ridge have all left it and are trotting back toward where the men with the long spears wait in the vale."

"You have done well, cat brother," Bili beamed back. "Wait where you are until you can see me and Prince Byruhn nearby. Come you. then to our folk and someone will buckle you into your armor and put on your fang spurs. We soon must fight."

# CHAPTER III

The road widened a bit at the crest of the ridge, and it was there that the king, his grandson and his son, along with their principal lieutenants, sat their restive mounts staring down at the valley-spanning formation of the Skohshuns, their foemen. Of them all, only Prince Byruhn and a couple of his nobles had ever seen a formed-up Skohshun pike line, but as this one was almost twice the size of the one against which they had so vainly flung themselves last autumn, even they were impressed, mightily impressed.

The big men stood a bit over a yard apart, it seemed, in lines that stretched unbroken from half up the slope of one of the flanking hillocks to half up the slope of the other. And there were a hellacious lot of them. Bili's quick, battlewise eye told him of at least a hundred pikemen in each line and as many as ten of those lines, one behind the other in ordered ranks.

The overlong pikes were all grounded and stood up from the lines like a narrow forest of branchless saplings, with the near-nooning sun a-sparkle on the honed, polished, foot-long points that capped the eighteen-foot hafts. Also reflecting the bright sunlight were the scale breastplates and simple steel caps of the Skohshuns and the gold and silver and brass animal figures that capped the staffs of the line of standards at the rear of the formation, while the standards themselves rippled slightly in the breeze that blew fitfully down the vale from the north.

Shrunken with the distance, a few mounted men—nobles and officers, probably—could be seen riding up and down the forefront, ceaselessly dressing the formation, assisted in this by men on foot bearing shorter polearms and wearing more armor than the common pikemen.

From their elevation, the New Kuhmbuhluhners could see that although the front ranks were straight and unbroken—like lines carved accurately in soft wood by a sharp knife in a sure hand—the formation was more jagged in the rear. More depth existed at the road and in level areas which might prove a good location for a full-scale charge of the New Kuhmbuhluhn horsemen, while the lines were reduced in depth in other places—such as behind the abattis in the streambed and on the brushy, steep slopes of the flanking hillocks.

The pickets who had quitted the ridgeline upon the approach

33

of the first battle were to be seen between the foot of the ridge and the formation, formed in a precise column and running easily toward the slope of the western hillock. Even as the king and his party watched, a Skohshun horseman spurred from a point at the foot of that hillock leading a riderless horse. As the other pickets continued on afoot, their leader paused long enough to swing up into the empty saddle, then followed the first rider upslope and into the hilltop camp.

For all his understandable impatience, the brigadier saw to it that Sergeant Winchel, who had commanded the advance observers, had a pint of foaming beer before officially rendering his report to the waiting knot of officers.

Still redfaced and streaming sweat from the long run in the heat of the sun, the broad-shouldered, thick-bodied man stood at rigid attention, his eyes fixed unwaveringly on a point directly ahead of him, and rendered his report in short, terse, toneless sentences.

"Sir! The enemy are all across the ford. There are three mounted units and one of foot. Only some half of the horsemen are heavy-armed . . ."

There were sighs of relief and a few exchanged grins amongst the officers at this, all silenced and wiped off by an imperious wave of the brigadier's horny hand.

"I'll have silence, gentlemen, if you please. We've damn-all time, as it is. Go on, sergeant."

The sergeant continued in the same dehumanized voice. "There seem to be no bowmen or dartmen or slingers among the foot, and no horse-archers. The numbers of the horsemen are a total of fifty to fifty-five score; the foot are half that number or less."

"Could you see any units that appeared to be dragoons— mounted men armed with infantry weapons, sergeant?" rasped the brigadier.

"Sir! A few, perhaps ten score, in the third mounted unit might have been such, but all in both of the leading units were cavalry—either heavy or light."

The old officer nodded once. "Well done, sergeant. You may return to your unit. Dismiss!"

As the beefy noncom spun about and stiffly marched from the pavilion, the brigadier allowed himself the luxury of a thin smile beneath his drooping mustaches. "It would appear, gentlemen, that our old trick has worked yet again in the case of these New Kuhmbuhluhners. They apparently lack either the numbers or the weight to truly endanger us, and their leaders were obviously so stung by the cunning words of our herald that they put their brains and war sense up on the shelf and left all their missilemen at home.

"If God so wills it and all goes well, goes as I planned it, our arms should win us a new homeland, this day.

"To your commands, gentlemen. The foe is in sight!"

Although Bili of Morguhn had no way of knowing it, while Skohshuns and New Kuhmbuhluhners faced each other across the expanse of that narrow mountain vale, far and away to the southeast, three men squatted around the dismembered remains of a serpentine creature and conversed, while constantly waving at the hordes of buzzing flies that shared their interest in the decaying flesh.

Dr. Mike Schiepficker laid aside a four-inch scalpel and whistled soundlessly through clenched teeth, then addressed the man across the table from him. "Well, you were right about its being no reptile, Jay. In close to a thousand years of off-and-on study of zoology, I've never seen or heard of any reptile this primitive. But it's no worm either, despite outward appearances; no worm has a bony spine or such well-developed internal organs. Offhand, with only the dissection of this single specimen behind me, I'd say it is an amphibian."

The other man's eyebrows rose sharply in disbelief. "An amphibian, Mike? Three meters long? And we've killed even longer, bigger ones before you got up here. I've been around for as long as you have and I've never heard of any amphibian this size. Not even half this size."

Schiepficker nodded. "Then you never saw or heard of the Japanese giant salamanders? They ran to lengths of just under two meters, very broad and stocky and heavy, too; heavier by far than this beast was. And this thing's ancestors did have legs. Look here, see that small, flat bone? That is an atrophied scapula—a shoulder blade. And back here . . ." He moved down the table and utilized two pairs of forceps to spread the lips of the incision that ran the length of the long, slimy body. "See that? And those? They're what's left of a functional pelvis and the bone structure of rear legs. This creature's very distant forebears may very well have looked a great deal like salamanders."

"That still doesn't answer the main question, Mike. Just what is this thing? A mutation of some sort, as David—Dr. Sternheimer—thinks?"

"No, I don't think so, Jay. There once was fair evidence that something the descriptions of which sounded amazingly like this inhabited certain portions of Europe—the Bavarian Alps and Sweden, as I recall. The Germans called it a *Tätzelwurm,* I believe, saying they inhabited caves, mostly. But not much was known of the beasts, as I say. And I never heard even rumors of anything like them in the Western Hemisphere."

"You say these are scavengers, basically?"

The second man nodded. "The first things we noted when we began to uncover the remains buried when that line of cliffs collapsed were that every trace of flesh, skin, cartilage and the smaller bones were gone and even a good bit of the cured leather, while the larger bones and bits of wood or metal to which leather had been attached were scored with scrapes and deep gouges. The peculiar teeth of the first of these things we killed fitted some of those scrapes and gouge marks perfectly, Mike.

"But I think they're predators, too. I know damned well they're vicious as all hell and next to impossible to kill without virtually blowing them apart. And any bite they deliver always results in a serious infection."

Schiepficker shrugged. "That's often true of the bites of flesh-eaters, Jay, most especially of those which indulge principally in carrion. Not that I'm necessarily ruling out the possibility that the creatures are venomous; it's a trait that many amphibians have, after all. Some kinds of toads used to be boiled down and rendered into arrow poison, you know.

"Well, if you and your man there will assist me, I'll get the still-intact parts of this specimen into the preservative before this heat rots it any further. I'd like to have two, maybe three, more of the critters to take apart, but don't detail any men to hunt them out until you get as much of that salvage work done as is possible. You know how important Dr. Sternheimer considers the primary mission of your present expedition to be, Jay."

General Jay Corbett did indeed know. This was his second attempt to bring back to the J&R Kennedy Research Center the packloads of millennium-old artifacts which the labors of his current command were slowly recovering from beneath the untold tons of shattered rock—books and technical manuals and schematics, dismantled machinery and electronic equipment and spare parts, miles and miles of wire of differing gauges and resistances, transistors, silicon chips and a vast multitude of items the uses of which he could only guess. And that was not even mentioning the precious metals—gold in both coin and bars, silver, several kilos of industrial diamonds, leaden containers of radioactive substances, a few flasks of quicksilver, five kilos of platinum and smaller amounts of other, much rarer metals.

Two years before, Jay and two of the Center scientists—Drs. Erica Arenstein and Harry Braun—their minds transferred into Ahrmehnee bodies, had journeyed far northeast, into the Ahrmehnee *stahn*, to rouse that entire fierce race into a full-scale invasion of the western *thoheekahtrohnee*—or duchies—of the Confederation, as part of a centuries-old scheme to so weaken the upstart Confederation as to allow the Center to reestablish the United States of America, of which long-defunct political entity they considered themselves to be the last legitimate portion.

While on a related mission into the Hold of the Maidens of the Moon Goddess—a race of warrior-women distantly akin to the Ahrmehnee—Dr. Arenstein had discovered that not only was the Hold squatting atop a barely quiescent volcano, but that the side of the mountain was honeycombed with caves, many of them far too regular in form to have been natural in origin, and that these caves were the repository of a hoard of items of twentieth-century technology, more precious than rubies to the Center.

Upon being presented this god-sent opportunity to obtain the priceless trove, Dr. David Sternheimer, the Center Director, had organized and dispatched north a sizable pack train and the force to guard it, along with necessary gear and certain explosives and related devices requested by the three agents in the north.

With the bulk of the Moon Maidens away in the Ahrmehnee *stahn*, making ready to join with the male warriors in the invasion of the western marches of the Confederation, Dr. Arenstein and her people had returned to and been welcomed in the Hold. Of a night, they had coldly murdered their immediate hostesses, signaled those hidden outside the Hold, who then had crept up on and knifed or strangled the sentries, and finally used radio signals to release the contents of previously concealed canisters of a powerful gas.

When it was safe to do so, the men and beasts filed through the entrance tunnel—all equipped with face masks which filtered out the noxious, sleep-inducing fumes. Reaching the caves, they began to dismantle, gather and speedily pack the entire contents of the caverns onto the mules and ponies, stowing the more fragile items in special containers brought north for that very purpose.

When all was in readiness for the long journey southward, two explosive charges were laid and equipped with timed fuses. One, the smaller, was for the purpose of sealing the entry tunnel; the other, a far larger one, was for the purpose of sealing the vent of the volcano which underlay the entire glen of the Hold. The thinking of the scientists was that if this vent was sealed, a small volcanic eruption could well result and thus conceal the fact that the Hold had been stripped of its treasures.

But one or both of them miscalculated. The eruption, when it occurred several days later than anticipated, was anything but small. It blew the Hold and most of the mountain off the face of the earth, sending white-hot chunks of rock—ranging in size from invisible dust particles to multi-ton boulders—far up into the sky to fall to earth many kilometers distant. Nor were the rocks and the far-ranging forest fires they caused all or even the least of the calamities.

A powerful series of earth tremors rocked and racked the entire region, changing the courses of streams, shaking down some mountains while raising new ones and, in at least one instance, reducing a long, wide, high and previously inhabited plateau into so many square kilometers of dusty, shattered rocks.

This plateau had been called by the Ahrmehnee the Tongue of Soormehlyuhn, and the principal north-south trail to the westward of it had run under the beettling bluffs of its westernmost flank. And the bulk of the pack train had been strung out along that very stretch of trail when the tremors had brought the entire line of bluffs crashing down upon men and beasts alike, crushing out the lives of the living and sealing their corpses and the inanimate treasure beneath untold tons of stone.

And for the survivors of this disaster, the quakes and fires had been only the beginning, a mere prelude to weeks to come of danger and horror and, for some, death.

Burdened from the beginning with burned or injured men, and menaced also by hundreds of rude, crudely armed but no less dangerous, pony-mounted savages who called themselves Ganiks and practiced, among other degeneracies, senseless and insensitive torture of prisoners and cannibalism, Jay Corbett had finally taken the most of the surviving force to hold the mouth of a narrow defile. In so doing, he hoped to allow the two scientists, the wounded, the pitifully few remaining packloads of loot from the Hold of the Maidens, the packload of fast-dwindling medical stores and a minimal escort of sound troopers under the command of the highest-ranking noncommissioned officer, Sergeant Gumpner, a bare chance at escape and survival.

Dr. Harry Braun had once been married to Dr. Erica Arenstein and had alternately loved her and hated her ever since—through hundreds of years and scores of bodies. She loathed and despised him and had many times deliberately done the very things that she knew would hurt him or arouse him to fits of public fury.

Braun had suffered a severe compound fracture of the leg when the first tremors of the earthquake caused his big saddle mule to fall with him still in the saddle. After treatment and splinting by Erica—who held an M.D. among her other degrees—the injured scientist had been narcotized and borne in a jury-rigged horse litter for the first few days of the southward journey.

But then the pressing danger from the Ganiks became more severe and Corbett had decided to try to shake the pursuit by cutting cross-country through the brush and thickets, hacking out a passage laboriously with sabers and axes. It had been necessary to put Braun astride a mount and tie him into the saddle. He had taken it into a mind already fuzzy with fever-induced delirium and drugs that Erica and Jay were deliberately, maliciously and with jolly sadism torturing him, especially in light of the fact that Erica had found it best to cut his dosages of anesthetics if he was to have enough to last the rest of the journey.

As they all rode hard up the narrow defile, leaving Corbett and his riflemen facing hundreds of Ganiks in the forlorn hope of saving what and who could be saved, Braun slowed, then dropped behind and, when Erica came up to him, pled piteously with her to dismount and tighten his girth, which he could feel slipping. But when she did so, he drew his big-bore belt pistol and tried to shoot her. When the weapon jammed, he pistol-whipped her into unconsciousness, then rode on and left her to either die or, far worse, be taken by the Ganiks. The story he gave out to Gumpner was that Erica had been killed by a small party of Ganiks in the defile and that he had been able to get off but the single shot at the marauders before his pistol malfunctioned and he could only ride on.

When he had decided to make his stand, Corbett had been convinced that it would certainly be the last stand for him and the riflemen he commanded. For all that the horde of barbarians were primitively armed even for this time and place, there were just too many of them; far more of them than he and his force had of cartridges for their rifles. But he had been wrong.

Due to some wildly implausible turns of good fortune, he and his force had beaten off charge after charge of the screaming, wild-eyed cannibals, piling up three to four hundred dead or dying Ganiks with well-aimed shots and explosive bullets.

But it had been a near thing—or so it had seemed at the time. They had been down to a scant handful of cartridges per man when the Ganiks were suddenly reinforced and, encouraged by the fresh forces, had mounted yet another full-scale charge. But when this one, too, had ended as had all the earlier ones in bloody butchery and defeat, those Ganiks still unhurt, some two hundred or more, had mounted their horses and ponies and ridden away to the northwest without a backward glance.

After a far-ranging reconnaissance of the Ganiks' line of withdrawal to be certain that it was really such and not simply a ruse to draw them out of their well-defended defile, the exhausted riflemen had butchered a Ganik pony and camped the night in the grassy, well-watered area just to the north of the mouth of the defile. Then, next morning, they had pushed on southward in the wake of the smaller, more vulnerable party.

It did not ease their minds to discover signs that a sizable mounted party of Ganiks was spurring on along the same trail between their force and the smaller one. But luck still rode with them. They surprised the contingent of Ganiks camped along the trail and had cut most of them down before some were fully awake. Two or three, no more, escaped in the darkness, afoot and unarmed. Their leader was captured alive but unconscious, victim of a blow from Jay Corbett's mace.

Some presentiment had caused Jay Corbett to spare the life of the middle-aged, bald, bearded and indescribably filthy cannibal chief, and he had never had cause to regret his action, far from it. Old Johnny "Skinhead" Kilgore had proved himself worth his weight in diamonds to Corbett and every other trooper of the survivors.

The Ganik's knowledge of game and hunting, of wild but edible plants and of plants having natural medicinal qualities had kept them well fed and healthy for almost all the remaining journey. He had quickly and easily shed most of his Ganik ways and become one of them. He made friends easily, and his unquestioned expertise as a woodsman soon had earned him the respect and trust of all the troopers.

But if he and his newfound mates fared well, the murderous Dr. Harry Braun surely did not. When Gumpner halted his small command for the night, after the wild ride from the defile, in a sheltered, easily defensible glen, Braun was alternately screaming with pain and lapsing into unconsciousness. Upon lifting him down from his saddle and examining him, Gumpner found the injured, splinted and bandaged leg immensely swollen and horribly discolored for its entire length—toes to crotch—with the toes and part of the foot turning black.

When Corbett joined Gumpner, the officer decided to do what little he could in the absence of a trained doctor by opening and draining the infected leg, and this he did with the assistance of Gumpner and a few others.

In the aftermath of the crude surgery, Braun surprisingly seemed to be improving, and when the horses, ponies and mules had grazed out the glen, Corbett had felt few qualms about moving on with the injured scientist. But Braun's condition had gradually deteriorated under the strains of daily travel, and when Old Johnny Kilgore and a hunting party found a promising, grassy, well-watered spot some kilometers west of the trail, Corbett had had the unit go into camp there.

At various times, when drugs or delirium had dulled his conscious mind, Braun had ravingly relived his cold-blooded murder of Erica Arenstein well within the hearing of every man in the column.

A week or so of bedrest, injections of antibiotics and nourishing foods, combined with the solicitous care of the two troopers assigned to attend him, had almost restored Braun completely. Then, like a thunderbolt, Corbett and Gumpner discovered that the foot of the broken leg was becoming gangrenous.

As a group of troopers on a deer hunt had recently seen landmarks that told them they were but a few days' ride from Broomtown Base—their home and the northernmost bastion of Center activities—Corbett decided to send Braun on ahead, mounted on a big mule and escorted by a Sergeant Cabell, Old Johnny Kilgore and a trooper, with led remounts and orders to get the scientist to Broomtown alive so that he could have his mind transferred into a whole, healthy body before his injured, diseased one died. Cabell, the trooper and Johnny were chosen because they and their charge were just then the only men in all the company who were not sudden victims of illness that left them infant-weak, feverish and racked with bone-rattling chills.

A few days along the trail, in a raging tantrum because Cabell would not immediately inject him with one of the last few dosages of opiates, Braun shot the well-meaning noncom out of his saddle. But as he turned his attentions and his smoking pistol on Old Johnny, the old cannibal sped a wickedly barbed wardart into the thigh of the scientist's good leg and then, regretfully, put another into the chest of the trooper just as that man fired a rifle at him.

In the fresh agony of the sharp iron blade deep-seated in his flesh and grating on the femur, Braun dropped both pistol and reins, and the mule set off at a flat-out run toward the south, with the screaming man firmly strapped into the saddle.

Old Johnny had returned to the campsite in time to tend the

stricken men and nurse some of them back to health, but it was long weeks before they were capable of marching on to the base. There they discovered that Dr. Harry Braun had, after everything, been dragged in alive by friendly natives and had reported that all of the remainder of the expedition were long dead, that he was the sole survivor.

It had long been an ill-kept secret that Dr. David Sternheimer had nurtured a deep and abiding love for Dr. Erica Arenstein for centuries, and when once he had learned from Jay Corbett the truth of her murder, his vengeance had been savage. Not only had Dr. Harry Braun been summarily stripped of all his privileges and rank, his mind had been forcibly transferred from the new, healthy body to another one—a body a good deal older and slowly dying of colonic cancer. Then he had been assigned menial, degrading duties in a place where Sternheimer could keep an eye on him.

For most of the following year, careful and meticulous preparations had been made both at the Center and at Broomtown Base. Then, in the spring, a large, well-armed and lavishly supplied force of Broomtown men had set out for the site of the buried pack train under the overall command of General Jay Corbett. Gumpner, now a major, was in command of the battalion of troopers and the civilian packers, while another civilian, Johnny Kilgore, led the scouts assigned to the new expedition.

They bore everything thought to be needful for retrieving the lost treasures. There were explosives to blast the huge boulders into movable sizes, sledgehammers, picks, shovels, crowbars, axes and other hardware, cables and strong cordage and chains, as well as collars and draft-harness sets for the big mules. A number of the troopers were trained experts in the use of the explosives, and not a few of the civilian packers had been drafted into the expedition from their normal occupation of stone-quarrying.

The memory of the vast hordes of bloodthirsty Ganiks had not faded from the minds of the planners, either. The men of the battalion were far better armed than had been the few who had defended that defile. In addition to the rifles and pistols, the sabers and axes and bayonets and dirks, there were machine guns, mortars, shotguns, and both hand and rifle grenades.

There were not just one but two of the big, long-range radio transceivers, each complete with its heavy, bulky battery pack and bicycle-powered generator for recharging. In addition to the regular once-per-day broadcast, Jay Corbett had Sternheimer's *carte blanche*. He could call in to either Broomtown or the Center when and as he wished to do so.

Although he was almost the antithesis of a superstitious man, Sternheimer had grudgingly admitted to Jay that he had had several unexplainable dreams that made him think that Dr. Erica Arenstein was still alive somewhere up in that wild country, and he had almost begged the general to watch carefully for any signs of his lost love.

Privately, Corbett felt certain that the missing woman was long months dead, and he did not quite know what to make of the emotional pleas of the normally cold, distant, correct and objective Director, but he had finally agreed to keep his eyes peeled for a trace of Erica Arenstein, then had shoved the matter to a far recess of his mind.

It had been shortly after the first blastings that the first of the monsters of the ilk of that one now stinking and covered with feasting flies on the table had manifested itself. They averaged three and a half meters in length and a thickness of thirteen centimeters, were annulated and covered with a thick, viscous slime. Seen at a distance, they might have been taken for huge earthworms. But at close range, when their beady eyes and wide mouths filled with double rows of sharp teeth became evident, it was clear that this was no worm.

They were aggressive and vicious, could move as fast as most snakes and had jaws powerful enough to easily sever a finger or a toe or to tear off sizable amounts of flesh. No one had ever heard one of the creatures utter any sound, but they were unremittingly fierce and devilishly hard to kill. Even with most of its body blown loose from the head by explosive rifle bullets, one of them had still managed to propel the head close enough to a quarryman to clamp the dying, tooth-studded jaws down on his foot, shearing right through the tough hide brogans to the flesh beneath.

Aware of the Director's long-held interest in unusual animals, Corbett had reported these creatures to the Center on his daily report and had suggested the dispatch of a trained man to properly examine them. Dr. Mike Schiepficker had been coptered up far enough for a mounted escort of troopers to meet him.

Actually, Corbett reflected, a large armed escort had really been unnecessary, this time around, and he could not conceive of any explanation for it, not one that made any sense. Nor could Johnny Kilgore, who had ranged farther afield and seen more.

Where, just bare months in the past, there had been a country aswarm with large and small mounted war or raiding parties of savage Ganiks, they had seen none, not one single living Ganik, and the one dead one they had chanced across had been many days' trek southward of here, that one killed by a bear. Their woodland camps sat tenantless—some of them, according to Johnny, had been attacked and/or burned, the signs were there—and even the plateau which had recently been home to thousands of the cannibal raiders was now utterly deserted, now affording a habitat only to a herd of scrubby ponies and other wild creatures.

And, again according to old Johnny, not only had all of the bunches of outlaw Ganiks disappeared from their usual haunts, but all of the families of Ganik farmers were gone as well, their farms and farm buildings sitting empty and obviously unworked for many months.

So the machine guns and mortars reposed still in their crates and cases in the rear of the supply tent, and the only shots anyone had fired hereabouts had been at game or to dispatch specimens of these huge, wormlike beasts in and about the work site.

When the last portions of the creature that Schiepficker intended to save had been immersed in the preservative and the containers sealed, the zoologist washed and dried his hands, then nodded to Corbett.

"Thanks again for your help, Jay. Now I guess we'd best get on the horn and tell Sternheimer of my findings and suppositions."

But even as the two men left the tent, a trooper trotted up, red-faced and streaming sweat in the heat. He rendered the abbreviated hand-salute of a cavalryman, then panted, "General Corbett, sir, Major Gumpner says come at once. Old Johnny Skinhead is back again. He's brought him a prisoner, another Ganik what says Dr. Arenstein is still alive, or was a month ago when he left her, leastways."

# CHAPTER IV

The valley was narrower at the foot of the ridge than it became farther northward; therefore, the descending columns of New Kuhmbuhluhn horsemen found it necessary to ride on some hundred yards before there was room to extend to full battle front. Both the advance and the extension were accomplished at a slow walk, partly to spare the horses and partly to minimize confusion, the fiercely independent and often unruly noblemen of New Kuhmbuhluhnburk never having been fond of or amenable to unit discipline or drills.

Following a recently conceived plan, Prince Mahrtuhn Gilbuht led his Second Battle toward the enemy's left, his ranks of horsemen spanning the distance from the eastern bank of the stream, across the road and to the foot of the flanking knoll. King Mahrtuhn led his own First Battle up the center, his ranks extending from the western bank of the stream to about halfway to the western knoll. Prince Byruhn's smaller Third Battle could only cover the remaining distance by reducing the depth of the formation. Once formed to royal satisfaction, King Mahrtuhn's massed trumpeters winded the call and the three battles began their advance.

For their part, the Skohshun formation remained just as they had been when first the Kuhmbuhluhners had crested the ridge for all the time it took the cavalry to descend, form up and start forward. Then, drums rolled, and the first two ranks of pikemen knelt and angled their long weapons so as to present an unbroken succession of foot-long, polished-steel pikeheads—half of them about brisket-high, half of them about head-high, where the horses could easily see them. Most of the ranks behind lifted their pikes to shoulder level, holding them with the points at a slight angle downward from the horizontal, ready to stab or thrust. The rearmost ranks of pikemen simply stood in place, their weapons still grounded, ready to fill the positions of fallen comrades in the ranks ahead.

Arrayed on the far right of the Third Battle, the right flank of Bili's condotta was some twenty yards distant from the left flank of King Mahrtuhn's First Battle, and the young *thoheeks* could have wished it were twice that distance or even more. The worst thing that could happen to him and his people, even worse than not being supported in meaningful force at the proper time,

45

would be to have a covey of hotheaded noble arseholes charge along the same stretch of front that Bili was attacking just as he had commenced his attack; but he could do nothing more, now, than to maintain as much distance as possible from the First Battle and pray Sacred Sun that such did not occur.

Observing the disciplined precision of movements, the calm, professional impassivity of the pikemen up ahead, then recalling the ill-controlled, moblike aspects of the royal battles with whom he now rode, Bili could not conceive of any possibility of King Mahrtuhn's winning the battle looming close, and he mindspoke his principal lieutenants.

"Remember my words of last night, all of you! Barring the most impossible variety of miracle, the New Kuhmbuhluhners haven't the chance of a wet snowball in a red-hot skillet, not against foot of that caliber yonder. Do that which we planned, *but no more* unless we are substantially reinforced . . . and I greatly doubt that we will be."

He broke off the farspeak, then, and mindspoke his huge black stallion, Mahvros. "It will be up to you, my brother, to see to it that all of the herd comes to me and my fighters immediately I mindcall you. Will Mahvros do that, for his brother?"

The big warhorse beamed assurance and undying love, even as he and every other horse in the three battles commenced a jarring gallop in response to the summons of King Mahrtuhn's trumpeters.

With a deafening cacophony of screaming horses, shouting, roaring, shrieking men and clashing metal, the First and Second Battles and two-thirds of the Third crashed against the pike line. Many horsemen were thrown as their mounts refused to impale themselves on the flashing points ahead. Others fended off seeking points with shields while hacking savagely at the tough oaken or ash hafts with sword or axe, or made to transfix the pikemen with lances that were mostly so much shorter than the pikehafts as to be worse than useless.

Standing in his stirrups, Prince Mahrtuhn Gilbuht swung his heavy axe with both big hands at a probing pike even as another point was jammed with force through the eyehole of the stallion's chamfron. With a shrill scream of mortal agony, the massive destrier reared, his steel-shod forehooves flailing empty air, while his rider fought to maintain his seat. Then another pikepoint was jammed its full length into the unprotected belly of the horse and the beast tried to back off the hellish steel, lost his balance and came crashing down, pinning his royal rider beneath his ton and more of weight.

On the left, Prince Byruhn had learned well his hard lessons on how to deal with a pikeline, nor had he carried out to the full his royal sire's orders. He led his nobles in riding up and down the glittering hedge of steel, just beyond their easy reach, swerving closer in no set pattern to hack at the hafts, while his mountaineer axe throwers picked off pikemen, here and there, with accurate casts of their deadly hatchetlike missiles.

Bili's condotta began the charge in company with all the rest of the New Kuhmbuhluhn horsemen, but ten yards out from the closest pikepoints, the condotta came to a practiced halt. They dismounted, unslung bucklers from off their backs, drew their swords and sabers and advanced at a trot in three-quarter armor with closed helms. When they were almost within touching distance of the bristling array of pikepoints, each third or fourth warrior allowed blade to dangle on knot and withdrew from behind the buckler what looked at a distance to be a head-sized ball of brown cordage.

The brigadier reined up a lathered horse beside where Colonel Bruce Farr sat his own mount. The brigadier's lined old face was red, and there was frantic haste in his voice.

"Colonel, your drummers must order your left-flanking companies to immediately ground pikes and draw shortswords! They . . ." Then he groaned, "Oh, God help us all, now it's too late." Then he mouthed nothing save snarled curses as he stood in his stirrups to see over the heads of his embattled pikemen.

The colonel rose himself, and what he saw shook him to the flinty core.

Taking a good grip on the dangling cords, the men and women cast the specially woven nets in such fashion that they ensnared a maximum number of the thrusting points of the third through eighth ranks of pikemen. Then, after hacking down or thrusting into the two ranks of kneeling pikemen, they fell onto their backs and began to swiftly worm their way under the points and hafts of the lengthy weapons. Knowing that their very lives depended upon it, they moved amazingly fast, and soon their already-bloodied blades were chopping, slicing, stabbing at the unarmored, unprotected thighs and loins, hips and bellies, arms and faces of the pikemen.

Skimpily armored and with both hands being occupied in keeping the long, heavy haft of the pike in place, hampered from any easy movement by both the weight of the pike and the close-packed formation, the helpless men could but scream and drop, dead or dying. At length, some of the men whose points were ensnared anyway dropped their hafts and drew their shortswords.

Most of them never even got close enough to blunt their edges on their opponents' armor-plated bodies, however, for the broadswords and sabers were sufficiently longer to have point in face or throat or an edge hacking at neck or arm before the pikemen's sidearms could reach striking position.

Bili lopped off an arm still grasping a pike just above the cuff of a mailed gauntlet, then turned to confront a man who had already hacked once or twice at the backplate of his cuirass. But before he could strike, the point of a pike struck hard at his breastplate, slid down the groove of its fluting and plunged into the lower belly of his erstwhile opponent.

A mighty, full-strength hack of Bili's heavy blade all but severed the haft and its iron-strip reinforcings. The force of the blow did tear the point, sideways, out of the unfortunate's belly, ripping a wide opening that spilled his intestines out to dangle like a bloody sporran between his widespread legs.

The brigadier slapped at a pikeman with the flat of his sword, shouting, "Damn you, whoreson! Ground your pikes—you had no order to present! Ground pikes, all of you! Thrust into that melee, you're as likely to spit one of your comrades as any of those Kuhmbuhluhners."

He turned to the regimental commander and snapped, "Dammit, colonel, where are your short-haftmen? Halberds and warhammers, that's all that can put paid to those murdering bastards."

Farr shrugged helplessly. "Sir, the earl ordered almost all of my short-hafts to reinforce the section of the line in the streambed. Only some few sergeants remain with me."

To the knot of aides who had followed him, the brigadier shouted, "One of you . . . Lieutenant Bryson, ride to Colonel Pease and bring back all his shorts at the double. The rest of you, dismount, adjust your gear and draw your swords. You too, Colonel Farr, *and* your staff officers and sergeants. We've all got better armor and longer swords than our brave pikemen. I can't just sit here and watch them butchered out there."

Suiting his actions to his words, the old warrior swung down from his saddle, lowered and carefully secured his visor, then tightened the knot on his wrist before drawing his long sword. At a limping run, he led his scratch force through a lane opened in the two ranks of uncommitted pikemen.

\* \* \*

When there were no more throwing axes, Prince Byruhn drew back some fifty yards from the pike line and surveyed what he could see of the overall combat. The dust and the distance made the area assigned to Prince Mahrtuhn Gilbuht, his nephew, faint and unclear, while to his immediate right, the First Battle was become a swirling mass of mostly mounted New Kuhmbuhluhners and unmounted Skohshuns armed with poleaxes, warhammers, short pikes and greatswords industriously hacking and stabbing and slashing at each other just a bit out from the pike line.

Due principally to the great clouds of roiling dust that this combat had raised, he did not for a long moment notice that just to his left of this broil, there was a jagged gap of some thirty yards' width in the lines of pikes.

Roaring gleefully, the mighty prince whirled his overlong battle brand high over his helmeted head and led his battle directly into that undefended expanse.

As Bili withdrew his nicked, dulled blade—now cloudy with sticky, red blood from point to quillions—from just below the breastplate of a gasping, wide-eyed pikeman, the back of his helmet was struck so hard that the force of the buffet all but drove him to his knees. Staggering slightly, he turned to face a swordsman in three-quarter armor of an alien pattern.

Shieldless, the Skohshun was swinging his sword with both hands, and his greater than average strength was evident in the crushing, numbing force of his blows. Bili caught and deflected two more sword swipes on the face of his buckler and tried to deflect another down the flat of his blade while fetching his new opponent a shrewd buffet in the exposed armpit with the steel-shod edge of the buckler. But Bili's much-abused blade shattered and broke off some foot below the quillions.

Gasping a breathless snarl, the young *thoheeks* slammed the convex center of his smooth-faced buckler full onto his foeman's visor with all the strength of his sinewy left arm, even as he used his booted right foot to jerk the man's left leg forward. Despite the flailing of his arms, the Skohshun lost his balance and fell heavily onto his back. His unlaced helmet went spinning off to reveal the red face of an elderly man with flaring white mustache. Before the old man could move, Bili had taken a long, quick stride and kicked him in the side of the head, then appropriated his victim's sword.

As he straightened, however, he saw a file of men trotting up behind the lines of uncommitted pikemen, led by a mounted officer. These men all wore full helmets and half-armor and were armed with pole weapons of more conventional size than the bulk of the Skohshun army.

*"Withdraw!"* he urgently mindspoke his lieutenants. "All disengage and withdraw, at once!" Then, to his stallion, "My brother, watch close and be ready to bring up the herd as soon as we clear the pike line."

But it was not to be, not then, not yet. The members of Bili's condotta had fallen back only a few yards when they first felt the fast-approaching thunder vibrating up through the soles of their boots, then found themselves dodging the galloping horses of Prince Byruhn's Third Battle.

With swords and lances, with axes, maces and warhammers, the prince and his men smote down any Skohshuns Bili's force had missed, then rode through the two files of uncommitted pikemen to hotly engage the newcome poleaxemen to the rear.

At the hilltop command post, from which he could see the entire length of the battlelines, Senior Colonel Sir Djaimz Alpine waited far longer than he should have for the return of the brigadier and the four or five staff officers who had trailed him when he had so suddenly called for his horse, mounted and ridden down into the rear areas. At some length, he beckoned over a young ensign.

"Grey, ride down there and don't come back up here until you've found the brigadier or, at least, word of what he's up to."

*"Sir!"* The pink-cheeked boy stamped, spun about, and set off at a run for the picket lines, his armor rattling, his left hand holding his scabbarded sword free of his churning legs.

Even as the ensign set his big gelding down the hillock, a lieutenant of foot reined in a foaming, hard-ridden mount before the headquarters and flung himself from the sweaty saddle to salute Sir Jaimz, then relay the question of his colonel.

"Of course not!" snapped the senior colonel brusquely, "Any hot pursuit of mounted foemen is always undertaken by our own mounted troops. Colonel Phipps knows that. He is to stay where he is, maintain the pike line. *Dismiss*!"

As the lieutenant remounted, Sir Djaimz once more turned to and looked along the nearer, western flank of the lines . . . and felt his blood run cold! The line had been severed, not just battered, but severed. Even as he watched in horror from his eyrie, armored New Kuhmbuhluhn horsemen were riding right through Farr's regimental lines, hacking down pikemen as they went, to engage the short-haftmen in the rear and spread out to take other units in the flank. Where in thirteen hells was the brigadier?

Colonel Sir Edmund Grey, father of Ensign Thomas Grey, had died of wounds after the big battle with the New Kuhmbuhluhn heavy horse, last autumn. Thomas, his eldest living son, had then been in training. This was the fourteen-year-old boy's first battle . . . and his last.

Even as he spotted the riderless horse of the missing brigadier hitched with several other saddled mounts to a low, spreading bush, a yelling, screaming horde of armored New Kuhmbuhluhners chopped and slashed their way through the last two lines of Colonel Farr's regiment, then split into three integuments—one to savagely attack a force of short-haftmen and the officer leading them, one to ride against the rear and right flank of the next regiment east—that of Colonel Herman Taylor, Ensign Grey's godfather—one to do likewise against the next regiment west, which meant that that unit was riding directly toward Thomas Grey.

The oncoming enemies looked huge, far larger than men should rightly be, monstrous; their weapons were splotched and smeared with fresh, bright-red blood, their armor and horse housings splashed with it. Young Ensign Grey's mouth was suddenly dry as ashes and his tongue seemed cloven to his palate, and breathing was exceedingly difficult. He seemed all at once to be suffering a flux of his bowels, and a painfully distended bladder did not in any way help matters. But he never even considered flight. He drew his sword, after lowering and securing his visor, and rode on.

Earl Devernee, technically the overall commander of the Skohshun army, as well as the hereditary leader of the Skohshun people, usually and wisely left decisions of a military—and especially of a battlefield—nature up to the brigadier and his staff,

Just before this battle, however, he had been urgently approached and bespoken by his first cousin, Colonel Harry Potter, and convinced by the officer that his understrength regiment stood in more danger of attack in their stream-spanning position than the brigadier was willing to credit or admit. The earl had used his seldom-invoked personal authority to strip several regiments of most of their short-haft fighters, then had assigned the lot of them to reinforce his cousin's pikemen. In the cases of at least three of the affected regiments, this unexpected abrogation of the painfully detailed planning of the brigadier and his battlewise staff was to result in a very high butcher's bill.

While Prince Byruhn and a few score of his mountain axemen took on the hastily formed ring of poleaxes and other short polearms, two of his most trusted counts led the bulk of his Third Battle in crashing, crushing charges against the now-exposed flanks of the two regiments to either side of that unfortunate one chosen by Bili Morguhn as the target for his new, unorthodox tactics.

Utterly lacking the customary screen of flexible and better-protected short-haftmen, the long-pikemen—hampered with a necessarily tight formation and heavy, unwieldy arms—were as helpless as fish in a barrel and went down in droves, spitted on lances and spears, hacked by swords and axes, their skulls sundered or bones crushed by maces or warhammers. Those few who escaped death or serious injury were the less disciplined men who dropped their pikes and fled. All of the well-trained, veteran pikemen died or fell in their assigned places.

Senior Colonel Sir Djaimz Alpine, completely unaware of the earl's ill-advised last-minute reassignments of personnel, could only assume that the force of New Kuhmbuhluhn cavalry was larger and stronger than it appeared at the distance to have ridden over and downed the well-armed and -armored flank screens of the special troops.

To one of the waiting officer-gallopers, he said, "My compliments, please, to Colonel Powell. He is to bring up his regiment at the double with all pikes presented and, when he has cleared the way, his regiment will plug the gap in the line where Colonel Farr's regiment was posted."

The first galloper was barely on his run toward the picket lines when Sir Djaimz was rattling off instructions to another and inwardly cursing the absence of the brigadier, even while blessing the old man for his years of patient tutelage and often impatient and profane example.

With the Third Battle actively engaging most of the still-standing Skohshuns within reach, the withdrawal of Bili's condotta was quick and easy. Mahvros and those few humans assigned as horse holders brought up the horses promptly. Bili and the others first saw all the wounded mounted and those unable to mount tied securely onto their mounts before themselves mounting and drawing back a hundred yards or so.

Standing in his stirrups, Bili could see the entirety of the pike lines, and what he saw was in no way heartening. To his right, the First Battle still seemed to be attacking, hacking fiercely if generally ineffectually at the unbroken pike hedge, King

Mahrtuhn's Green Stallion banner waving at the forefront of the fight.

On the other side of the stream, however, there was no battle. The pike hedge stood firm behind uninterrupted lines of glittering steel points. Of the New Kuhmbuhluhner force which had attacked them—Prince Mahrtuhn Gilbuht's Second Battle—only the bodies of dead or dying men and horses remained on the field before the pikes.

Then, Rahksahnah, sitting her big mare beside him, touched his steel-sheathed arm, mindspeaking, "Bili . . . the king!"

The young chief of Clan Morguhn snapped his gaze back to the area of the First Battle's unavailing engagement to see King Mahrtuhn—recognizable by his richly embellished armor and gear—lolling limply in his saddle, supported at either side by members of his bodyguard, neither of whom looked sound and whole themselves. As they led the monarch's limping charger from proximity to the dripping pikepoints, the horse bearing the Green Stallion Banner followed in its accustomed place, despite its empty saddle.

However, few if any of the remaining bulk of the First Battle seemed to be aware of the wounding of the king. They continued to vainly hack away at the Skohshun formation, losing man after man and horse to precious little avail.

None of it made any sense to Bili. Spotting the chief hornsman of the royal trumpeters on the outward fringes of the broil, the young *thoheeks* galloped Mahvros over to the man.

"Blow the recall!" he ordered shortly.

The middle-aged musician turned slightly in his saddle and, with a ghost of a sneer, stated, "My orders come from King Mahrtuhn, alone, my . . . lord mercenary."

A big, powerful hand in a blood-tacky gauntlet grasped the hornman's richly embroidered surcoat and half-dragged him from his saddle, slowly shaking him the while.

"King Mahrtuhn," snarled Bili, "has been severely wounded and is being borne from the field. I, Bili, Duke of Morguhn, command you to blow recall at once, while there is still something left of the First Battle. Put that damned horn to your lips or I swear that you'll be lacking lips, and head, entirely, sirrah!"

Intimidated to the point of stuttering terror by the towering, grim and blood-splashed nobleman-officer, the chief hornman gasped out the call to his subordinates, but it was they who ended up blowing it, for his lips were trembling too severely to shape the notes properly.

\*     \*     \*

Fortunately for his Third Battle, Prince Byruhn spotted the fresh regiment of pikemen trotting down the valley when they were still sufficiently distant to allow him time to collect his scattered horsemen and withdraw them through the much-widened gap in the Skohshun lines. Otherwise, he and they might well have been trapped behind those lines and cut down, piecemeal.

A few yards out from the Skohshun formations, Duke Bili rode up to him. "Byruhn, your father, the king, is sore hurt, maybe dead, for all I know. I've had the recall sounded for his battle, since their tactics were accomplishing nothing of a positive nature. There's no sign of your nephew or his battle; they must have withdrawn earlier. The command is now yours, obviously. What are my lord's orders?"

Byruhn sighed and looked behind, where the lines of the Skohshun pikemen were reforming precisely even as the fresh regiment moved into place in the gapped formation.

"Get to hell out of here," he snapped, "before they are formed up to countercharge, as they did last autumn. It has all, everything, been wasted, today, young cousin. But then, we—both of us—knew that it would be, eh? So much for old-fashioned, senseless pursuit of an outdated honor. Now let's get what force hasn't been frittered away back to New Kuhmbuhluhn-burk, wherein the terrain and the odds will be on our side for a change."

But the Skohshuns did not countercharge. Bili's last view of them from the crest of the ridge between the blood-soaked valley and the river showed them still in their place, the forward lines of pikes still at "present." But the Skohshuns' rear area was a seething boil of activity, and the constant passings back and forth of riders up and down the western hillock led him to believe that some important person of that alien army had his headquarters thereon.

No sooner were the New Kuhmbuhluhn survivors across the river and back into camp than Prince Byruhn set every sound man and woman to the task of breaking that camp and forming for a march back to New Kuhmbuhluhnburk. There was much grumbling and grousing on the part of the exhausted warriors, but Bili could see the points: to stay here was to invite an attack by the numerically superior Skohshuns, and cavalry was of little account as a defending force; also, there was the matter of the wounded—including King Mahrtuhn—all of whom would be immeasurably better off in the care of Pah-Elmuh and the other Kleesahks skilled at healing, and while a night on the march might kill some of those wounded, so too would a night of

suffering on hard pallets in camp under only the rough-and-ready
care of their comrades and a horse leech or two. And there were
plenty of spare horses to bear horse litters. Over half of the force
that had ridden into that ill-conceived attack were now dead,
wounded or missing, but only about a fifth of the horses were
dead, missing or seriously enough hurt to require being put down
or immediately tended.

A litter was fashioned of King Mahrtuhn's cushioned camp bed,
and the still-unconscious monarch—stripped of his hacked and
bloody armor, boots and gambeson, his visible wounds cleaned
and bandaged—was gently placed therein. Prince Mahrtuhn
Gilbuht's crushed and mangled corpse, wrapped in the silken
folds of his personal banner, was securely tied atop the load of
one of the wagons, on Prince Byruhn's order.

They marched through the night, under a bright half-moon,
with Bili and the hale members of his condotta providing flank-
and rearguards. A bare score of Skohshun dragoons had splashed
across the ford when the camp was finally struck, the site
deserted and most of the slow-moving column a good mile on
the road to New Kuhmbuhluhnburk. But the small unit of cavalrymen never made any attempt to close that distance. Indeed,
they deliberately halted several times to maintain it whenever the
column found it necessary to slow or pause. It was obvious that
they were but a scouting force, not seeking to harry or fight, and
none in Bili's condotta or in the main column had the mind or
the energy to try to take a fight to them.

Bili had sent the prairiecat Whitetip racing ahead to the nearest
point from which the big, talented feline could farspeak the
Kleesahk Pah-Elmuh, in order that the huge humanoid and his
ilk might meet the column before it reached the mountain city.
With the king comatose, his chosen heir dead and Prince Byruhn
in full command of the shattered remnants of the royal army,
there was no longer any need to conceal the fact that he had had
the big cat accompany the force.

Pah-Elmuh and five other Kleesahks met the battered column
at the fourth hour after dawn, still some twelve miles from New
Kuhmbuhluhnburk. Pah-Elmuh himself made directly for that
litter holding King Mahrtuhn, knelt beside it and, with his
eyelids closed, lightly ran his gigantic palm the length of the
royal body, from feet to head.

When he finally looked up at Prince Byruhn, there was both
pain and sadness commingled in the depths of his oval-pupiled
eyes. "King Mahrtuhn no longer lives, Lord Prince. His body is

cooling and has begun to stiffen. I grieve with you. He was a good and a just sovran.''

The massive, hirsute creature swiveled his bone-ridged head on his short, thick neck, looking about. "Where is your nephew, Prince Mahrtuhn Gilbuht? He must be told that he now is our king.''

"No, Pah-Elmuh," Byruhn sighed. "Poor young Mahrtuhn will never wear the crown of New Kuhmbuhluhn, not now. He died on the field, and his body is back there on a baggage wagon. I suppose, Steel aid us all, that that means I must be king." He sighed again, more deeply, then added, "And I must be the very last of my line, I fear me, for my nephew had not yet sired any sons, and, as well *you* know, I . . . I dare not breed.''

# CHAPTER V

*Ahrkeethoheeks* Hahfos Djohnz, Warden of the Ahrmehnee Marches, looked up from the letter he had been reading and leaned back in his desk chair, his elbows on its arms, his hands idly toying with the leather tube in which that letter had been rolled.

The middle-aged-to-elderly man who stood before his desk did so at rigid, military posture of attention, for all that of all his clothing and equipment, only the plain, functional sword and the businesslike, unadorned dirk he wore looked at all military. True, his clothing, boots and armor were all plain enough, but their rich quality betrayed them—no army ever issued, or could afford to issue, such material.

The shadow of a smile flitted over the lips and eyes of the seated officer. Then he remarked conversationally, "It's obvious that civilian life agrees with you, Djim Bohluh. So why must you go a-traipsing off into the unknown western mountains, eh? Not that I'm of any mind to refuse you, not with the backing of your insanity that this letter indicates you to have, I'm not."

His pale-blue eyes fixed on a point above and beyond the head of Hahfos, the older man began, "Sir, with the lord *strahteegos'* permission, Bohluh, Djim, has—"

He ceased to speak suddenly, as the seated man began to laugh. "Oh, knock it all off, Djim. I'm no longer a *strahteegos* and you're no longer a sergeant. Pull up that chair yonder, help yourself to the ale or the wine and let's discuss this like the civilians we both now are. There, that's much better."

Hahfos poured himself a measure of wine and indicated that his guest should do likewise. The cups were large, of massive, chiseled silver and decorated with the golden bear that was become Hahfos' personal ensign as well as that of this new sept of Clan Djohnz.

"Djim Bohluh sits because the lord *strah* . . . ahh, *ahrkeethoheeks* requests it. If it pleasures him, fine . . . but it still ain't right and fittin' fer a common man to sit and drink and all with a noble off'ser, and Djim Bohluh knows it, sir."

Again, Hahfos' easy laugh rang out. "Djim, Djim, times have changed, but I guess that in your stubborn, loyal old heart you never will, and I can't but respect you for it.

"But look you, man. You are come to me as the official

57

emissary of the *tahneestos* and acting *thoheeks* of a Kindred Clan. Your letter of introduction—as if a letter to introduce you to me were needed, hah!—is signed by the High Lord Milo himself, not to mention a prince, two *ahrkeethoheeksee*, five *thoheeksee* and a number I've not yet counted of *komeesee*, *vahrohnoee*, *vahrohneeskoee* and city-lords.

"Your second letter, this Confederation-wide safe-conduct, is signed by both the High Lord Milo *and* the High Lady Aldora Linszee Treeah-Pohtohmas Pahpahs. Djim, you have powerful friends in the very highest of places, nor are you exactly a mendicant beggar. Your letter of credit from the Confederation treasury contains no limit as to amount, nor do you seem to be at all impoverished in your own right. That sword, for instance, it's an Yvuhz, isn't it? Prince-grade, perhaps?"

The older man shrugged. "No, my lord, duke-grade."

"What?" said Hahfos sarcastically. "*Only duke-grade? Shameful!*" Then in his normal tone, "Even with the sizable pension for your Golden Cat, you'd have to live on air for a good five years to save enough to buy a sword like that."

"But I . . . but Djim Bohluh dint buy the sword, my lord."

In mock horror, Hahfos asked, "You *stole*, Djim? A good, honest, honorably retired veteran of the Confederation Army stole?"

Old Djim forgot himself long enough to show worn yellow teeth in a sly grin. "Near enough as, my lord. I won the dirk and the sword, too, off the captain of the bodyguards of the ambassador of the King of Pitzburk, up to Kehnooryos Atheenahs."

Hahfos, too, grinned. "Two dice or five, Djim?"

"Five . . . and my old dicecup," the oldster replied.

"And beautifully, unnoticeably tapered, without a doubt," laughed Hahfos. "The old army game, played by a past master. Didn't the poor barbarian bastard even suspect he'd been had?"

"Not until that next mornin'," answered Bohluh. "Summa his frin', they come up t' me and 'lowed as how I hadda give back his thangs or faht him. So I fit him, down to the guards barricks, thet aftuhnoon. He won' worth a damn with a shortsword and a army shield, but the bugger had guts, put up a dang good fight, he did."

"Did you kill him, Djim?" inquired Hahfos, as the old man paused to wet his throat from the contents of his silver cup.

"No sir, my lord, jes' smashed his kneecap and mashed in his nose and all, both of 'em with the shield, too, never evun laid the shortsword to any part of him won't armored, I dint."

"I assume, to have been an officer of the ambassador's guards, this man must have been a nobleman of the Middle Kingdoms. So what was the upshot of your crippling him, Djim?''

"Wal, my lord, sir, the ambassador'd been watchin' I come to fin' out. Raht then and there, he offered fer to hire me to go up nawth to Pitzburk and teach shieldwork to his king's whole dang army. I tol' him I'd have to thank on it, but I couldn' do it nohow til aftuh I done a job fer the High Lord and High Lady. He gimme this here ring and said whenever I wuz to come to Pitzburk, to give it to enybody at the palace and ast fer Archduke Brytuhn.''

Hahfos whistled softly. "Sun and Wind, man, that's the king's half brother. As I said earlier, you have powerful friends in high places." He paused, then asked, "He knighted you, too, didn't he, Djim?"

The broad, beefy old man flushed. "Don' mean diddly, my lord, sir, not in the Confederation, it don't. 'Sides, it ain' like I *earned* it or nuthin', like I done fer to git my Cat.''

"Oh, but it does mean something, Sir Djim Bohluh," said Hahfos gently. "It means a great deal. As for earning it, the archduke obviously felt you deserved it for a notable combat. And I'm more than certain that you earned that and more many times, when there was no officer surviving to bear witness, over the forty-odd years you soldiered in our army. Djim, even in officer circles, you were a living legend; you'd have been an officer yourself, had you not been such a boozing, brawling, profane, insubordinate rakehell, when in garrison. But that's all years agone, Sir Djim, I'm no longer an officer of that army and you're no longer a sergeant. However, I'll issue you this one, last command: start wearing that order, today, now! It may not mean much to you, yet, but it will mean a great deal to the only disciplined troops I can just now let you have to take west with you. They're all Freefighters from the Middle Kingdoms, one and all, and I've no slightest doubt but that they'll be happier following the banner . . . you do have a banner? Well, never you mind, you'll have one before you leave here; these Ahrmehnee women are marvelously skilled at all manner of embroidery.

"Anyhow, these Freefighters would rather be led by a Knight of the Black Bull of Pitzburk than by anyone else present in this area, I'll wager. There are a hundred and ninety-two of them— all dragoons, well mounted, well armed, good soldiers, as their type goes. Of course, you'll need guides, translators, and it just so happens that I can help you there, too.

"You'll dine at my home tonight, and I'll there introduce you to Freefighter Captain Guhntuh and a couple of Ahrmehnee warriors I think you'll like. Oh, and Sir Djim, be sure to wear that ring and your order, eh?''

When the Ahrmehnee messenger, a Taishyuhn tribesman, had departed Sir Geros Lahvoheetos' house-cum-headquarters to dine with Soormehlyuhn distant-cousins, the young knight drained off his jack of brandy-water and, while absently refilling it from the ewer, remarked, "A Knight of the Order of the Black Bull of Pitzburk, that Ahrmehnee said, Pawl. On his way down here with nearly tenscore Freefighters, three more Moon Maidens and more than threescore Ahrmehnee warriors he's paid the rent on from a couple of the *dehrehbeh.*

"I could understand it if it were old *Komees* Hari or even the High Lord sending us reinforcements, but what the hell is a nobleman of Pitzburk doing down here?"

"Sir Geros, lad," replied the gray-haired, fiftyish Freefighter officer, "Duke Bili's dam, you must remember, is a daughter of the Duke of Zuhnburk. That means that he has relatives of varying degrees of kinship all over the Middle Kingdoms. No doubt some of the returning Freefighters took word of his disappearance in these mountains up to Pitzburk, and this is the response of some cousin or other . . . and he must be a well-heeled cousin, son Geros, for you know these Ahrmehnee don't rent their fighters cheap."

"But, damn it all!" swore Sir Geros, "We could have marched tomorrow . . . or the day after, anyway. Why in hell must we wait another fortnight or more for this damned Pitzburker?"

Captain Pawl Raikuh took his own jack down from his lips and said, matter-of-factly, "Because the addition of him and his force will give you something on the order of six hundred swords at your back, that's why; this Pitzburker comes well dowered indeed, Sir Geros. I say that despite the fact that I'm a native Harzburker, and as is well known, we Harzburkers own damn-all love for any shoat out of the Pitzburk sty."

He sighed, then, cracking his prominent knuckles loudly, added, "All the same, I'll feel considerably better to be riding off into those mountains and into the lap of Steel knows how many more Ganiks in the company of six hundred rather than a mere four hundred fighters, Pitzburkers or no.

"Yes, Sir Geros, you'd be well advised, I think, to wait for this Black Bull knight . . . for a moon, if necessary."

Captain Djeri Guhntuh had grown old in professional soldiering—which was adequate statement of his luck, survival instincts and combat skills. He was well over fifty years of age, only some ten years younger, truth to tell, than was Sir Djim Bohluh. Unlike most Freefighter officers, he was not noble-born, though years of command under, with and over born nobility had rubbed a certain amount of polish onto his bearing and manner. He was quite simply a born leader of men and a well-proven combat commander; soldiers all followed him or heeded him automatically. The same was true of old Sir Djim, and the two men recognized their mutual and close similarities on first meeting. Before they finally rode forth from the principal village of the Taishyuhn Tribe and headed southwest, they were become fast friends and they shared command with a natural ease.

As they wound their way through the territories of the various tribes which constituted this southern branch of the Ahrmehnee *stahn,* their native contingent grew, apace, as the Ahrmehnee-wise march warden, Hahfos, had bade them expect. The messenger sent ahead to Sir Geros Lahvoheetos—thought to still be bivouacked in Behdrozyuhn lands with his own force of Freefighters and Moon Maidens—had alerted any Ahrmehnee warriors with itchy feet or a need for hard money that a low-lander with a need for fighters and the wherewithal to pay their hire was coming.

At nearly every sizable village there would be a contingent of them, swarthy, big-boned men in exquisitely fashioned coats of mail and open-faced steel helmets with cheek guards and segmented nape guards of hardened leather. To Sir Djim and his Freefighters they seemed all alike—big noses and black eyes, slashing swords and cursive daggers, spears and small, round, hammered-bronze bucklers, the leathern cases of darts and throwing sticks finely tooled and richly decorated, like the saddles on their big, bred-up mountain ponies, sleeping robes rolled and tied on the crupper, warbag and an occasional cookpot hung from the near side of the pommel, axe from the off side.

As the numbers of Ahrmehnee warriors began to seriously outnumber the company of Freefighters, Captain Djeri Guhntuh began to privately question the worth of so many irregulars and openly doubt the feasibility of hiring on more of the same.

But Sir Djim Bohluh welcomed—most cordially welcomed, indeed—every Ahrmehnee tribesman he could sign on. In the more than forty years he had soldiered with the Army of the Confederation, he had heard of and seen men just like these hike the very best regulars into the ground, then suddenly turn and beat those same finely equipped, well-led regulars to a frazzled standstill. Whole battalions—and at least one entire reinforced regiment—of Confederation infantry had marched into the Ahrmehnee lands in hot pursuit of raiders to never again be seen, to disappear completely, and assignments to the always-under-strength garrisons of forts along the borders of Ahrmehnee lands had been, in Sir Djim's soldiering days, considered to be a virtual death sentence by the rank and file of the Confederation Army.

Nor was there any need to carry load on packload of beans and grain for the mounts of these irregulars, as there was for the warhorses of Captain Guhntuh's Freefighter dragoons. The mountain-bred ponies were quite capable of staying in good flesh off nothing more than grass, rougher herbiage, even tree bark, if necessary. That these ponies' riders, too, expected to live off the land was attested by the small amounts of rations they brought with them, nor did Sir Djim doubt that they could do just that.

But Bohluh was nothing if not shrewd; he let it be widely known that he agreed with Captain Guhntuh, but allowed himself to be "persuaded" by the leader of his original force of Ahrmehnee, one Bahndahr Taishyuhn, to hire on any tribesmen passed upon by that worthy—a fortyish man with the scars of a veteran and the look and bearing of a natural killer. And so when at last he and his force approached the unmarked border of Behdrozyuhn lands, he lacked the numbers of warm bodies he might have led, but he felt assured that all or most of those he did lead were of better than average quality. He had ridden out of Taishyuhn lands with about two hundred and fifty effectives; he would join Sir Geros with nearly five hundred.

Brigadier Sir Ahrthur Maklarin still felt as if he had been ridden over, trampled by an entire brigade of heavy cavalry. Each and every necessary movement still brought a choked groan or a snarled curse from betwixt his swollen lips. On the left side of his head, just behind and above the ear, was a hard knot the size of a turkey egg. That New Kuhmbuhluhn bastard had smashed the boss of his buckler so hard into the brigadier's face that it had actually bent the cold-hammered steel of the visor, breaking the old officer's nose, mashing his lips until they split and spouted blood, loosening all of his front teeth and chipping four of them and all but breaking his jaws. While he had just lain there, half stunned, the dirty by-blow had kicked him in the head—the old man recalled that, clearly. And to add insult to injury, some issue of unspeakable filth had stolen his fine sword, which blade had been his father's, before him.

He had been found by the regiment sent into the gap left by the virtual extirpation of Colonel Bruce Farr's regiment. A litter had been quickly fetched and he had been carefully borne up to his pavilion and the staff surgeon summoned. That worthy had speedily ascertained that, although his patient was one mass of bruises and contusions, scrapes and the occasional cut or split in the skin from crown to soles, a broken nose, loose teeth and three fingers that might or might not be broken were the worst of the old man's injuries. He left him in the care of his staff and aides and hurried back to the scores of seriously wounded men who awaited him.

Well knowing his superior's nature, Senior Colonel Sir Djaimz, immediately it was clear that the New Kuhmbuhluhn force was truly withdrawing from the field, had come to the brigadier and, when he found him both conscious and rational, had sketched the calamitous events of the day.

To all intents and purposes, one entire regiment of pikes—Colonel Farr's—had ceased to exist. The colonel himself was gravely wounded, and it would be long before he took the field again, if ever he did. The two regiments which had flanked Farr's—Taylor's and Gambel's—had been so badly mauled as both to be down to about half the effectives listed before the battle. The regiments to the west of the stricken three had all taken heavier than usual losses, most of them from a variety of small throwing axe identical to those which had exacted similar losses in the autumn battle of the year past.

There had been few if any missiles employed by the other two attacking forces, both of which had been easily held off by the pike lines and severely bled as they had attempted to hack through by main strength. But those who had thrown the deadly little axes had never closed in any strength until a way for them had been cleared by those who had come in afoot.

Unable to then speak clearly or without much pain, the brigadier had thought to himself, "Humph, well, our herald's cozening didn't work on all of them, obviously. Hope the canny bastard who led those axe throwers was killed. Wonder if he's the same fucker who chewed us up so badly last year? Speak of last year, have to talk to our prisoners from last year again, too, along with those from this set-to . . . if we captured any, that is. Far more men attacked us than I'd thought they'd be able to scratch up.

"And as for prisoners, what about that strange, dark woman and her band of scruffy scum we captured in our glen? *Rifles!* Our Skohshun legends speak of them or something similar—they used to be common, apparently, in our lost homeland. God in Heaven, if I had enough of them I could go through this land like a hot knife through butter! But she doesn't know how to make them . . . or, at least, she *claims* she doesn't, nor even how to make the charges and projectiles for them. She does say that she could lead us to where a fair number of the rifles are buried, but from the maps she drew up, we'd have to go directly through the very heart of New Kuhmbuhluhn to get there.''

Sir Djaimz continued his report. ''All save three of the short-hafts from Colonel Pease's regiment are dead or seriously wounded, but with the exceptions of Farr's, Taylor's and Gambel's sergeants, no other shorts were lost.

''However, the loss of officers was exceptionally high. Colonels Farr and Taylor are wounded, Colonel Gambel is dead. A total of seven other officers are fit for duty from the entire before-battle complement of those three regiments. Five of the six staff officers who rode with you down to the rear areas are dead. Lieutenant Bryson is wounded; so too is Ensign Grey. I'd sent the lad down to find you. Instead, he apparently essayed to stop the New Kuhmbuhluhn horsemen headed for Gambel's regiment, single-handedly; the surgeon had to take off one of his legs at the knee, but he thinks he'll live.''

''Poor valiant little bugger,'' thought the old man, then, ''Oh, Jesus, Lady Pamela, his mother, will ream me out a new arsehole for this! Fine piece of female flesh, there, that woman . . . if only I were twenty years younger . . . ten, even . . .? But she'll not stay widowed long, if I'm any judge of these matters. Now young Tom can be honorably retired into the reserve and get to work siring a new generation of Greys on some likely chit.''

After a brief but noticeable pause, Senior Colonel Sir Djaimz said gravely, ''Although not in the same way, thank God, we have been flanked, taken in the rear, before—several times within my memory and probably many more than that in your own, sir—but our losses have never been this heavy before, mostly for the reason that the short-haftmen were there to do their principal task, that of defending the otherwise highly vulnerable rear and flanks of the pike lines for a sufficient time for men to ground pikes, turn about and form a hedge of two fronts or a porcupine, whichever seemed best at that time and place.

''Now, sir, while I am not necessarily saying that that would have worked in this case, not against a mixed force of both heavy horse and light horse plus a contingent of heavy-armed foot, I do state categorically that our chances to avoid such a bloodletting as our arms have this day experienced would have been far better had we had our shorts in the proper place when they were needed.''

"You'll rise high, my boy," thought the brigadier, "either in rank or by your neck from the end of a rope. You know damned well just who, just which noble arsehole, is directly culpable for this calamity, know as well as do I.

"It's really my fault, though. I should've foreseen something like this happening under the circumstances. I knew that that damned Potter was displeased with the alignments, and I knew he is a cousin of the earl, and I knew that the earl—unlike his old father, God rest his soul—does dote on playing at war captain, when he finds or makes himself the opportunity.

"So, it's going to be entirely up to me to gingerly chew our esteemed leader out for his tragic folly, this time. Sir Djaimz here obviously wouldn't dare do so; he has too much to lose to chance incurring the earl's disfavor. At least my place is secure.

"But I'll put that particular chore off until I can speak clearly and precisely—there must be no misunderstanding of aught I say to him.

"Well, I suppose that the next, logical step is going to be to march on New Kuhmbuhluhnburk itself, and call on it to surrender . . . not that I think the fiesty bastards will, mind you. No, I'd wager we end up besieging them there . . . unless the place is weak enough to fall by storm, which I doubt on general principles. Odd, that no scout of ours has ever been able to get an actual sight of that city and come back to us with the tale. Even our herald was not allowed close enough to give us any idea of the defenses of the place. But I must plan to act on the assumption that New Kuhmbuhluhnburk is at the very least defensible and well garrisoned and, being a mountain city, probably has sources of unpollutable water inside the walls, as well.

"And so, Ahrthur Maklarin, that leaves two options: entrench and throw zigzags close enough to tunnel and undermine a likely stretch of wall, or simply hunker down on the spot and try to starve the buggers out, if we can't find a traitor or two to open a stray gate to us of a dark night.

"From last year's crop of prisoners and from those we captured when we took our glen, I get an impression that out from the foot of the capital there spreads a long, wide and exceptionally rich plain. Conceivably, we could live well off their own lands while besieging their city. But as we've here learned to our sorrow, not all of these New Kuhmbuhluhners think or act alike. There's a wide streak of shrewd canniness runs through some of the leaders, so no doubt but our folk up in the north will be on short rations, are our men on the siege lines to be fed for however long it takes to achieve a capitulation. But it can and must be done. Our folk are tough, accustomed to privation, and they and their forefathers before them have done the like before to support a field army. They will not conceivably stick at doing it all again, not to gain a prize so rich as these lands, this Kingdom of New Kuhmbuhluhn.''

The Skohshun army stayed in place, remained in the camps they had come to call Twin Hills for long and long after the disastrous battle. The seriously wounded, if they lived through it, were wagoned back to what they called Skohshun Glen and the wagons returned with foodstuffs, beer and other necessities of field life.

Long before he could even sit up straight without blinding pain, the brigadier had reassumed his command. The young Earl Devernee had taken his oral birching with far better grace than Sir Ahrthur had foreseen. Apparently he had been shaken to his innermost core of being by the sanguineous results of his intemperate decisions of that morning before the battle. This fact cheered the battered old man mightily, for he had much yet to do and he had not relished the thought of an ongoing feud with his nominal superior whilst he went about his necessary tasks with the army.

Of the three, lonely prisoners—all wounded—taken in the aftermath of the battle, two were New Kuhmbuhluhn nobles, and they gave him precious little information he had not had ere this. The third, once stripped of armor, proved to be a dark and lovely *woman;* but she could not or, more likely thought the brigadier, would not speak any comprehensible tongue. Her racial similarity to the woman prisoner up in the glen struck him early on, so he suddenly decided to have all of the prisoners brought down to the camps, thinking that he might well find a use for them between here and New Kuhmbuhluhnburk.

As regarded the army, there was no rebuilding of Colonel Farr's regiment possible, not without stripping the last reserve pikeman from the glen, nor could all the vacant places in the ranks of the other two regiments be filled in. Therefore, he had Farr's regimental banner sent back in the same wagon that bore the wounded officer himself; it and he would become a part of the reserve establishment until/when/if there were enough trained bodies to again fill that unit out.

The few pikemen and shorts left of the "disbanded" unit were parceled out as replacement fillers where needed. As for the remnants of the regiment of the late Colonel Gambel, the brigadier retired that banner, too, and merged the survivors with the regiment of Colonel Taylor. It seemed to him the quickest and simplest answer to the problem, and he was itchy to get the army reorganized and on the march toward New Kuhmbuhluhnburk before the foemen had the time and the leisure to concoct any unpleasant surprises for him and his.

His mounted messengers kept the roads and trails dusty between Twin Hills Camps and the captured glen, while his messages kept the glen and a large number of its inhabitants as busy as so many ants. But the Skohshuns were familiar with this kind of activity. Almost every war season within living memory it had been the same drudgery of preparing their men for war and providing for them whilst they campaigned; the only activities held of more worth were those of agriculture and animal husbandry, and even these were closely related, of course, to the welfare of the troops in the field.

Unsatisfied with reports from various of his subordinates, the brigadier himself took the time to interview, to debrief first the commander, then several of the officers and other ranks of the dragoons who had trailed the defeated army of New Kuhmbuhluhn all the way to the capital. But to a man their observations of the city and its environs made no sense, had little similarity one to the other, yet these men all were trained, experienced scouts.

The brigadier found the whole business to be most unsettling, but he moved on to other affairs, rationalizing that he and all the rest would be there to see the city and countryside soon enough.

When Dr. Schiepficker had completed his oral report and surrendered the microphone to Corbett, the officer said, "If you're not sitting down, David, I strongly advise that you do so, now."

"*Erica* . . .?" came the hoarse, hesitant whisper. "She . . . she's . . . you've found her . . . her . . .?"

"It would seem, from what a Ganik that Johnny Skinhead brought in had to say, that up to about a month ago, she was alive and the captive of some group or tribe calling themselves Skohshuns. Their lands are well up to the north and the west of here, somewhere close to the south bank of the Ohio River, I'd say, on the basis of current information. Apparently, they are newcomers to these mountains, invading—migrating, really—from north of the river. Instead of relying on cavalry as do most groups hereabouts, they seem to have developed truly effective infantry, along the general lines of the Swiss or German *Landesknechten* and—"

"Dammit, Jay," fumed Sternheimer impatiently, "the very

last thing I want to hear right now is your assessment of their culture, military or otherwise. The one, the only thing I want you to tell me is when you are going to move to rescue poor Erica.''

Corbett sighed. "David, which is the most important thing to you, to us, to the Center, just now—salvaging our loot from the Hold of the Moon Maidens or marching off God alone knows how far into completely unknown country on a mission which already may be pointless? If it's the former, which of my Broomtown officers should I leave in charge of the salvage operation while I take a reinforced company north? If it's the latter, what would you suggest be the provisions made for Dr. Schiepficker and the other civilians while the rest of us go charging to the supposed rescue with the entire battalion?''

"Oh, God damn you, Jay Corbett!" Sternheimer snarled with intense feeling. "Of all people, you know how I feel about Erica. You also know how important, how very vital that salvage mission is to us at the Center, and I—

"Wait! I've got the solution. Why not leave Dr. Schiepficker in charge?''

Corbett sighed once more. "David, David, Mike Schiepficker is a gifted zoologist, he's even a decent rifle shot, but I doubt if he could easily tell the difference between a blasting cap and an increment charge. Whoever remains in charge,-in my place up here, must have a good grounding in explosives and blasting, along with a military background and the ability to command. And, David, I can think of but one man down there who meets the explosives qualifications.

"If you want me to go north after Erica, put Dr. Braun's mind into a decent body and get him and Colonel MacBride from Broomtown up here to me, yesterday. The sooner they are here with us, the sooner I can leave with a special force. You'd better lay on the biggest copter for the job, too, as I'm going to be wanting MacBride to bring along some additional weapons and equipment.''

"No," Sternheimer began petulantly. "I don't think Harry Braun should—''

Corbett cut him off brusquely. "David, I don't think you understood me. Those are my terms; they are nonnegotiable. This is not a mission I really want to undertake, you see. I'm doing it for you, as a personal—a very, very personal—favor. I'd much rather complete this project, here, before undertaking anything else, and unless you immediately meet my conditions,

I'll do just that.'' He paused, then added, ''Do I make myself clear, this time around, David?''

Now it was Center Director Sternheimer who sighed. ''Yes, Jay, your meaning is quite clear. I'll set things in motion, down here. You can make arrangements with Broomtown Base. Out.''

# CHAPTER VI

After the good laugh they all had had at thoughts of the probable effects on their besiegers of Sir Yoo Folsom's explosively cathartic beer, *Thoheeks* Bili, his officers and their entourages left the palace portion of the citadel complex to stroll the full circuit of the walls of the besieged mountain city of New Kuhmbuhluhnburk, of which he was become de facto ruler, king in all save name.

The existing situation failed to please Bili in the least. He entertained no scintilla of desire for suzerainty over this isolated montane pocket kingdom, his overriding ambition being to get himself, his wife and child, and those lowlanders who had followed his banner so valiantly and so long back east into first the Ahrmehnee *stahn,* then the lands of the Confederation.

But he was become what he was become simply through unavoidable circumstances. Because his father, then-*Thoheeks* Morguhn, lay ill and hovering near to death, he had been called to return to his patrimonial lands from the court and army of the King of Harzburk, whereat he had dwelt and trained and served from his eighth through his eighteenth years. That he had ridden back to Morguhn a proven warrior, a Knight of the Order of the Blue Bear of Harzburk, was a most fortunate happenstance, for he had ridden his telepathic warhorse into the very epicenter of a social earthquake. His homeland was being ravaged by a blood-soaked rebellion ostensibly organized around and for the purposes of a long-suppressed religion practiced by the previous owners of the lands, the Ehleenee, but actually plotted and orchestrated by Witchmen, agents of an ancient evil far to the south.

After the rebellion had been bloodily put down in Morguhn, the surviving rebels all fled west into the neighboring duchy, where they completely wiped out the *Thoheeks* of Vawn and all the loyal Kindred through assassinations, treachery and, finally, blatant atrocities. Aroused noblemen and their retainers from all over the vast Confederation had then marched into Vawn with a large segment of the regular army of the Confederation and quashed the rebels there as well.

But barely was the one war over and done than yet another was of direst necessity begun. This one, too, was caused by the Witchmen. At their scarcely needed instigation, the Ahrmehnee tribes—whose ancestors had once held the lands now comprising

the western duchies and had been driven out of them and into
their present mountains by the Army of the Confederation—and
the Maidens of the Moon Goddess—fierce Amazon warriors who
were distantly related to the Ahrmehnee—were massing in previously unheard-of numbers, assembling about the village of
their chief of chiefs, the *nahkhahrah,* for a raid in force against
the already devastated western lands of the Confederation.

The Undying High Lord Milo Morai—one of the group of
near-immortal mutants who had first formed the Confederation
and now ruled it—had opted to strike the Ahrmehnee before they
could strike him and his lands. He had launched the forces at his
disposal—Confederation regulars, both horsemen and infantry,
Confederation noblemen, their retainers and the numerous
Freefighters or mercenaries many of them had hired to flesh out
the followings behind their various banners.

Bili, a natural commander and leader of men, as well as the
owner of rare and infinitely precious extrasensory gifts, had
impressed the High Lord early on in the Morguhn rebellion, and
so, despite his youth, the *Thoheeks* and Chief of Morguhn had
been entrusted the leadership of the southern tine of the fork on
which the High Lord meant to impale the always troublesome
Ahrmehnee for good and all.

Bili's force had been all cavalry, including most of the
Freefighters—all of whom practically worshiped him because,
having fostered for so long in Harzburk, he seemed more like
one of them, more like what they all innately expected a fighting
nobleman to be than did the pampered, effete-seeming, luxury-
loving Confederation nobles.

He had split his available forces into squadrons, balancing as
far as possible the numbers of well-equipped and -mounted but
often less than war-wise Confederation nobles with an equal
quantity of the hard, lean, scarred Middle Kingdoms mercenaries
whose profession was war. Then he had sent these squadrons to
reave and despoil their way north and east, through the very
heart of the richest, most densely populated of all of the Ahrmehnee
tribal areas.

And those squadrons had gone through the hills and dales and
vales and villages like the proverbial dose of salts! With few
adult males about to oppose them—most of the hale men of
fighting age being assembled in the north, ready to invade the
Confederation—the squadrons had burned and killed, raped and
robbed, butchered livestock and ruined those foodstores they had
not the pack animals to steal and bear away. They had despoiled
their gory paths about halfway to their northern goal—the village

of the *nahkhahrah*—when Bili was recipient of a telepathic order from the High Lord which halted the depredations and sent most of the force back whence they had come.

Bili had felt the long-familiar tingling and had automatically relaxed his mind to enable easier reception of the farspeak.

"Bili, our war with the Ahrmehnee is ended," the High Lord had beamed. "Get word to all your columns immediately to retire back on the Trade Road and return to Vawnpolis through the *thoheekahtohn* of Baikuh. You are to take a squadron and ride northwest. You are seeking a largish mule train which is led by three of the Witchmen . . . well, one of them is a woman. And, speaking of females, if you intercept a force of armored, horse-mounted Ahrmehnee women, do not be surprised—they are after the same quarry as are you.

"While I'd like to have at least one of the Witchfolk alive, don't you take unnecessary chances; remember all I've told you of them and their wiles and their exceedingly deadly weapons, weapons which can punch right through even the best grades of plate armor from a thousand or more yards away.

"Now the treasures they carry on their pack beasts are rightfully the property of the Ahrmehnee female warriors of whom I just told you. I understand that they are all virgins, but forgiving them that, the man who's seeking a rich wife could scarcely do better, to my way of thinking.

"And by the bye, Bili, the *brahbehrnuh*, their hereditary leader, is reputed to be a proud, handsome, long-legged creature named Rahksahnah. She is of a long-lived, vastly gifted race, and she should throw good colts and fillies, many of them. Think you on that matter, my boy.

"As for the machines and unfamiliar, long-range weapons the Witchfolk carry, I would prefer that they all be smashed, then dumped in a river or a deep lake.

"You'll be far, far west, Bili, so it's possible that you'll chance across Mehrikan-speaking barbarians called the Muhkohee. They are reputed to be sly, treacherous, savage eaters of human flesh. Even these wild Ahrmehnee fear them, lad, so beware.

"Sun and Wind keep you all, Bili, Come back first to the *nahkhahrah*'s village when you are done."

Since mindspeak—telepathy—was a rather common talent among the Kindred nobles, Bili had had scant difficulty in reining in and turning about his packs of wardogs, all save one, an all-Freefighter squadron containing no mindspeakers; to this one he sent gallopers.

Choosing only the very best of his reserve squadron—the

warriors, the best horses, the best armor and weapons for them, with a very abbreviated pack train—Bili set off in the indicated direction but on a course designed deliberately to intercept a maximum number of the retiring squadrons. From these, as he met them, he chose again the best of the best, frequently intimidating Confederation noblemen into "loaning" their better-quality harness and weapons, their finely bred, extensively trained and highly intelligent warhorses to less well equipped and mounted Freefighter officers and troopers. These actions in no way endeared him to said noblemen, but then, they would not be riding west with him, either.

They moved as fast as the limitations of horseflesh would allow and they were many days' march into the unknown far western mountains when one of the advance-scouting prairiecats found a few hundreds of Moon Maidens and Ahrmehnee warsage she imparted in the few moments before she finally died of her grievous wounds alerted Bili that his allies-to-be stood hard pressed by the barbarians called Muhkohee not far ahead.

They had increased their pace, backtracking the dead Maiden's course, and had finally ascended onto that plateau that the Ahrmehnee called the Tongue of Soormehlyuhn. There they found a few hundreds of Moon Maidens and Ahrmehnee warriors standing at bay and beset by a horde of thousands of the shaggy, stinking, ill-armed, pony-mounted Muhkohee.

After sending his archers to take up positions on the top of that cliff against which the battered defenders were ranged, Bili led his squadron of heavy horse down a steep, shaly, treacherous slope in a charge that crashed squarely into the right flank and rear of the smelly primitives. A second charge, from the other side, this one reinforced with some hundreds of mounted Moon Maidens and Ahrmehnee, along with the now-shaftless archers, utterly broke the mob of barbarians and sent them fleeing as fast as their ponies could bear them down the length of the plateau with Bili's now heterogeneous command in hot and bloody pursuit.

Then, as the exhausted men and women and cats and horses were wending a weary way back from the western edge of the plateau over which the surviving Muhkohee had escaped the gory and vengeful swords, sabers, spears and axes, Bili's extra-sensory abilities alerted him to fast-encroaching danger in time for him to see the squadron mounted and off the southern end of the Tongue of Soormehlyuhn scant minutes before a tremendous earthquake shook it into rubble.

The young *Thoheeks* of Morguhn had endeavored to keep his

command together despite the horror and terror of the natural catastrophes. But in the zigzagging race to escape the hot, crackling, intensely smoky forest fires engendered by a fall of hot ashes and superheated boulders from the skies, the group had become sundered into two or more smaller groups. When, at long last, they had left the fires behind them, Bili had found himself in alien and most likely hostile territory in company with a mixed contingent of Ahrmehnee, Freefighters, Moon Maidens and a sprinkling of fellow nobles of the Confederation, both Kindred and Ehleenee. A day later, two of the prairiecats and a trio of Ahrmehnee ponies had joined them, but that had been all, nor could he seem to make farspeak contact with any of his missing friends or relatives.

Early in the first morning of their encampment in the tiny vale they had found in the smoky dusk of the previous evening, the Silver Lady, the goddess reverenced by Ahrmehnee and Moon Maidens alike, had communicated with the leader of the Moon Maidens and given the order that—since their hold was now destroyed and all their folk dead—they were to give over many of the ways of the hold and choose and mate with the men with whom chance had thrown them. The *brahbehrnuh*, or leader, Rahksahnah, had chosen *Thoheeks* Bili.

But hardly had the two young warriors shared the first sweet embrace of their mating than Bili was warned telepathically by a prairiecat that a mixed force of horsemen and infantry was fast approaching the mouth of the vale. It was a near thing, true, but no battle took place there, and, after some discussion on various matters, Prince Byruhn had persuaded Bili to bring his force from the dangerously exposed position he occupied in the vale and partake of the safety and hospitality of one of the New Kuhmbuhluhn "safe glens," Sandee's Cot.

During the very first meeting between Prince Byruhn and Bili, both of them sitting their big warhorses in a mutually arranged and sworn Sword Cult Truce, Pah-Elmuh, the leader of those huge, hairy hominids called Kleesahks, had knelt and hailed Bili as "the Champion of the Last Battle." Some year or more later, Bili still did not fully comprehend the full import of this title, but he had become accustomed to the reverence with which both he and Rahksahnah were treated by the many Kleesahks and had likewise become accustomed to being addressed as Lord Champion by them.

Bili and his followers had originally only intended to bide at Sandee's Cot long enough for the forest fires to burn themselves out, then to ride back into the Ahrmehnee *stahn*, but Prince

Byruhn had, by most devious means, prevailed upon him and them to stay in New Kuhmbuhluhn at least long enough to help him rid his country of the despicable race of Ganiks, outlaw elements of which the lowlanders knew as the Muhkohee.

This Bili and his hard-bitten little band had done with the aid of Count Sandee and a few of his men and some score of the huge Kleesahks. They were wintering in Sandee's Cot, awaiting the spring thaw to make their way back east, when, once again, Prince Byruhn had come to call and, being this time hard pressed by the Skohshuns in the northwest, had once again set about the same devious mode of "persuading" the lowlanders to ride back to New Kuhmbuhluhn and throw their weight and warlike skill against this new foe of the kingdom.

And so they all had ridden north with the spring, and Bili had pledged his and their services to King Mahrtuhn and the House of New Kuhmbuhluhn until the Skohshuns were defeated. Now, King Mahrtuhn and his designated heir, his grandson, Prince Mahrtuhn Gilbuht, lay dead in the rock-carven crypt of the dynasty, deep within King's Rest Mountain. Poor Prince Byruhn—now King Byruhn, much against his desires and keenly aware of a hoary prophecy that Byruhn would be the name of the very last king of his dynasty—now lay comatose in his old suite in the palace, struck down through accident on the walls during the first attempted storming of them by the Skohshuns.

The prince was not and had never been a mindspeaker, but in order to protect his thoughts from those who did happen to own that gift, the Kleesahks had long ago taught him how to erect and maintain a powerful mindshield. Apparently this shield had been raised into place at the time the catapult missile, a large, heavy, round boulder, had rolled off the rear of an engine platform and fallen to strike the prince and crush his thick helmet. Now, with that impenetrable mindshield firmly locked into its accustomed position, Pah-Elmuh could not reach the stricken monarch's mind in order to instruct it how to begin repairing the brain's internal damages.

And so Prince Byruhn lay upon the great bed in his suite, administered thin broths and other liquids through a flexible tube that Pah-Elmuh had somehow contrived to get down his throat into his stomach. Byruhn could not swallow and would soon have died without that tube, but as it was, the flesh seemed to be wasting away from his big-boned frame day by day.

Three days after the tragic accident, those members of the royal council who had survived the costly battle had come to Bili, who, based upon one of King Byruhn's orders, was already commanding the garrison of the city, and implored him to serve as royal regent during the new king's recovery and convalescence. Promising them an answer in two days, Bili had discussed the weighty matter with Rahksahnah, the lieutenants of his condotta, those New Kuhmbuhluhners he had come to respect, Pal-Elmuh the Kleesahk, even, finally, with the prairiecat Whitetip; then he had summoned the councilors and informed them that only if both they and the commoners' council agreed to his tenure and his terms would he accept the regency. They had, all of them, of all stations.

Bili of Morguhn had had a part in sieges before, both in the defensive and the offensive roles, and he often thought that if defend a city he had to do, this city and citadel of New Kuhmbuhluhnburk were ideally suited and situated to make its commander's task relatively safe, easy and comfortable, while at the same time causing a maximum of discomfort, peril and frustration to the besieging forces.

Despite the vast hoards of foodstuffs for man and for beasts which he had been made aware were stored in the side of the mountain against and into which the city and the citadel were built, Bili had assembled and addressed the native Kuhmbuhluhn landholders—those still alive and active after the battle against the Skohshun pike lines—and told them all to return quickly to their lands. They were, one and all, to strip those lands of all provisions that could be easily carted or herded to the city, butchering or burning or otherwise rendering unusable everything that must perforce be left behind to the tender mercies of the encroaching Skohshuns.

He did not tell them to bury their valuables; he knew that they would do that anyway. Nor did he tell them not to bring their noncombatant dependents behind the walls of New Kuhmbuhluhnburk. He simply pointed out that no matter how well supplied, close-crowded cities under siege were most prone to breed terrible plagues against which there existed little if any protection. Most of the landholders ended by sending their families, servants, some of their retainers and large portions of their herds and flocks up into the surrounding mountains—safe and familiar to them, foreign and potentially dangerous to the Skohshuns.

When the defeated army, bearing their dead royalty and their many wounded, had passed through the gates of the burk, not a one but was certain that the Skohshuns would be under the walls within bare days; but their unanimous assessment had been off by the better part of a month, and by the time the enemy column finally appeared on the plain below the city, it had only been necessary to bring in the herds and flocks then at graze on the nearer reaches of that plain, man the barbican and slam shut the ponderous gates. All else was in complete readiness for a protracted siege.

Two months, or the best part of that amount of time, had now gone by since the arrival of the Skohshuns on the plain, and in the four major assaults essayed against the burk, not a single one of the alien soldiers had gotten farther than the stout, stone-built barbican or the verge of the gorge behind it. The attackers had managed to get all of their wounded back down the mountain each time, but they had left a plentitude of dead bodies to constantly inspire the garrison and the inhabitants of New Kuhmbuhluhnburk. Morale within the beleaguered city could not have been higher, and Duke Bili and his retinue were roundly cheered by populace and soldiers alike each time they appeared on the walls.

But, although none then knew, it was not to last.

The first good look that Brigadier Sir Ahrthur Maklarin got at the fortress-city of New Kuhmbuhluhnburk had sent his spirit nosediving into the lowest reaches of his boots. He had occasionally heard rumors and fables of impregnable cities; now, to his horror, he beheld one that surely deserved that appellation.

It was abundantly clear even from a distance that there would be no undermining of those walls of massy stone, not unless one had the fantastic ability to undermine the very mountain itself, for that city was not just built on but built into the very fabric of the mountain.

He also realized that to think of surrounding and interdicting New Kuhmbuhluhnburk was pointless in the extreme, for ten times his available force could not have adequately manned the works and trenches it would have taken to completely circumscribe the sprawling base of the mountain, and that was precisely what it would take to seal off the approaches to that city with any certainty of success in the undertaking. Therefore, he chose what appeared to be a good, level site and set his regiments to the hard work of digging a deep, broad ditch and packing up the residual earth firmly so that palisade stakes could be there implanted when enough trees from the surrounding mountain slopes had been felled and trimmed and snaked back to erect that wooden wall which would defend his encampment.

Stones—and there were all too many in the soil of the plain— were graded by size and laid aside as ammunition for the engines, whenever the engineers got around to assembling the things.

Within the perimeter of the huge camp, the first things to be set
up were the kitchens. Latrine and refuse pits quickly followed,
then horse lines, wagon parks and supply depot. Only then were
the disciplined, well-organized troops allowed to begin pitching
the camp proper.

The herald sent to demand the surrender of the burk came
back with the news that both King Mahrtuhn and his heir, Prince
Mahrtuhn Gilbuht, had fallen in the battle, and that the present
king of New Kuhmbuhluhnburk was one King Byruhn. The
herald reported that he had been well received and most lavishly
entertained by one Duke Bili of Morguhn, who seemed to be the
overall commander of the burk garrison, as well as by a number
of nobles and officers.

The brigadier had scanned the written message brought back
by the herald, cursed feelingly, then dropped the sheet and
allowed it to roll itself back up. "This King Byruhn is blunt
enough, I'll say, blunt to the point of insult." Then the old man
addressed the herald, saying, "Well, man, you've now been
closer to that pile of rock than any of the rest of us to date. Can
you give us a clearer picture of just what types and degrees of
fortifications we're up against than you could after your last
visit, last year?"

The herald, a retired officer of about the brigadier's own age,
shifted on his stool, using both hands to move his stiff leg into a
more comfortable position, then replied, "Sir Ahrthur, yon sits
an exceptionally tough-shelled nut, and it may well be that we
simply lack the strength of jaws and teeth to ever crack it. To
begin, the only road up to the place switches back twice in the
ascent, which bodes ill, you can imagine, for attacking troops
thus longer exposed to the arrows, slingstones, pitchpots and
whatnot sure to be raining from the walls onto them. Also, the
roadbed is of timber corduroy, and, despite the sand and dust
coating them, I could ascertain that the timbers are well soaked
with inflammable substances."

One of the colonels remarked depreciatingly, "Very clever,
but what do they do after they have once burned the road, eh?"

The brigadier nodded. "Yes, Colonel Potter, that particular
trap can be sprung but the once . . . but how would you like to
be on it when they chose to fire that roadway?"

Then, "Go on, Sir Djahn. What of the outer works and the
walls themselves?"

Grimacing with pain, the herald shifted his stiff leg to yet
another position, then shook his white-haired head and replied,
"Worse than the road, if possible, for us, Sir Ahrthur. The

barbican, though it looks to be hard against the gates from here, on the plain, actually is separated from walls and gates by a deep, narrow, but sheer-sided crevasse that runs along most of the front face of the burk walls. What the barbican is actually there to guard is the bridge over that crevasse, although it is really not necessary, for the span is fitted with great iron hooks at its outward end which can only be for the fastening of cables or chains to raise it."

"This crevasse," demanded the brigadier, "you say it's narrow? Well, how deep is it would you estimate, Sir Djahn?"

"The bottom is uneven, Sir Ahrthur, but I'd say that seventy feet deep would be a good average depth. And it seems to serve as a seasonal streambed, as well—there are watermarks on the sides, well up them, too.

"Now to those city walls. I can scarce credit the witness of my very own senses, Sir Ahrthur; had I not seen them close on, touched them, walked upon them, I would not believe that such walls could be built by mortal man. But they are there.

"The lower half to two-thirds of those walls are not walls at all, not laid masonry walls, rather are they the living stone of the mountain itself, left in place when the flattened-bowl shape of the city area was carved out of what once must have been a shelf on the flank of the mountain. In places, this remnant is thirty or more feet in thickness at ground level, with one- and two-story habitations carved out of its inner face.

"The upper reaches of the walls, the battlemented portions of them, are composed of worked slabs so huge as to cause one to wonder at how they ever were quarried, transported or laid into place, much less so beautifully squared, smoothed and fitted as to not need mortar or cramps to hold them in their order. The masonry battlemented wall varies from fifteen to about twenty-five feet in height and is a good twenty feet in width across the top.

"As regards towers, there are only those you can see from here—a pair flanking the gates and one at each corner, but not much higher than the burk walls, themselves, and really only raised platforms for stone-throwing engines."

The brigadier raised his bushy eyebrows and smoothed one of his drooping mustaches with a thumbnail. "What of that high tower that seems to go near to the summit of the mountain, Sir Djahn?"

"It's only a half-tower, Sir Ahrthur, built directly into the flank of the mountain itself. It was obviously built as a keep, and I would hate to have to attack a garrison in it, but the New

Kuhmbuhluhners just now are using it and the vast labyrinth of passages and chambers bored into the bulk of the mountain for magazines and stables. The crypt of their kings is in that mountain, too, which is why it is called King's Rest Mountain. That crypt is most impressive, but even more impressive is a huge, deep, spring-fed subterranean lake within that mountain that supplies all of the water needs of the city and garrison."

"And this garrison, Sir Djahn?" inquired Sir Djaimz, the senior colonel, "What are your impressions of it, as regards quantities and qualities of troops, leadership and morale?"

"The titular leader and commander is, of course, King Byruhn, Sir Djaimz. He is a huge man who towers a good foot above average height and weighs, I would say, well in excess of twenty stone, though he is a veteran warrior and owns precious little if any fat on that big-boned frame. However, he seems preoccupied with some weighty matter and devotes little time to the garrison, leaving that to his senior captain, one Duke Bili of Morguhn, a lowlander mercenary from the east."

Colonel Potter smirked. "Mercenary, hey? How much do you think he'd cost us to say . . . leave a gate open one dark night?"

Sir Djahn shrugged. "I got to know him rather well, colonel, and I doubt me he could be bought for any price, not with his word already pledged to King Byruhn."

Potter laughed. "Come, come, Sir Djahn, every mercenary has a price; for that matter, every man has a price."

The herald eyed his questioner coldly and asked, "Is it so, colonel? Then what, pray tell, is your own price?"

"Now damn your eyes, Sir Djahn!" Potter's chair crashed over as he came to his feet, his hand seeking the hilt of the sword he was not wearing just then, his features beet-red and working in rage.

The brigadier's broad, callused palm slapped the table explosively. "Damn *your* eyes, Colonel Potter! Sit down and hold your tongue. Sit down, sirrah!"

Sulkily, Potter righted his chair and resumed his seat, staring malevolently from beneath his brows at Sir Djahn, but remaining silent, as ordered.

The brigadier nodded. "Now, let us continue the debriefing, gentlemen, if you so please." He looked to Senior Colonel Sir Djaimz.

That officer asked, "All right, Sir Djahn, give us a thumbnail sketch of this Duke of Morguhn and the general command structure within the garrison of New Kuhmbuhluhnburk. How many of the nobles were disaffected by this condottiere being placed over them?''

"None, it would appear, Sir Djaimz. This Bili of Morguhn seems to be a univerally popular officer and man. As regards my impressions of him, well . . . he is above average height, though not so tall or heavily built as the king—six foot two or three, I'd venture to say, somewhere between fifteen and seventeen stone weight—a thick-bodied man, though not fat, nor in any way clumsy of movements.

"He wears the Order of the Blue Bear of Harzburk, and his accent, too, is of the Middle Kingdoms, though his duchy seems to lie in the Ehleen Confederation. How he and his condotta came to fight for New Kuhmbuhluhn, I have no idea, but it seems that this is the second year of their contract. Last year they served in the southerly reaches of the kingdom, I was told, against some primitive savages called Ganiks.''

The old brigadier nodded again. "Oh, yes, the cannibals. I've heard legends of how the ancestors of the modern-day Ohyohers drove that tribe across the river, years agone. But go on, Sir Djahn.''

"Bili of Morguhn looks quite young, but I doubt me not that that look is deceiving, for he is obviously a trained and vastly experienced warrior and leader, both in fieldwork and in siegecraft. He seems well along in the task of welding the garrison of the burk into as well-run and efficient a force as his own, small condotta.''

"Thank you, Sir Djahn,'' said Sir Djaimz. "Now, this garrison, what numbers are we facing, what are they armed with?''

"As might be expected, polearms, mostly reworked and rehafted agricultural implements from the looks of them, though some fair number are weapons made as such to begin, too. From the appearances, every able-bodied man in the city is being drilled in the use of those polearms, that or given lessons in the operation of crossbows and staff slings.''

"A citizen levy, yes, that's routine, expected, in any threatened city,'' said the brigadier. "But what of trained bands, full-time troops? How many in this condotta, eh?''

"About two hundred, Sir Ahrthur, perhaps a quarter of those either hornbow archers or expert dartmen. The royal footguards number some five score and are armed with short pikes and poleaxes. There are the New Kuhmbuhluhn nobility, of course, though not so many as I would have expected; I am told that their battle casualties were quite heavy, which you can believe or not, as you will. Two thousand horsemen could have been hidden in the warren they've made of that mountain and I'd never have known it. But it would seem that while the walls will be well manned, few of those manning them will be much experienced.''

# CHAPTER VII

Behkah, though she of course yearned to be back with her man, was of the opinion that she might have fared much worse than she had since these Skohshuns had captured her, wounded and helpless, on the battlefield. Once recovered of her hurts, she had been kept fettered and under day-and-night guard in one small tent, while the captured Kuhmbuhluhners were housed in another close by. But she had been adequately fed, visited daily by one of the surgeons and encouraged to walk under guard as much as she wished. But she had not been raped yet, or afforded any ill treatment, save by a white-haired old man who had slapped her face a few times before her act had convinced him that she did not speak any Mehrikan at all.

Nor did her fellow captives seem to have been ill used in any way, though of course she could not speak to them, not without giving away her linguistic deception.

She had heard her guards discussing the possibility of captives who had been taken earlier being brought to the encampment and housed with her and the rest, but that had not come to pass by the time the entire Skohshun army—prisoners included—took to the road and marched on New Kuhmbuhluhnburk.

As amazed as Behkah had been at the neatness and orderliness of the first encampment she had seen of these Skohshuns, she was no less amazed at how fast the encampment before the walls of New Kuhmbuhluhnburk went up. Within less than one full day, the fosse was dug out, the rampart raised and the tents pitched in serried rows, the prison tents too, near to the center of the rectangular camp.

The prison routine recommenced for her and the others, and on her walks about the bustling encampment, she often looked up at the burk, straining her eyes vainly, wondering if one of those tiny figures on the battlements of the walls was her dear Frehd, wondering if ever he thought of her or if he now mourned her as dead.

On the march and here in this new camp the Skohshuns had not borne their heavy, unwieldy, overlong pikes; rather had they been carried, in bundles of several hundred and carefully wrapped against rain or dampness, in long, narrow, stake-bed carts. Officers and pikemen alike all wore their swords and dirks, naturally, but unless going out to forage, few bore polearms of any description, she noted, though stacks of them were scattered about ready to hand when and if needed. Nor, with the exception of helmets, was armor much in evidence, again save that worn by woodcutters and foragers leaving the encampment.

After the first few days, Behkah gave over trying to keep count of the numbers of felled trees dragged across the plain and into camp by teams of horses, mules and huge plodding oxen. Once topped, tall, straight trunks were set deeply into the packed earth inside the fosse, just far enough apart to force an attacker to squeeze through sideways; short or crooked trunks were quickly rendered into faggots for the cooking or watch fires, or shaped into double-pointed stakes and set into the floor of the fosse to impede attackers.

Nor were even the smallest branches allowed to go to waste, she noted wonderingly. Of the nights, with little or no light, the skillful fingers of pikemen wove them into latticework fences to enclose the horse lines, officers' tents and latrines, even one for the area around the tents of the prisoners. They also fashioned smaller-mesh frames to hold conifer tops and tips over which to spread their cloaks or blankets. She and the other prisoners were provided with these camp beds, as well.

Then, early one morning, still another foraging party set out with their wagons, but it was not yet midday when they returned, all wreathed in happy smiles, three of the wagons creaking under, the teams groaning with the weight of, barrel after barrel of some liquid, all of which were off-loaded at the supply area.

The young surgeon, who had faithfully called each day since their capture on her and the imprisoned Kuhmbuhluhners, failed to come for almost a week, and when he finally did arrive, he looked tired and drawn with care and worry. Behkah overheard him telling the other prisoners that half or more of the camp had suddenly come down with a violent, painful and debilitating flux of the bowels. The senior surgeon, he had gone on to say, feared an onset of the dreaded camp fever and was taking such precautions as he could—insisting that all potable water be briskly boiled, among other expedients, and recommending that the other ranks be afforded extra rations of beer until new sources of water could be found, especially since the discovery of a considerable quantity of large barrels of beer hidden away by some nameless New Kuhmbuhluhner farmer had swollen the beer supply appreciably.

When they came out onto the plain before the besieged city, Dr. Erica Arenstein breathed a sigh of utter relief. She had done a goodly amount of walking and hiking in this current body before the Skohshuns had captured her and a fairish amount since, curiously exploring the glen, under guard. So the march down from the glen to the siege camp, executed as it had been at the best steady pace the draft oxen could be prevailed upon to maintain, had been little exertion to her.

But to her entourage of Ganiks, who had seldom in their adult lives walked any farther than the nearest pony or horse, the march had constituted a form of slow torture. Only when kicks and blows, cuts of stockwhips and ungentle proddings with polearms failed to elicit a response of some sort was a fallen prisoner ever grudgingly tumbled onto the load of a wagon or a wain.

Nor was the simple fact of unaccustomed exercise the only or the worst problem undergone by the Ganik bullies. All of their boots had been taken in raids or after ambushes or battles, and consequently most were more or less ill fitting. Moreover, they were all horsemen's boots, poorly suited for long-distance marching, nor had the primitive Ganiks ever used any sort of stocking or foot wrappings. Before the first day of the march was half done, their feet were become one excruciating mass of blisters, burst blisters and oozing sores. By the nightfall halt, even the strongest of the bullies were gasping, or crying out in pain at every limping pace, their lacerated feet squishing audibly in quantities of their own blood.

After she and the handful of Kuhmbuhluhn prisoners taken after the battle of the previous year had done the little of which they were capable for the suffering men—bathing their feet with a mixture of vinegar and water, then putting them to soak in such containers as were available filled with more water laced with more vinegar and some salt—Erica stalked across the camp to confront the officer commanding this column, with whom she had had some harsh words earlier in the day.

Supply and reinforcement trains were mostly commanded by a sergeant, an ensign, a lieutenant, perhaps larger or more important ones by as much as a captain, but Colonel Potter was a colonel and a regimental commander, as well as a blood relation of the earl. The soldier gossip was that his present assignment was a form of punishment for some misdeed or other. Erica could well believe that rumor, for from her first meeting with the pompous, bandy-legged little officer, she had found him possessed of all the charm and human warmth of a bull alligator combined with the patience of a rattlesnake with a toothache.

This dusk, she found him dining with the only other two

officers in this column, a junior surgeon—his rank roughly the equivalent of a captain—from the glen reserves, and the boy ensign "commanding" the three hundred reserve pikemen being marched up to fill out the ranks.

An orderly at first halted Erica, but a snarled word and a wave of one of Potter's greasy hands saw her passed to stop before his improvised dining table. There was a wicker-covered demijohn beside the colonel's stool, and his ill-coordinated movements and slightly slurred speech told the woman what that demijohn likely contained.

"Well," he smiled coldly, "gentlemen, we are honored with a visit from our female-sawbones prisoner, with her overbig mouth and her loose, flapping tongue."

Then, to Erica, "What sort of outrageous demands and stipulations did you come to present me this time, woman? Chilled wine and rare roast beef, is it? Or perhaps feather beds for you and your unsavory crew for the night?" He laughed humorlessly, but Erica noticed that neither of the other two officers joined him—the teenaged ensign industriously applied all of his efforts and attention to his dish of boiled pork and potatoes, while the surgeon fiddled with his cup and looked embarrassed.

"No, colonel, the rations are adequate of quality and ample of quantity," Erica answered quietly and seriously. "But I must inform you, I fear, that none of my men will be capable of marching for at least a week. So badly are their feet injured that they will certainly be too swollen in the morning for them to get into their boots."

"Oh, really? How truly dreadful," said Potter mockingly.

Realizing in advance that appeal to this sarcastic little man was pointless, Erica still felt that she must go on the record with her objections. She had told it all to Potter, alone, earlier in the past day, but now these other officers could bear witness.

"Yes, colonel, as I mentioned this midday, the boots of my men were fashioned for riding, not for extensive walking. Moreover, they are unaccustomed to marching, having spent most of their lives in a saddle. Besides, Brigadier Maklarin's message said that we were to be 'conveyed' to him, as I recall."

His narrow, pockmarked face twisted in anger, a feral gleam in his beady eyes, the colonel leaned across the table, heedless of the cup he overturned. "Can't march, hey? Can't get their poxy boots on, you say? Well, by God they can march without boots, barefoot, damn them! And any one of them not on his feet when I pass through in the morning will never need to worry about marching or anything else again, not in this life! D'you get my meaning, you insufferable sow? Conveyed, indeed! It's more than enough that a wain had to be put to carrying your ratty gear and a tent. I'm damned if I'll waste more wheeled transport on so scurvy a lot as yours!

"Now, get out of my sight and leave us to eat our dinner in peace. Female or no female, if you intrude on me again, come to me without my summons, I'll have you stripped and well striped, woman!"

Much later, well after darkness had closed about the camp, the junior surgeon appeared with two other Skohshuns outside the tent into which Erica and all the rest were crowded. One of the Skohshuns bore a lantern, and by its dim and flaring light the young man cursorily examined the feet of the Ganiks. In his wake came the third Skohshun, bearing a wooden tub from which he scooped large handsful of some strong-smelling, greasy unguent with which he liberally coated the Ganiks' feet. Then the surgeon took the lantern while the first man swathed each foot carefully in a square of clean linen cloth.

Beckoning Erica outside, the surgeon said, "Doctor, back in the glen, I never had the time to come and meet you, but I have heard much good of you, of the unsolicited medical work you did for our people, the new and most successful techniques you introduced. For this, if for no other reason, I deeply regret the shabby way in which Colonel Potter is misusing you and your followers. But, alas, nothing that I can say will in any way sway the man, now. When once we reach the siege camp, well, that will be another pot of beans.

"He . . ." The Skohshun surgeon looked about before going on in a lower-pitched, conspiratorial voice. "Three large wagons and one wain were assigned to transport all you prisoners and your effects, as well as supplies for you for the trip, to include two tents of this size and a smaller one for you alone. I know this order for fact because my own orders followed on that same sheet, all signed by the brigadier's adjutant.

"Now the proper numbers of vehicles are in this column, so I can but assume that the colonel found some other loads to fill those wagonbeds that were to convey you and the men. Whatever those loads, they're obviously something he's damned edgy over. Hell, maybe it's all whiskey, for the man's been drinking steadily all the day long, and he's still at it this night.

"But drunk or sober, Potter is no whit less dangerous, doctor. Those pikemen and that child officer will obey him blindly, will maim or kill all of you, if he says the word. That's the inbred discipline of our people and our army, for he's a colonel and his mother was a Devernee. So please do nothing to provoke Colonel Potter, I beseech you.

"I agree with you, with your prognosis. Those men will not be able to don their boots tomorrow. My assistants have gone back to the main camp, and when they return they will have a quantity of rawhides and leather lacings with which to fashion rough brogans for your followers. Tomorrow night, I'll have them bring enough woolen foot wrappings for all of your men. Their boots can be carried in the wain. But they must march, doctor, one way or the other, for now that that evil little man has publicly stated the intention, he will kill or have others kill every one of your men who is not on his feet on the road at dawn.

"But he will suffer soon enough for these misdeeds, doctor. You have the sworn word of a Devernee on that."

Then he disappeared into the surrounding darkness.

Jay Corbett found the Dr. Harry Braun who was coptered up to join him with the special weapons and his replacement military commander, Colonel MacBride, a Broomtown man of late middle age, a far cry from the arrogant elitist he once had been. The body was different, naturally, but Corbett and all the other original Center people had long since grown accustomed to seeing their colleagues in new bodies. Under the best of circumstances, they had to transfer into new, young bodies on an average of every twenty-five years.

No, it was not the new body; Braun's entire bearing and personality seemed to have altered quite perceptibly. For all of the muscular grace, the youth and radiant health of that handsome new body, Braun's eyes seemed to hold fear, terror, really, and the memory of long-drawn-out agony. His arrogance was become courtesy to the point of diffidence, and this courtesy seemed to extend to everyone, even the Broomtown men and old Johnny, whom he formerly had patronized in even his best moods.

When this new and very different Dr. Harry Braun tried to thank Corbett for persuading the vindictive David Sternheimer to release him from the torturous imprisonment in that suffering, slowly dying body, he began to weep and, in the end, could only gasp "Thank you" over and over again between shuddering sobs. Embarrassed at the display of—in his mind, unmanly— emotion, Corbett left the tent as soon as he decently could, thankful that none of his men had witnessed it, giving as excuse the many and most urgent matters to be discussed in a very circumscribed time with Colonel MacBride, which was all true enough.

Pat MacBride, at least, was unchanged, still being the same man that duty and Corbett had long ago shaped. Not too different from what his father had been, and his grandfather before, thought Corbett. Jay had trained and worked closely with all of them, as well as with still more ancient MacBrides who preceded them, for Pat was the fifth generation of MacBrides who had soldiered for Broomtown and the Center. Nor was he the last, for his eldest son, Rory, was a captain in Gumpner's regiment, two of his younger sons were sergeants and his youngest was presently in the training unit at Broomtown Base.

When he returned to his tent, it was to find the grizzled, prematurely gray officer, a cold pipe clenched between yellow teeth, studying Corbett's handwritten list of the personnel and equipment for the northbound expeditionary force which he was calling Operation Erica.

Looking up at Corbett from beneath brows still coal-black, the big-boned man asked bluntly, "Why no long- or intermediate-range transceivers, sir? Those handhelds will be useless for anything more than twenty miles away, even the new type."

Corbett shrugged and sank onto his cot, the only other place to sit in the spartanly furnished tent. "For what purpose, Pat? We're going to be burdened with a long enough mule train, as matters stand—the heavy weapons and their ammo, extra ammo for the rifles and the grenade launchers, rations, grain for the animals, medical supplies, those explosives and pyrotechnics, and so on. I just cannot see burdening another mule or two ponies with one of the big transceivers."

"But what if you get into big trouble, sir?" MacBride continued. "Admittedly, your reinforced company has the firepower of a battalion, or better, but you still could run onto more than even that could handle. You've always told officer trainees to keep at least one ace up the sleeve. Where's yours, sir?"

Corbett grinned wolfishly. "Throwing my own words back at me, eh, Pat? Well, never you worry, old friend, my aces are in place when needed, and you and this contingent down here are not one of them.

"Your orders, as I said back down the trail, are simple and direct to the point: retrieve every bit of material you can of those buried packloads, repack them and get them started south to Broomtown with a reasonable guard under command of a reliable officer of your choice, with Dr. Schiepficker as a supernumerary.

"You and the remainder of the troops are to stay up here with Harry Braun for a maximum time of three months. If I'm not back by then, I won't be, ever.

"As regards Dr. Braun, he seems a changed man, but I am disinclined to accept him at face value. Watch him carefully. If he should snap back into his bad old ways, just recall that he has no authority of any description. *You* are the sole commander of this operation in my absence. Dr. Braun's only function is that of explosives expert, aside from the fact that he and Dr. Schiepficker are expected to aid in evaluation of devices and parts for them that you get from under those rocks. If he causes you too much trouble, you'll have written authority from me to either confine him or to shoot and kill him. Okay? And don't worry about what the Council might say about it, Pat. David Sternheimer hates the doctor's guts. If you have any personal qualms, just recall how Braun cold-bloodedly murdered Cabell, last year. He was a nephew of yours, wasn't he?"

MacBride just nodded, his lips set in a grim line, a steely glint in the depths of his brown eyes.

Corbett went on, "I mentioned in passing those long, wormlike things. Well, Schiepficker's principal reason for being up here is to study them, so cooperate with him insofar as you can, without getting any men hurt or killed in the process. If he tells you he's got to have one alive, tell him where to go and precisely what to do with himself when he gets there. There is simply no way that that could be done safely. Those creatures are strong, incredibly hard to kill, and as vicious as a rabid wolf; their jaws easily lop off fingers and toes and their bite is invariably septic. Oh, and don't get any of that slimy mucus they're covered with in your eyes, either; it seems akin to the secretions of poison toads.

"Well, Pat." Corbett stood up. "You might as well have your gear brought into this tent. It's where you'll be living in my absence. My force will be moving fast and as lightly as is possible, all things considered, so a tent and a camp bed will be luxuries I can't afford. There's room enough for us both to sack in here tonight. Gumpner and the force and I'll be off at dawn."

More than a month before that morning when General Jay Corbett led his force out of the camp by the landslide, another, considerably larger mounted force had crossed the ill-defined border from the southernmost reaches of the Ahrmehnee *stahn* into the unmapped, unknown and sinister lands to the west. This column was as heterogeneous as was the condotta of Bili of Morguhn. Middle Kingdoms Freefighters rode with petty nobility of the Confederation, with fierce Ahrmehnee warriors on their bred-up mountain ponies, with Maidens of the Silver Lady in their antique-pattern armor.

The Maidens were led by a woman who had been one of the missing *brahbehrnuh*'s lieutenants, one Rehvkah, who bore the scars of the serious wounds she had taken during the great battle against the Muhkohee on the Tongue of Soormehlyuhn. The Freefighters followed two renowned officers of their own ilk, Captains Djeri Guhntuh and Pawl Raikuh, this last him who had commanded the famous Morguhn Company of Freefighters throughout the hotly fought campaigns in the duchies of Vawn and Morguhn, then into the bitter invasion of the southern portions of the Ahrmehnee *stahn*.

Because the *dehrehbeh* of the Behdrozyuhn Tribe of the Ahrmehnee had been at long last persuaded to stay at home and restore order and prosperity to his twice-invaded, twice-shattered, extensively fought-over tribal lands, those of his tribesmen who rode with this column and the several hundred Ahrmehnee warriors from other tribes had chosen several of the more experienced and famous of their number to act as the Ahrmehnee lieutenants for him who was leader of the entire column.

Two knights rode in the lead, followed closely by their bannermen and attendants, who led the sumpter mules which bore their arms and armor. They jogged along side by side, the elder forking an iron-gray gelding spotted on the rump with darker gray, the younger on a big red-bay mare. They were engaged in the very same argument that had occupied them from almost the moment they and their two units had joined at the Behdrozyuhn village nearly a week agone.

"And I says horse turds, Sir Geros!" growled the elder from the deep chest of his big-boned, thick-shouldered, rolling-muscled body. "Don't matter diddly what kinda he-cow thang thet Pitzburker hung awn me, I'm jest whut I allus was: Big Djim Bohluh, the meanest, drinkin'est, cussin'est, fightin'est, fuckin'est soljuh the Army of the Confederation evuh had an—"

"Yes, you see, Sir Djim," the younger, slenderer, flat-muscled man put in eagerly, "that's just what I mean. You are an experienced soldier, a veteran of many years with the army. You know what orders to give and just when and how to give them. Me, I needs must be watched over and prompted by Pawl Raikuh, else I often would be lost in matters of a military nature; but you, now, you would know it all. That's why I think you should be the paramount leader of this force, not I. Why can't you agree?"

"And I'll say 'er one more time, Sir Geros, suh," Sir Djim said tiredly, a touch of exasperation in his voice. "I wuz a damn good sergeant . . . when I won't drunk, I means. But I won't never no of'ser, dint never wawnt to be one, *won't* be one, now, neethuh. You say you younger nor me? Wal, the las' ten, fifteen years I's in the Reg'lars, ever dang of'ser I had ovah me was younger nor me, so you won't be gettin' no cherry, see.

"As for not knowin' whatall to say or whin to say 'er, shitfire, man, you got all you need in thet Raikuh. Of'sers don't *give* orders, mostly, Sir Geros, they tells they sergeants whatall they wawnts done and the sergeants gives the troops the friggin' orders, thet's SOP in eny dang army. If they good of'sers, they watches and listens and learns from they sergeants, thet's the way it allus been.

"You wants me to be one your sergeants, I'll do 'er, Sir Geros, and happy as a hawg in shit, but I ain't gonna take ovuh runnin' thishere hashup, and you wastin' Sacred Wind tryin' to tawk me into it."

Farther back in the column, two other men rode side by side. These two were about of an age—a bit younger than Sir Djim, but considerably older than Sir Geros. They were alike too in other ways, some easily visible, others far less so. Both were Middle Kingdoms-born—though one was base and one of noble antecedents. Both had begun their soldiering as common troopers and clawed their way to command positions in the best tradition of their violent calling. Both had had the experience of fighting through the rebellion which had begun in Morguhn and ended in Vawn, then had served in the campaign against the Ahrmehnee which had followed hard on the heels of that rebellion.

The words of old Sir Djim, often nearly shouted, had drifted back to where Raikuh and Guhntuh rode. Guhntuh shook his head, saying, "Pawl, if you have the influence you seem to have over Sir Geros, for love of Steel, ask him to lay off Sir Djim and resume his command. That old man has stated nothing less than the unadorned truth, by his lights, and no argument by Sir Geros is going to change his mind.

"Archduke Hahfos of Djohnz privily informed me that Sir Djim is at least sixty years old, possibly half a score more than that—no one save him really knows, it seems."

Raikuh grinned. "Yes, I remember that story. Whilst Bohluh was a staff NCO with the Confederation Army headquarters at Goohm, he so 'doctored' the records as to slice fifteen to twenty years off his official age. Had he not been a Golden Cat man and thus easily remembered by the Undying High Lord Milo, he'd most likely have gotten clean away with it, too, and died in the ranks of old age.''

"Well," stated Guhntuh, "I'll say this truth to anyone who wants to know it: For a man of such advanced age, he is without question the strongest, most active and supple, most personally pugnacious oldster I've ever run across. He can fence my top weapons master into the ground with almost any weapon you care to name, and can and will drink you, me or anybody else under the table. He knows curses I've never heard and can curse for a good hour without repeating himself once. While I've never seen him really fight—"

"I have," remarked Raikuh, nodding. "He was seconded to my Morguhn Company just before we stormed those undermined salients outside Vawnpolis, and for want of time to think of another posting for him, I assigned him to help to guard the then-bannerman, Sir Geros, at that time a sergeant. I recall only bits and snatches of that action, of course. After all, I was fighting, too. But my recollections of him were of cool, almost detached precision of a near-mechanical nature in his strokes and parries and thrusts with that broad, heavy shortsword, even while he used that big, wide shield to protect not himself but Sir Geros. He sustained some near-fatal hurts that day, and when he was wagoned back into the Duchy of Morguhn, I assumed I'd seen the last of him. Steel, but he must be tough, all whipcord and boiled leather!''

The other captain briefly showed an expanse of gapped, yellowed teeth. "He is that, right enough, colleague; belike the tens of thousands of gallons of spirits and ale and beer and wine he's imbibed over the years have pickled him to the consistency of campaign pork, and it takes a good man to cut a chunk of that stuff with a razor-edged poleaxe. Moreover, for a gentleman of later years, Sir Djim has got a better nose for scenting out easy women than far many a younger man. He found at least one in every Ahrmehnee village we rode through on our way down here; swived them all right and proper, too, or so I'm told. The old boar even got into one of the three Moon Maidens what rode down with us, if you can credit trooper rumors, and the way their captain, that Rehvkah, looks at him sometimes, when she figgers nobody be watching her . . . ? Well, it leads a man to wonder why is all.''

"I'd keep a locked jaw on that, were I you," warned Raikuh. "I've seen Moon Maidens fight, too, and every one of them is much younger and much faster than either you or me, friend.''

Guhntuh shrugged. "If that should ever come to pass, I'll take my chances. I fear no mannish woman, no matter how fast or young. But the rumor I mentioned is none of my business, either, true enough. But I've had damnall success with the few convalescing Maidens who were at the Taishyuhn village over the last year or so; I'd come to the conclusion that they all were man-hating lesbians.''

Raikuh's head bobbed once in the affirmative. ''Most seem of that peculiar persuasion, Djeri, but a few seem more normal. There is one of whom I can think that I *know* would tumble with Sir Geros did he but slightly crook one finger . . . but he hasn't, to date. Nor do I think he's bedded any of those hot-blooded Ahrmehnee girls who've been panting after him for so long. You know, sometimes I wonder and worry about him.''

Guhntuh grinned slyly. ''Lahvoheetos? That's Ehleen, ain't it, Pawl? You know what lotsa them Ehleenees is like. Mebbe he's just pining for a little boy's bottom?''

''I think not,'' said Raikuh in a tone that brooked no demur. ''Before he was ennobled, Sir Geros and I were as close as two brothers. Were he bent in that direction, I would've known it long ago.''

''Mayhap his passion is war, fighting, killing,'' suggested Guhntuh. ''I've known men who would rather kill, see lifeblood flow out, than eat, drink, sleep *or* screw.''

Again Raikuh shook his head. ''Not our Sir Geros. He's at the base a very gentle man. He only turned to Steel when it became obvious to him that he'd die otherwise. He was heartsick for over a week after the Ahrmehnee and the rest of us executed all those captured cannibals in that village business of which I spoke yesterday; he knew it had to be done, but he could never have done it or ordered it done.

''No, I've come to the conclusion that he's simply overshy, needs a really aggressive woman, probably. Given enough time, I'm sure he'll find himself one.''

Captain Pawl Raikuh's prescience was well known, but he rode completely unaware of just how accurate was his last sentence regarding the eventual seduction of Sir Geros Lahvoheetos.

# CHAPTER VIII

Lieutenant Kahndoot slapped right palm to left side of breast-plate smartly—a Freefighter cavalry salute long ago adopted by all members of Bili of Morguhn's condotta—as he and his inspecting entourage approached the section of wall she commanded this watch.

Many of the Moon Maidens had telepathic abilities, unknown and unutilized until their exposure to eastern mindspeakers. Kahndoot was one such, which had been one reason that Bili had wanted her as a lieutenant of the condotta.

He now mindspoke her, beaming, "All is well here, little sister?"

"Little happening up here, oversized brother," she replied silently, with a touch of equally silent humor. "But down below, the enemy are scurrying hither and yon like ants on an overturned hill. Another wagon train just arrived on the plain, along with two, maybe three hundreds of pikemen. Perhaps they mean to attack again. I hope so—things are deadly dull here."

He smiled, beaming back, "Yes, if they come again, we'll just serve them another heaping helping of what we gave them last time. We have at least as many stones as they have men for us to squash with them. This is a variety of siege warfare that I can easily live with—no fear, no hunger or thirst, no worry about mines under the walls or towers, no enemy engines that can range the city, a competent garrison, along with a loyal and uncomplaining populace. Now, if only King Byruhn were still hale and about . . ."

"He shows no improvement, then?" she beamed. "I had begun to think that Pah-Elmuh and his Kleesahks could heal anyone of any injury."

"They explained it all to me, little sister. What it all boils down to is that they cannot breach his involuntary mindshield, and therefore they cannot order his mind to begin the self-healing process, so he well may die."

"And if he does," probed Kahndoot, "you will accept the crown, brother Bili?"

"Oh, no, little sister, not me; I have lands and family and dependent folk far and far to the east. I have no designs on this cold, stony little kingdom."

"Then who, brother? It is said he is the last member of the royal house."

"I know not," Bili admitted. "I suppose it will be up to the council—what's now left of them in the wake of that stupid battle—to choose a new king. But it won't be easy, for all of the nobility are related to King Byruhn in one way or another, though all about equally distant in relationship. There will surely be a long period of anarchy in the land before a strong man finally seizes control, and I neither want to nor intend to be here to see it. Immediately these Skohshuns are scotched, it's me for home."

She sighed audibly. "Would that I might say such, brother. But we Maidens, we now have no homes, no families to which to return; for us now, one strange place is as good as another. We had hoped that here, after what Prince Byruhn had told us . . . but what good are the assurances, the promises of a dead man, or of one soon to be dead?"

Bili the Axe had no answer to that question.

Of nights when there were no other wounded to tend, when no childbirth was imminent to occupy him, Pah-Elmuh the Kleesahk took his rest in King Byruhn's chamber, trying in every way he could to reach the monarch's mind through that seemingly impenetrable mindshield, so that the huge body could have the opportunity of healing its hurts before the lack of proper food weakened it enough to die.

Near the rising of the old moon on a night, he lay supine on the pallet he had devised. After over an hour of vain mental probing of the comatose king, the hirsute humanoid was teetering upon the edge of sleep when the silent call came.

"Pah-Elmuh!" Bili's powerful mindspeak was immediately recognizable to the Kleesahk. No other pure-blood human he ever had encountered had so strong a telepathic talent. "Pah-Elmuh, it is Rahksahnah. Her waters have broken and . . . it's too early, isn't it?"

"I come, Lord Champion," Pah-Elmuh beamed. Sighing gustily, he arose from his pallet, once more examined the unconscious king, then strode toward the chamber door. He now was of a mind to regret that he had helped the Lady Rahksahnah to delude Bili as to just how far along her pregnancy was or had been at the time she insisted upon riding out to war, for this Lord Champion just now had more than enough worries cluttering his mind and this new one was pointless, needless. As he paced down the corridors in the direction of the suite of the Lord Champion, the massive Kleesahk mindcalled his two assistants.

Behind him, the soft beams of the risen moon bathed over the recumbent form of Byruhn, King of New Kuhmbuhluhn, lying like one of the carven images of his ancestors in the crypt buried in the bowels of King's Rest Mountain, only the movements of his chest as he shallowly breathed showing that a spark of life still glowed within his body.

In the chambers of the Champion, Pah-Elmuh and his Kleesahks wasted no time, shooing out all humans save only the Champion himself, and a brace of trusted, experienced palace midwives.

After resting the palm of his hairy hand briefly, lightly, on the young woman's distended abdomen, he smilingly reassured both her and Bili, mindspeaking, since such was far easier to his kind than trying to shape human speech with tongue and palate ill suited to that task.

"Nothing is amiss. The two babes simply are ready to emerge."

Bili's cornsilk eyebrows rose in the direction of his shaven scalp. "*Two* babes, Pah-Elmuh? You are certain?"

The Kleesahk kneeling beside the wide bed smiled, then beamed, "Oh, yes, Lord Champion, two babes—one male, one female, both perfectly formed, alive and healthy. They each are, of course, smaller than was your son, born last year; but, even so, as ill suited to proper childbearing as is the Lady Rahksahnah's body, as much as was her suffering last year ere I was able to come to her, I think it were better that the two babes be removed as I finally had to remove your son from her body."

Bili nodded, wordlessly, beaming, "You know best, Pah-Elmuh. What benefit needless suffering, say I?"

Once more, Erica sat with Brigadier Sir Ahrthur Maklarin. Anger, disgust and a tinge of embarrassment were mirrored on the old man's lined face as he spoke.

"Madam, you have my deepest apologies for the actions of Colonel Potter. Most reprehensible. He will suffer dearly on account of what you and Reserve Surgeon Devernee have here recounted this day. My orders to him regarding you, your men and the New Kuhmbuhluhn prisoners were explicit and written out in plain English, so it will be on his head, alone, that he chose to so flagrantly disobey them.

"The suffering he inflicted upon your men was senseless and cruel in the extreme. Moreover, there was no cause for their injuries in the first place, for he might have asked, determined that they owned inappropriate footwear and had them all issued pikemen's boots to replace their own riding boots, did he intend to march them rather than follow his original orders."

His tone became softer, then, as he gently asked, "The . . . the injury to your face—more of Colonel Potter's work?"

Erica's fingers went involuntarily to the scabbed-over cut running almost from ear to chin across her cheek. "No, not Potter," she grimly replied. "That supercilious little bastard Ensign Hollister. He was supervising the beating of one of my men who had fallen, lay already senseless on the road. This beauty mark was my punishment for objecting to that beating; the fledgling sadist did it with that riding crop he carries for a swagger stick.

"I'll tell you, Sir Ahrthur, if he hadn't had armed, grown men at his beck and call, I'd have killed the little son of a bitch right there!"

The Brigadier riffled through the stack of notes made by his adjutant during the questionings of the woman and the reserve surgeon earlier, then asked, "That was the man who was beaten to death?"

Erica Arenstein shook her dull, dirty, matted head. "No, the man they beat to death was not one of mine, Sir Ahrthur. That was one of the Kuhmbuhluhners, an older man, and from the look of him, not in the best of health to begin. No, all they did to my man was to break his upper arm and crack some ribs. But another of my men is now blind in one eye, thanks to another bite of Hollister's whip."

The brigadier sighed sadly. "What could have gotten into that boy? Beating, tormenting, maiming helpless, unarmed prisoners! That is not, has never been the Skohshun way. Were you or your men mistreated, in any way ill used whilst you all were held in the glen, up north?"

Again, she shook her head. "Not once, Sir Ahrthur, not by anyone, for all that we had killed a good number of your cavalrymen before we were captured. Aside from the facts that we were disarmed and our movements restricted, we might well have been your guests rather than your prisoners."

The old man nodded slowly. "Just so, madam, just so. I can but imagine that Potter's evil poison infected young Hollister to his detriment, for I have known many Hollisters over the years and never have I found one to be aught save a decent, honorable gentleman. Immediately you have departed, I think I must have a few serious words with the boy. Potter can wait, he's under strict arrest in his tent. He'll keep for the nonce.

"But now, madam doctor, to the reason I had in mind for having you and your men wagoned up here. These rifles of yours—how far can they cast a projectile and still kill a man with it? Understand, we Skohshuns had such weapons at one time, but that was centuries ago, at the least, and our old legends don't really impart much of a serious, military nature with regard to our ancient firearms."

Erica shrugged. "I know of kills that have been made with rifles of this type at ranges of two thousand meters. You see, Sir Ahrthur, the bullets have a small but most effective explosive charge incorporated in them. A hit almost anywhere on a human body will kill quickly from shock alone, while the chunk of flesh that would be blown out of an arm or a leg would lead to almost certain death from loss of blood. But as I have already told you, I could no more make or show you how to make these weapons and ammunition than I could flap my arms and fly. Nor are there enough rifles to arm even a squad of your troops, and I think that there's all of some hundred rounds of ammunition left for the rifles we do have."

The brigadier said dryly, "One hundred and fourteen of the longer, slenderer ones. And I take it that that man of yours I had armed, mounted, supplied and released never returned from his journey to this place wherein he might find more of the projectiles for these rifles?" At her negative headshake, he asked bluntly, "Do you think, then, that he deserted you and his mates? That he went hotfooting back to wherever you all came from?"

She replied, "No, I don't think so, Sir Ahrthur. For one thing, there's no longer any place for him to return to. The New Kuhmbuhluhners exterminated those of the Ganiks they did not or could not intimidate into moving south, out of New Kuhmbuhluhn. No, I'm more of the opinion that Bowley is dead. After all, it offered to be a very dangerous trip, especially for one lone man, no matter how well mounted and armed. He was a brave man, a very brave man, to undertake the trip at all."

"It may be as you say, the man is dead," nodded the old officer. "Then I must make such use of you and your men and rifles as the limited number of projectiles will allow. If you agree to my plans, you will no longer be prisoners, but rather my allies. Remember, we Skohshuns are at war with the very kingdom that drove out or slew your own folk."

It was on the tip of Erica's tongue to state flatly that the bestial Ganiks certainly were not her folk, thank God, but instead she asked, "What did you have in mind, Sir Ahrthur?"

The creature's eyes were of no use in the stygian dark of the labyrinthine corridors. Claws clicking on the stone pave, it followed the conmingled scents of the various twolegs—human and humanoid—that had trod these ways before it. It was weak with hunger; its long-empty stomach rumbled and growled. At last, there was a dim glow of light from far up the corridor, light . . . and an odor of fresh blood.

Softly whining in starved anticipation, the creature padded in the direction of that light, following the mouth-watering scent of the blood, only to stop in frustration bare yards from where its sensitive nose told it was the source of the delightful odor.

Not only was the way obstructed by a pair of massive metal-bound and -studded doors, but on this side of those doors stood no less than six big twolegs. Their bodies, their heads and parts of both pairs of their extremities were all sheathed in shiny metal, while their forepaws held the shafts of deadly-looking spears and poleaxes.

Snarling its disappointment, the creature finally found a way to pass these big, dangerous twolegs unseen. Within its primitive mind, it harbored but the one image: food, hot spurting blood and tender, quivering flesh to fill the gaping, demanding emptiness of its shrunken belly, to give renewed strength to its pitifully weak body and legs. Mayhap the very next twolegs it encountered . . . ?

But there seemed to be no small, weak, vulnerable twolegs anyplace the creature went, only more and more of the big, strong, metal-sheathed ones, always several of them together. It was getting desperate enough to attack even one of these, could it find a single one, alone. At last, it did find a lone twoleg and was upon the very verge of rushing in for a quick kill when the twoleg victim-to-be suddenly opened one of the movable wooden barriers, took two short steps into the dark night beyond that barrier and abruptly began to swiftly ascend a wooden device that quickly put him beyond the reach of the creature's jaws and teeth. But the barrier had not swung shut and the creature was quick to slink through the opening.

Bili of Morguhn and his entourage did not go their usual route on the morning after the birth of his twins; rather did they follow the city guardsmen through the streets to the spot whereon what was left of a body had been discovered. And there was not much of it left—the partially defleshed and tooth-gouged skull, a few vertebrae, the pelvis, the still-shod feet, a gnawed and incomplete femur and the scattered, shredded, blood-soaked clothing.

Although many guardsmen and curious citizens had tracked about the area since the grisly discovery just after dawn, some few of the presumed killer's paw prints, stamped on the smooth stone in dried blood, still were in evidence. Bili and two of his officers squatted around one of these.

"Wolf, right enough," said the young *thoheeks*. "But did ever you see wolf spoor so large? I've hunted the most of my life and I've never seen such. Why, that beast's feet are more than a hand in length!"

Freefighter Captain Fil Tyluh nodded agreement with his leader. "But how does my lord suppose the thing got over the walls, and them both lit and patrolled, then out again without someone seeing it?"

"I don't know . . . yet," said Bili grimly. "But I mean to find out, and that soon. Send a runner up to the palace and fetch back a brace of the late king's tracking hounds. We'll find out what part of the walls that damned wolf went out over, at least."

But he did not. The veteran hounds refused to track. After a brief, tentative sniff or two of the ensanguined area, they both tucked tails between legs and huddled close together, their sleek bodies trembling, hackles raised, whining in clear terror.

"What the hell kind of mongrels did you bring me?" Bili demanded of the royal hunter who had fetched the canines to the scene.

The grizzled hunter shook his head in obvious puzzlement. "M'lord Champion, Bearbiter and Bruindeath, here, they be King Mahrtuhn's favoritest bear dogs. It's many a big bear—six-hunnerd-, seven-hunnerd-pounders, too—they's held till the hunt could come up to them. Afore this here today, I'd've laid my life that they wasn't no critter in all these mountains neither one of them hounds was afeered of."

Bill shrugged his armored shoulders. "Well, take them back to their kennels. They're no good for my purposes." Then he mindcalled, "Whitetip, cat brother?"

The powerful mindspeak of the prairiecat responded. "I have just seen and mindspoken your new kittens, brother. If they had the proper amount of fur, I could possibly admire them, for they are assuredly big enough. The Lady Rahksahnah is learning, at least. This time she had only the two, but that still is better than one. Maybe next time she will throw you a respectable litter—three, four, perhaps five."

"Whitetip, a very large wolf got into the city last night and killed and ate a young woman. The hounds seem afraid to try to track the wolf from the place where it slew and ate. How is your nose this morning? I need to know just where it came across the walls."

"I come, brother," beamed the cat.

But when the monstrous feline had sniffed at the place whereon the killer had obviously lain—this fact attested by the presence of several coarse, reddish-brown hairs stuck in a thin smear of dried blood—he wrinkled his nose and beamed, "Are you certain this was done by a wolf, brother chief? It smells like no wolf I've ever scented. Like no other animal, for that matter."

"Could it have been a man, cat brother, laying false paw prints, perhaps?" In Harzburk, Bili recalled, a man had once tried to conceal a murder by dumping the body in a forest, then stamping around and about the corpse while wearing a pair of wooden-soled boots cunningly carved to resemble the feet of a bear. But that malefactor had been apprehended before he could burn the telltale boots, had confessed under torture and was then impaled in the central square of the burk.

"No, brother," the big cat demurred. "While there *is* the vague hint of man smell to it, there is mostly something else, not really twoleg, not Kleesahk at all, but not really an animal smell, either. It is simply beyond my experience."

"Well, can you at least follow it, cat brother?" asked the young commander. "Scent it to where it left the city?"

"I think I can," agreed the cat, "unless there is more than the single trail to follow."

But the prairiecat did lose the trail at a point near the palace kitchens where some scullions had recently dumped pails of inedible slops and soapy water to allow them to run out the drain that pierced the corner of the curtain wall.

Bili gazed up at the nearly nine feet of smooth wall critically. "Well, I suppose it's possible—just barely possible—that the beast, whatever it is, could have jumped that high, gotten onto the battlements. But where could it have gone from there? Nowhere, unless it has wings. That's a good hundred-foot drop, and the cliff's too sheer for anything bigger than a lizard or maybe a mouse to find purchase."

Once again, there was no answer.

The big Ganik bully, Horseface Charley, had crept into the spot earlier decided upon just before dawn. Now he lay well concealed beneath an overhang of rock, his hands, face, hair, beard and clothing all oiled, then heavily sprinkled with rock dust and streaked with soot, his rifle similarly dulled. With him in his burrow under the overhang were a skin of watered wine, a quantity of Skohshun hard bread and jerked beef, a handful of dried fruit and a plug of chewing tobacco. But aside from his rifle and forty rounds of ammunition, he had brought along only its hanger-like bayonet and his belt knife—he was not there to fight, only to kill.

The slope on which he was situated was steep and the rocks he had piled before him not only helped to conceal him and his burrow but provided a rest for the rifle that was rock-steady in every sense of that phrase. As the sun rose, those piled rocks and the overhang combined to keep the burrow relatively dim and cool for the big man who lay on his belly, the rifle stock cradled against his right shoulder, sighting up the length of the barrel at one of the armored figures standing on the battlements of the main wall some five hundred meters distant up the steep hill.

The upper part of a body clad in cuirass and open-faced helmet leaned out in the crenel between two massive merlons, apparently to shout something to someone of the garrison of the barbican, then lingered as if awaiting an answer. In the interval, Horseface Charley settled the rifle's buttplate solidly against his clavicle, pressed his bearded cheek to the dusty stock, sighted carefully and slowly squeezed the trigger. The rifle roared and slammed the butt into his shoulder with considerable force. Horseface kept his keen eyes fixed on his target while he rapidly operated the bolt of the rifle, ejecting the smoking brass case and jacking a live round into the chamber of the piece. For a long moment, it seemed that his shot might have missed, but then the distant figure disappeared from the crenel far more quickly than it had appeared, as if jerked by a hidden rope.

Horseface Charley smiled contentedly to himself, worked his wad of tobacco around into another spot and began to sight up at another target.

Bili had barely returned to his palace office when the frantic mindcall came from Lieutenant Kahndoot. "Brother, one of the engineers, here on the top of the gate tower, has been killed. There is a smallish hole over one of his eyes and it seems that his head for some reason flew into pieces inside his helmet."

Half out of the sweat-soggy canvas pourpoint, Bili worked his arms back into the sleeves and thrust his head through the neck opening, called back the serving men to help him back into the just-removed armor. Two mysterious deaths in one morning, he thought wryly, were more than he cared for.

Accompanied by Sir Yoo Folsom, Captain Fil Tyluh and two guardsmen, Bili strode the length of the west wall and was just putting foot to the stairs that would take him up onto the top of the corner tower, when Kahndoot's mindspeak came again.

"Brother, two more have been slain in the same manner as was the first. Take care when you come not to expose yourself anywhere on the front wall. Both of these others died there."

Bili briefly recounted what he had been told by Kahndoot's telepathy, then he and the other four men entered the door to the low-ceilinged tower room, squeezed their way between the piles of catapult boulders, commodious siege quivers of darts, arrows and quarrels, racks of assorted polearms, bags of slingstones, forked shafts for pushing over scaling ladders and other impedimenta, to emerge at the similar doorway that opened onto the front or south wall. At a crouching run, they crossed to the open door to the gate tower and the waiting Lieutenant Kahndoot.

After Bili had carefully examined the three still-warm corpses, he shrugged, looking up at Kahndoot and his other subordinates. "I would think that we can safely assume that this is the foul work of the Skohshuns, who clearly are up to something down there and so want us to keep our heads down, be less alert than usual. As to precisely what weapon did the actual killing, I can't say, not without delving into that mess inside those helmets, but I imagine, since no one seems to have seen a slinger, that it was a prod—one of those crossbows that throws stones or leaden pellets. Now, true, I've never heard of or seen one of them powerful enough that its projectiles were capable of striking, penetrating with such power as this, but that is not to say that such weapons don't exist, for upgrading the effect of weapons is—as all of us know—a constant, ongoing process."

He arose, wiping his hands on the thighs of his trousers. "Lieutenant Kahndoot," he said aloud for the benefit of Sir Yoo Folsom and those others present who were not mindspeakers, "alert your people to keep as close a watch as possible on all approaches without unnecessarily exposing themselves to that prod or whatever. Come nightfall, I'll send a couple of the Kleesahks down there to try to find the hiding places of whoever is picking our men off this wall.

"Now, the barbican is, of course, the most vulnerable of all our defenses. Who is the mindspeaker there, this watch?"

"There is not one there, Dook Bili," said Kahndoot, who was always much more formal orally than telepathically.

"Damn!" His big, bony fist made a sharp crack in the palm of his other hand. "All right, for now, but in future there must always be at least one easily ranged mindspeaker in that barbican, and on every other watch detail, for that matter. For all our obvious advantages, this city still could fall, you know, do we conduct a sloppy, cocksure defense of it.

"Lieutenant Kahndoot, send an order to gap the main gates enough for one man to get through them. Send a runner—a mindspeaker, with orders to stay at that post for the rest of this watch—over to the barbican. He'll be safe enough on the drawbridge; it's not exposed. He's to pass on to the barbican commander just what I've told you. Be wary, but keep low enough to not make a good target for those prod men, and at the first sign of a looming assault, mindcall me, directly."

The broad-shouldered, thick-bodied woman saluted as Bili and his entourage departed, even while her mind was instructing a telepathic Moon Maiden runner.

After a late planning session with certain of his staff and of the royal council, Bili was just drifting off into much-needed sleep when one of the Kleesahks, Oodehn, mindspoke him.

"Lord Champion, we found the spot where the man lay who slew those upon the wall yesterday. What should we do?"

Bili pondered briefly. "If it appears that he might return, Master Oodehn, erect a cairn nearby as an aiming point for our archers and engineers. I'd liefer have the bastard alive, him and his new-fangled, extra-hard-hitting weapon, but he must be put out of action are we to maintain an effective wall watch."

The mindlink was broken by the Kleesahk, but before Bili's own mind could close, there came another beaming, this one from Pah-Elmuh. "Lord Champion, it will please you to know that King Byruhn's condition seems to have improved a little. His color is better and he seems to at last be taking more benefit from the milk, wine and broths we keep forcing into his belly. But still his mind is closed to me, alas."

Once again, old Count Sandee was entertaining strange low-lander noblemen at his hall and high table. One of his daily patrols from out the safe glen of Sandee's Cot had run across this column of invaders from the east, and the leader of the patrol, Phryah the Moon Maiden, had shown herself to them after recognizing sisters she knew among their ranks. When he had heard that this strange Maiden knew the present whereabouts of *Thoheeks* Bili, the *brahbehrnuh* and the two missing Ahrmehnee headmen, Sir Geros had not been at all loath to follow her and her patrol back to Sandee's Cot.

But at the first, Count Steev Sandee had been most loath to allow so large a force of armed invaders within his safe glen and had kept the most of them camped outside the Cot, just beyond its outermost defenses. But as it became clear to him that these men and women harbored no designs upon the glen or any other possession of New Kuhmbuhluhn, he had at last allowed them all entry and lodged the most of them in the huge, commodious tower keep down by the lake, for the Cot itself had room only for the nobles and the captains.

The old Kuhmbuhluhn nobleman spoke his mind bluntly, as had ever been his wont. "Sir knights, you and your force are well come into Kuhmbuhluhn at this time. For at this very moment, our good King Mahrtuhn, his chosen successor, Prince Mahrtuhn Gilbuht, and many another brave warrior of our beleaguered little kingdom lie dead, killed in battle against the northern invaders, the Skohshuns. Our capital, New Kuhmbuhluhnburk, is straitly besieged by this alien host, and King Byruhn, but recently crowned, lies gravely wounded within the city, while its defenses are commanded by that same stark young warrior-duke whom you came to find—Bili of Morguhn, him and all those others you seek after.

"Bare days before my patrol found you all, had I been in contact with the counts of certain other safe glens in these parts of our so-threatened kingdom, that we might form up such forces as we could scrape together to ride over the mountains to try to succor New Kuhmbuhluhnburk, to so sorely hurt the Skohshuns as to break their siege . . . or die trying.

"But, stripped as we were months agone to send arms, men, horses and supplies to the north, we could have raised no more than a scant two hundred swords, and too many of those with only mountain ponies to fork. However, now, with you and your hundreds of well-armed and -mounted fighters . . . ?"

Sir Geros answered the question readily. "My lord count, since it appears that *Thoheeks* Morguhn has felt your cause against these northern invaders sufficient to freely pledge him and his to the furtherance of the Kingdom of New Kuhmbuhluhn, how can I—the most humble of his followers—do less? I and my force are your men as of this moment . . . uhh, men and women, that is."

"Me and mine, too," Sir Djim Bohluh nodded.

Within the hour, Count Sandee had sent messengers galloping to all six of the other, southerly safe glens with the glorious news of the unexpected and most fortuitous reinforcements.

Led by Skinhead Johnny Kilgore and the other Ganik, Merle Bowley, General Corbett's column marched long and hard and made good time, coming to the environs of the glen wherein

Bowley had said Erica and the rest were being held in under two weeks. Then, Corbett took over.

A rocket and two mortar bombs demolished the massive gate to the glen and toppled one of the two flanking towers. Then Corbett sent Merle Bowley in under a flag of truce, threatening to visit worse destruction upon the entire glen and every living soul within it did not Erica and her party come out forthwith and unharmed.

# CHAPTER IX

Counter Tremain swallowed as much of Horseface Charley's boastful bragging as he could stomach, then burst out, "Shitfahr, Horseface, awl you sayin' is you's up thar awl the fuckin' day and you dint kill but three of them Kuhmbuhluhn bugtits, fer shore! By Plooshuhn, I could do thet good, I swanee, and I ain' nowhars near's good with a ryfuhl as you is."

And that, thought Counter morosely, was how he now came to be making his slow, careful way up the mountain to the spot that Horseface had described to take the Ganik marksman's place on the morrow, to lie almost motionless through all the hours of daylight in a hole scooped out of the rocky soil and shoot at any Kuhmbuhluhner foolish enough after the preceding day to show his head or body as a target.

In answer to Counter's rebuttal of Horseface's braggadocio, Erica had answered calmly, "No, he only killed three, but his killing of them served the purpose for which he was there. Even from down here in the camp, we could see that very few figures were visible on the walls, towers or barbican for longer than mere fleeting instants of time after those three were downed. And that is just what the brigadier wants—fewer and less vigilant watchers in those areas.

"As for your suggestion, Counter," she had smiled, "I do think that one day at a time up there is enough for any of you. Charley has blazed the way now, so you will go up tonight and take the position for tomorrow. If anyone does offer a good target, by all means do your damnedest to hit him, of course. But I doubt if more than one will, probably early on in the day, and when once they learn you're still shooting at them, they'll doubtless do a repeat of today—staying low and out of sight as much as possible.

"As I told Charley last night, if you move as little as possible, there's no way that you can be spotted, not with that silencer-flash-hider on the rifle. When we found that rig back at the landslide, I couldn't imagine what we'd ever use it for or when, but I'm very glad now that I brought it along anyway."

"But Ehrkah," Counter had protested, not in the least relishing the thought of a day lying motionless in a hot, cramped hole under a pile of rocks, "I ain' nowhars near as good a ryfuhl shooter as ole Horseface is. Chances is, evun if I's to shoot at airy one them Kuhmbuhluhners, I ain' gonna hit 'em. Naw, Ehrkah, I thanks Horseface, he awta go back up thar t'naht, not me.''

She had shaken her head of black, glossy hair and replied, "Counter, shooting, hitting, killing the men on those walls and fortifications is unimportant, really. The thing that is of importance is to keep them down and off the higher points altogether, if possible, so it's of little moment whether you hit them or not. No, you go up tonight and come back after dark tomorrow. Then Charley can do it again.''

And so, with the woods-wise stalking ability of the outlaw Ganik he had been for most of his life, Counter Tremain was making his cautious way up the slope, flitting from rock shadow into shallow depression and back to rock shadow, himself only a shadow in the wan moonlight. For most of the way the going was merely difficult, but in places it was so precipitous as to be almost impossible—several times he had to shuck off his new pair of Skohshun pikeman's boots, sling them around his neck and use his freed toes as well as his strong fingers to seek, find and use tiny cracks and crevices and invisible ledges to negotiate an advance over and up the smooth-seeming rockfaces.

But finally he was there, in the proper area. Booted feet first, Counter slid into the long, narrow hole and, after settling himself into the most comfortable position he could manage, began to pile up reachable rocks to form a rest for the barrel of his rifle. That done and the camouflaged weapon resting in place, the Ganik bully—still panting and copiously sweating from the exertions of ascent to this spot—rolled over on his back and unslung the waterskin with intent to refresh himself.

And that was when the thick, weighty slab of rock which overlay and covered his burrow seemed to float of its own volition upward, then huge-feeling but unseen hands grasped Counter's body, jerked it out of the hole and shook it as a dog would shake a rat, until all the world and all time roared about him in a barely seen black-red roaring and consciousness departed him all in a rush.

Nature had not endowed Paget's Glen as well as she had Sandee's Cot, so it had been necessary for the long-dead men, Teenéhdjooks and Kleesahks who had designed and constructed its defenses to carve off the outer faces of many of the hills. The stone thus quarried had been utilized for the walls to span the gaps between the hills, their towers and the approach fortifications, as well as the thick, lofty main keep within the glen.

Like the ancestors of Count Sandee, those of Marques Paget had, as soon as a more comfortable habitation was built, used the tower keep as a combination armory, stables and temporary guest-housing. Even so, it was not big enough by half to house the multiracial force now led by Count Sandee and Sir Geros. So only the Middle Kingdoms Freefighters inhabited it, while the Ahrmehnee and Moon Maidens camped by preference in the wooded hills just beyond the glen's outer defenses, spending most of their time in hunting, feasting on their kills, drinking the copious quantities of beer provided by their hosts and dancing around their fires far into each night to the wild, rhythmic music that was an integral part of the heritage of their race.

They stayed a week, then took to the trails again, reinforced by the hundred or so fighters of Paget's Mark. They then rode toward the second destination in their winding, roundabout advance— the safe glen ruled over by Count Rik Nalliss. Then, stronger by some seventy warriors—many of these a bit long in the tooth, but scarred by many a hard-fought campaign and more than willing to undertake another for their new king against the alien invaders—the column angled on northwestward in the direction of the next safe glen.

But Count Nalliss' contingent was the last large one; all of the latterly joined ones were of fifty men or less, usually less. Not even these trickles were refused a place in the slowly swelling ranks, however, Count Sandee and his fellow nobles being willing to accept any Kuhmbuhluhner who could fork horse and swing steel on behalf of King Byruhn.

So as the relief column began to toil up the southerly reaches of the range separating them from northern Kuhmbuhluhn and the besieged capital, almost fourteen hundred fighters followed the massed banners along the mountain track that Duke Bili and his condotta had traversed earlier that year.

For most of the way through that range, they found it easy to subsist on the flesh of wild ponies, deer and other game, along with roots and herbs, greens and wild fruits, while still maintaining a decent rate of march. But one and all they longed to reach the plain where, they hoped, there would be something other than rock-ale—water—and fresh breads.

Although many or most of the New Kuhmbuhluhn noblemen maintained the customs and usages of their rank on the march— being cooked for, served and otherwise waited upon by servants all had brought along—the lowlanders, both noble and common, were far less formal, so the scene and conversation that took place one night was not uncommon at all.

At a spot a little apart from the Freefighters and the Ahrmehnee warriors, old Sir Djim Bohluh and Captain Djeri Guhntuh sat facing each other across a cookfire and watched a sizable hare spitted on a green stick broiling over the coals wherein several wild potatoes baked in rock-hard clay jackets. The while, they slaked their thirst with an Ahrmehnee decoction—twice-baked journey bread ground into powder, stirred into hot water and flavored with crushed, dried herbs and juniper berries—that bore as much resemblance to decent beer or ale as did the hare to suckling pig.

Sir Djim turned the spit a trifle on the forked sticks that supported it and prodded at the hot flesh with one horny forefinger, remarking, "Should be done enuf to eat 'er, soon. Mebbe the hare'll git the taste of thishere horsepiss outen my mouf. Don't them Ahrmehnees know nuthin 'bout beer-makin'?"

The Freefighter officer grimaced at the taste of the contents of his own cup and nodded. "Oh, yes, Sir Djim, the Ahrmehnee brew excellent beer, ale, too, even small quantities of mead and fruit wines. The Archduke Hahfos is of the opinion that some of their meads and herb ales will eventually become a profitable trade item with the Confederation. Perhaps so, mayhap not; I'm a simple soldier and know damnall about trade."

Djim Bohluh set aside his cup, took out his pipe and the bladder of tobacco and set about the filling of the one from the contents of the other. "Djeri, it's suthin' I been wonderin' 'bout the *ahrkeethoheeks* fer some time, naow. He's from a good fambly, a noble, Kindred fambly, but he nevuh wuz rich; mostly he lived awn his ofser's pay, whilst he's in the Confederation Army, leastways . . . plus loot and gamblin' winnin's, o' course.

"But, lo and behold, there he be up in wild Ahrmehneeland, livin' like unto a black Zahrtohguhn prince. He wears silks an' satins an' the fines' leathers an' gol' an' jewl'ry, he lives in a house thet wouldn' be outa place in the bestes' parts of Kehnooryos Atheenahs or Theesispolis, eatin' the bestes' food awf silvuh plates an' awl, with a whole friggin' pl'toon of servunts to do fer 'im."

Guhntuh raised his eyebrows quizzically. "You two seemed to be old friends, when he introduced us, Sir Djim. Did you not ask the archduke himself how he came into such wealth?"

"I did jes thet," averred Sir Djim glumly. "But whutawl he said, it dint mek no sense, not neethuh time. Fust awf, he said as how it wuz his wife's dowry. An' thet whin ever'body knows how pisspoor them Ahrmehnees be. Then he come to tell me 'nothuh time, thet awl whut he had wuz give to him by a bar!"

Guhntuh chuckled. "What the archduke told you was nothing less than the unvarnished truth, Sir Djim. Both versions. Have you, perchance, heard the tale of how he first met his wife, the Archduchess Pehroosz Djohnz of the Bahrohnyuhn Tribe?"

Old Djim grinned appreciatively. "I met 'er—she be a raht toothsome bit, noble or not, an' thet's a fine, sturdy-lookin' lil colt she's done th'owed him, too. But how he met 'er? Naw. I'd figgered the High Lord, he'd done got close with them Ahrmehnee chiefs an' got one their get to hitch up with the *Ahrkeethoheeks* to mix the blood an' cut down the chancet of a rebellion, like. Thet's usual in settlin' conquered lands."

Guhntuh shook his head and, while taking out his own pipe and tobacco, said, "No, there is nothing at all usual about the tale concerning the archduke and her ladyship.

"You were not on that campaign against the Ahrmehnee *stahn*, Sir Djim, but you surely know of it? Whilst this duke you seek now had led his force to attack the Ahrmehnee from the south and the High Lord was driving straight up toward the village of the *nahkhahrah* from the east, the High Lady Aldora was leading a cavalry onslaught down from the north, and me and my boys, we was a part of her force.

"It was no real fighting for the early part of that ride, Sir Djim, because most of the Ahrmehnee warriors was all down south in and around the place that the *nahkhahrah* lived, all getting set to attack the Confederation. So we all rode through them tribal lands like a dose of salts. We robbed, we raped, we burned whole villages, butchered every head of stock we come onto, even them we couldn't eat. Them folks we didn't kill, we drove into the hills—legal bandits, we was. I could come to like that kind of warfare a whole lot.

"But, by Steel, we plumb paid for all of it, afore it was done! One morning early, right at false dawn, when we all was camped in a big clearing, the Ahrmehnees come to hit us—it was thousands of them, Sir Djim, all warriors, all screeching and screaming and howling like wolves, they was. I won't no captain, then, you understand, I was a lieutenant of a hundred of Captain Watsuhn's Freefighter squadron. But by sunup of that day, the old captain was dead, along with all the other officers except me and more than four hundred of our six hundred troopers.

"Of course, what was left of the High Lady's force did manage to beat them screeching devils off, elst I wouldn't be here, 'cause I'd took a dart through my thigh early on and I couldn't even stand up. But we didn't do no more marching or riding or raiding for a while, I can tell you that!

"Since it was a good, dependable water source there, the High Lady had some rough fortifications put up on that same campsite and set about reorganizing, and before she was set to move on in the campaign, the word come from the High Lord that it wasn't to be no more campaign, that the Confederation was at peace with them Ahrmehnees.

"Well, the High Lady seemed damned anxious for to get to where the High Lord was, for some reason, her and that reformed rebel, Baronet Drehkos. She took a force a little bigger nor our present one—mebbe, sixteen hundreds, and including me and my company—and we rode hard till we reached the Taishyuhns' main village."

Redstone pipe packed to his critical satisfaction, the captain lit a splinter of pine in the coals and began to puff the tobacco to life, continuing to talk around the stem of yellowed bone.

"Well, us Freefighters, we went into camp on that big shelf down below the Taishyuhn village, where Fort Kogh is, you know; the High Lady, she knew that us Freefighters weren't about to put up with none of that make-work, spit-and-polish shit like the Confederation Regulars, so she kept my company and the others separate from them.

"Anyhow, her that was to become her ladyship, Pehroosz, had come a-riding in with that Ahrmehnee Witchwoman what come to marry up with the *nahkhahrah*, Kogh Taishyuhn. While every Ahrmehnee around abouts was getting things ready for the big blowout wedding feast of the *nahkhahrah*, thishere Witchwoman, she sent her ladyship out into the hills for to dig up some special roots and an old boar bear chased her up a tree and was just set to go up after her when the archduke, who was out a-hunting deers, come by.

"I hear tell it was a near thing, that day. That damn bear chewed the haft in two right behind of the blade and the archduke had to meet bruin breast to breast and put paid to him with a damn hanger. And that was a flat, big-assed bear, too, Sir Djim—I seen the skin!

"Well, just before the bear had come at her, her ladyship had dug up a real old, corroded-up strongbox from the little hollow where she was digging roots for the Witchwoman, and she brung it back with her. I hear tell the thing was dang heavy, and for good reason, because when the old lock was forced and broke, it come about that that damn box was full up to the tiptop with little bars of solid, pure gold! Every one of them weighed a little over three ounces and they was all stamped with words in some language couldn't nobody—Kindred, Ehleen, burker or

Ahrmehnee—read. Anyhow, it was near forty *pounds* of gold in that box, Sir Djim!

"Well, being the kind of man he is, the archduke first tried to turn the newfound treasure over to the High Lord, but Lord Milo opined that it was found on Ahrmehnee land, therefore it was rightly the property of the *nahkhahrah*. But old Kogh said that according to the customs of his people, whoever found things like that was owner of them, but that as the archduke had saved her ladyship from the bear, he thought that the two of them should ought to split the gold between them. Well, that's just what they done, but as his lordship had already took a shine to her ladyship, them two was married on the same day the *nahkhahrah* was.

"That might've been the end of it all, too, but Archduke Hahfos come to wonder if it might've been more than the one box of gold up there in the hills, so he went back with a bunch of men with shovels and pickaxes and all. And the very first swing of a pick hit metal, Sir Djim. Won't nobody ever know, probably, the whens and wheres and hows of it all, but it was *hundreds* of them same kinda boxes, some of them not a full foot under the ground."

"All of them full of gold?" queried Djim Bohluh.

"Aw, no," replied Guhntuh with a shake of his head. "No, lots and lots of them had nothing inside but kinds of paper with writing and funny-looking pictures and all on them. But there was more gold—some in bars, some in gold coins and a whole lot in jewelry, jewelry like you never seen afore, too. And there was boxes full of smaller boxes and bags of cut jewels, unmounted, and pearls and opals. There was boxes of silver bars and coins, too, as well as some bigger boxes plumb full of old books from more'n a thousand years ago. At least, that's what the High Lord said—he wrote back in a letter to the archduke, after he'd done boxed up all them books and papers and sent them all up to Kehnooryos Atheenahs. He said too a lots of them papers was a kind of money they used back then in place of gold and silver, that or pieces of paper that said the fellers that had it owned part of manufactories and trading companies and suchlike.

"The High Lord Milo, he went on to say that some them books had been real rare and hard to come by even way back then, and he thanked the archduke over and over for getting them all up to him."

"The *ahrkeethoheeks* kept it awl, aside from whut he sent up to Kehnooryos Atheenahs?" asked Bohluh. "No friggin' wonduh he can live like he does!"

"No such thing!" snorted Guhntuh. "I doubt me if Archduke Hahfos kept a tenth part of whatall he found, valuewise. That palace he had built and lives in now, that ain't his, Sir Djim. In time that'll be the palace of Kogh Taishyuhn and the other *nahkhahrahs* after him. Then the archduke, he'll move up to a smaller place—the House of the Golden Bear—he has up in the hills, built on the spot where he met her ladyship and kilt the bear and found the treasure buried.

"A whole lots of that treasure has gone into the Ahrmehnee *stahn*—rebuilding villages, replacing livestock, dowering gals, enlarging and modernizing the Ahrmehnee forges what make that fine, light, strong mail, not to mention improving the few roads that was there to start and building new ones place of the tracks and trails, and all of it means work and hard-money wages for every swingin' dick in the whole *stahn* who'd rather work than fight. Them few fire-eaters was left is a-ridin' with us, you know."

The officer paused long enough to rake one of the lumps of clay out from the bed of coals, crack it off the potato with a sharp rap of his knife pommel, then slice the tuber open to steam and cool enough to eat, while he continued his discourse.

"You can believe it won't none of his lordship's doing, way he's come to live and dress and eat and all, not a bit of it. It was her ladyship won him over to acting the part of the rich, powerful, respected man what he is. I was there through it all and I can tell you the archduke, he was as damned discomforted as a hog in a scaleshirt for some little time, but her ladyship got her way, like she allus does, mostly. And talk in the villages is his lordship'll be the next *nahkhahrah*, once old Kogh Taishyuhn dies."

"But the *Ahrkeethoheeks* is of a Kindred house. He's no damn Ahrmehnee," stated Djim Bohluh flatly.

Guhntuh just nodded. "Yes, but the Ahrmehnee say anybody marries a Ahrmehnee is a Ahrmehnee because of it, you see, and that means his lordship is a Bahrohnyuhn. Then, too, he was formally adopted into the Taishyuhns by the *nahkhahrah* on account of saving her ladyship by killing that bear, see? So come down to it, he's more of a Ahrmehnee than most borned Ahrmehnees, being of two tribes and all. All the *dehrehbehs* likes him, so he'll likely be the next *nahkhahrah*, for sure. Steel keep him, he's some kinda first-class gent, he is!"

"The bastard carries himself well," thought General Jay Corbett, as he sat his mule facing Earl Devernee on his horse, "for all he's clearly scared shitless of our weapons. Hell, in his place I'd be jelly-kneed, too—after all, what chance have even the best-armed, best-trained schiltron of pikemen against rifles and hand grenades, not to even mention machine guns and mortars? Few as we are, he seems to know that we could go through his glen like Sherman went through Georgia."

Aloud, he said, "Mr. Devernee, I have no designs upon you, your people or your lands; all that I want is the unharmed persons of Dr. Erica Arenstein and her party delivered to my camp. So why didn't you just bring her and them out here with you? That would have been the simplest thing to do."

Earl Devernee was indeed terrified, as Corbett had sensed, but for his people, not for himself. Sight of what the aliens' horrifying weapons of war had done to that massive gate, to those sturdy, stonework towers flanking it, in a bare eyeblink of elapsed time had sent cold sweat trickling the length of his spine, set his nape hairs all a-prickle. That sinister sight had confirmed in his mind the uselessness of trying to fight with two understrength reserve regiments of pikemen and a bare handful of light cavalrymen.

He had been of a mind to insist that the woman and her minions stay imprisoned in the glen instead of sending them on to the brigadier, and now he wished he had done just that. He would have too, had he not still felt guilty for his act of family favoritism and the bloody, expensive carnage that that act had engendered at the battle.

"You might have sent that message with a herald, sir, before you destroyed my gate and one of my towers," he said to Corbett in reply. "Even in warfare, there are certain courtesies should be observed and honored."

"Would you have delivered up those prisoners had I done as you suggest, Mr. Devernee?" demanded Corbett.

The earl shrugged. "Not immediately, probably, but the way would have been opened for some sort of negotiations. Nor would there now be dead and wounded men to care for or bury."

"The way is opened now for far more than negotiation," Jay Corbett stated with the cold grin of a winter wolf. "And if Dr. Arenstein and the others aren't in my camp, alive and well, by sunup tomorrow, Mr. Devernee, my men and I are going to come in there and take them, and if that means the killing of every fighting man you own, we'll do that too. Am I understood, Mr. Devernee?"

"Your intentions could not be more clearly stated, sir," affirmed the earl solemnly. "But if these men in evidence hereabouts are all that you number, then you might have a care, lest you and they bite off a bit more than all of you can easily chew. Besides, the prisoners are no longer in the glen."

"If you've killed them . . ." began Corbett, menacingly.

But the earl raised a hand, saying, "Please, sir, we are not brutal barbarians, but civilized folk. Whilst they bided within the glen, the woman and her men were well treated, for all that they had most cruelly ambushed first an ill-armed party of woodcutters, then a patrol of dragoons, killing and wounding many men with their deadly, firespitting weapons.

"Brigadier Ahrthur Maklarin, who commands our field army, sent for them, that they might use those selfsame weapons to aid his men in the taking of a fortress-city to the southeast of here. So I am certain that they are now no less well kept than they were here, especially so if they are truly become our allies."

But Corbett shook his head. "Frankly, Mr. Devernee, I don't believe you. I reiterate: Have them all in my camp by dawn tomorrow, or what I do and order done to your people and that glen will be solely on your head."

"But I speak the full, honest truth, sir!" the earl expostulated. "How can you be convinced? Please, sir, tell me."

Lady Pamela Grey read the short letter conveyed to her by the leader of the aliens, then looked up from it at the dark-haired, black-eyed stranger. "A well-built man," she thought. "Strong and fast, from his looks. Thick as his wrists are, he could probably cleave a man from pate to belly with that saber he wears. And he's certainly gentle-born and -bred, for his air of command is entirely too natural for him to be else. Now, if only he were friend rather than foe . . . ?"

"Sir," she said coolly, "this is assuredly Earl Devernee's mark and seal. If you wish to truly search this glen, I shall see to it that you are in no way hindered, that all buildings or enclosures are gaped open to you at your pleasure. But I should think that the fact that the earl, our hereditary leader, was willing to voluntarily place himself a hostage in your camp might convince you that he is an honorable, a just and a truthful man."

"Were I in his place," said Corbett in a tone no less cool, stiff and formal, "were I the hereditary leader of a people, I certainly would prevaricate to protect those people; I could do no less for those who depended upon me, however much such a deed might compromise my personal sense of honor, madam. I think that your Mr. Devernee and I are much alike in that and in other ways, so, yes, I do intend to search this glen . . . and not only for living bodies, but for fresh graves, as well."

But she shook her head with a swirl of dark-blond hair. "You will find nothing recognizable in any grave in this glen, not a recent one, one dug since we conquered it. Only upon the field of battle, where large numbers of corpses are involved, do we practice inhumation; in usual practice, we cremate our dead, burying the ashes in pots or small caskets."

Corbett thought fast and lied glibly. "Even so, there will be proof if you people have murdered Dr. Arenstein, for a section of bone in one of her arms had been replaced with a silver one . . . unless it is your custom to rob the dead."

Fire blazed from her blue eyes. "Sir, must I say it again that we are not barbarians? We have enlarged a natural cavern to make a common crypt, and I shall be more than pleased to show you to it; you may open every casket, unseal every pot and sift ashes to your heart's content, if that is your desire. But I state here to you the fact that that woman and all of her companions departed this glen as part of a reinforcement and supply train bound for our army nearly two months agone. If you seek her and them, you must do such beneath the walls of New Kuhm-buhluhnburk, not here."

Bili of Morguhn handled the dusty, dirty device of wood and metal gingerly, so recently having seen the evidence of its deadly capabilities. Carefully, he laid it on the floor beside his armchair and regarded the enemy captive—now weighed down with heavy fetters—before him.

At last, after a searching appraisal, he said, "You're a Ganik, aren't you? What's your name?"

Counter spat on the floor at the feet of the seated man and sneered. "Go fuck yersef, yew skinhaidid cocksuckuh, yew!"

Bili sighed. "I would have preferred to keep this simple and civil, but obviously you Ganiks have no concept of civility.

"Master Oodehn," he bespoke the Kleesahk who had captured and brought back the prisoner, "put me a rope over that beam up there, then fetter this man's wrists behind him, tie one end of the rope to the center of the connecting chain and hoist him up by it. I want his feet about my height off the floor. I learned long ago, at the court of Harzburk, how to obtain cooperation from recalcitrant prisoners."

Counter, who had over the years taken such savage delight in sadistically torturing hundreds of men, women and children, proved, however, to have a very low personal pain threshold. His feet were not a foot off the floor when he began to scream, as his own body weight began to strain the muscles and ligaments of his shoulder joints to the tearing point.

Bili mindspoke the Kleesahk to lower the captive, but only to just where his toes could take a part of his weight. Then he said grimly, "Now you know that I mean business, Ganik, and that I have no intention of enduring either stubborn silence or insult from you.

"Now, once again, what is your name? Where did you get this weapon and how does it work? How many of them do the Skohshuns have?"

When, by dint of alternate demands and threats, plus a bit of reading of the contents of the prisoner's completely nonshielded mind, Bili felt that he had all of the information that Counter Tremain could give him, he mindspoke the Kleesahk, Oodehn.

"Can you wipe any memory of all this, from capture on, from this Ganik's mind, Master Oodehn?"

The huge hominid wrinkled his hairless brows in a very human way, beaming back, "No, Lord Champion, I doubt that I can. But I am certain that Pah-Elmuh could."

Pah-Elmuh had but just withdrawn the tube from the throat of the comatose King Byruhn, after having forced a small measure of a milk-and-brandy mixture into his stomach, when Bili's mindcall reached him. After beaming an affirmative response, he carefully cleansed the unconscious monarch's beard and mustaches, drew up the sheet and blanket and the silken coverlet over the nude body against a possible night chill, then made his way toward the chamber from which Bili had called him. As the entire chamber was bathed in the soft, silver radiance of the moonlight, the Kleesahk blew out the flame of the lamp as he exited the sickroom.

# CHAPTER X

Counter Tremain started and looked warily about him, but he could discern nothing anywhere near to the rifle pit that was to be feared. Shaking his head, he muttered under his breath.

"Dadgummit! Thet climbin' musta plumb wore this ole boy out fer to put me to sleep lahk thet. Gonna hev to be some carefuler awn the way back down, too, cawse both my dang ole shoulders is sorer 'n a dang boil. Hell, I'm sore awl ovuh!"

He checked his rifle once again, made certain that a round was chambered, that the magazine was full, the safety engaged and the calibrated rear sight set properly—all the things that Erica had taught him and the other rifle-armed bullies last year, far to the southeast when they had dug the weapons out from among the clean-picked bones beneath the rockslide.

That done, Counter rolled back onto his back, took a long pull at his waterskin, then settled himself to sleep the rest of the night away. His mission did not start until sunup.

At breakfast on the morning after the capture, mindwiping and release of the Ganik, Counter Tremain, *Thoheeks* Bili was apprised by the commander of the night watch that the huge killer wolf had once more penetrated the lower city and, this time, made its way into a house to seize, kill and partially devour its human victim. There were firm paw prints in a tiny garden plot near to the house, and, moreover, a neighbor had gotten a fleeting glimpse of the beast in the bright moonlight, his testimony confirming that it was indeed a rusty-roan wolf, though by size the grandsire of all wolves—past, present and future.

Eschewing his normal wall rounds, Bili went directly to the scene of this fresh outrage, and this time he took the big prairiecat Whitetip along at the start, for all that the feline was sleepy and lethargic after a night of prowling the environs of the Skohshun camp, spooking their livestock into near hysteria and otherwise making himself useful.

In the loose, damp loam of the garden patch were two clear paw prints—one of the near forepaw, one of the near hindpaw. Bili squatted and held his broad palm over the forepaw print, with one edge at the heel of that print. He whistled softly; an arc of toe print and three of the claw marks were visible beyond the other edge of his palm.

Moreover, the prints went deep, perhaps some half-inch, and these prints were headed toward the house, not returning with a belly load of human flesh. Nor had they been imprinted after a jump from some height—these were the even tracks of a walking beast. So that meant that the skulking killer was larger still than Bili had thought from the first killing—two hundred pounds at the very least, probably more—and the questioning of the man who had caught brief sight of the departing creature confirmed this estimate.

The off-duty pikeman had arisen early, principally to determine why his goats were so restless and noisy. As he had closed the house door and strode toward the pen where the two nannies, the young buck goat and the nursing kid milled and loudly bleated, he had seen a huge shape come sidling out of the doorway of the house next door to him.

"M'lord duke," he said to Bili, "I thought t'first 'twas one them ponies t' countryfolk brought into t' city; thet's how big 'twas. 'Twas shaggy, too, like a mountain pony, but when it cumminceted to trot up t' street, 'twas for sure 'twas no pony. I thought me then of y'r worship's cat, yonder, but no cat never moved like t' beast did, none what I ever seed."

"Could it have been a bear, soldier?" queried Sir Yoo Folsom, who stood at Bili's side. "True, they're somewhat rare down on the plain, but I've hunted and slain more than a few in the mountains. A couple of them were even reddish-brown, too."

The commoner just shook his close-cropped head. "No, m' lord, not lessen bears is starting for to grow curved, bushy tails, of late, and t' trot like t' big dawgs."

Bili nodded. "No, Sir Yoo, it's a wolf, right enough. No bear ever left prints like those in that garden mold. I too have hunted both species of beast."

Then, to the pikeman, "You're the only living man, so far, who's set eyes to that wolf, soldier. You've stated that such was its size that at first you took it for a small pony. Well what would you estimate was its actual height at the withers? As tall as this prairiecat, eh?"

"Aye, m'lord duke." The man's head bobbed. "Likely a tad more'n t' cat. But not so thick in t' body or laigs. T' wolf, it ain't been eating over-good, 'twould seem. I could see near ever rib and t' humps of t' backbone, too, in places."

Once again, Whitetip was set to the scent of the strange, huge, deadly beast. The trail ran straight up the street along which the pikeman had seen the creature. The street debouched into one of the fountain squares, and the beast had apparently paused to drink at the circular stone splash basin, like any other thirsty animal. But the watches had but recently been changed, this fountain square was commonly used to form up the guard reliefs, and, because the clean-swept stone pavement did not hold scent very well to start, the coming and going and tramping about of so many men had obliterated the trail at that point, much to the chagrin of the frustrated feline.

That afternoon, at the conclusion of their dinner, Bili discussed the matter with Rahksahnah and his officers at the high table, asking, in preface, "Sir Yoo, I saw one or two wolves when we marched through the southern range, last spring, but there were none on the plain, as I recall. How common are they hereabouts?"

The Kuhmbuhluhn nobleman shrugged and gave over cracking nuts in his powerful hands to answer, "They're seldom seen in even the foothills. Each time I've hunted them, or bears, either, we had to ride up into the true mountains to find them. Now, true, my old pappy used to tell often of certain severe winters when packs come down onto the plain, even howled under and round about the walls of this very city, but Mama allus told us younguns that he'd heard them same stories from *his* pappy and just tailored them to fit, sort of, to make him some good tales to tell us of nights.

"No, Duke Bili, wild critters is smart. Us Kuhmbuhluhners has been killing off wolves and bears and treecats since first we come to this here New Kuhmbuhluhnburk. They knows it and they sure ain't going to come close enough to get a arrow or a dart or spear run into them unless they is flat starving to death . . . like that pikeman said this great big wolf looked to be."

"Precisely." Bili nodded. "But why is this one huge wolf a rack of skin and bones? Think you on that, Sir Yoo, and you other gentlemen and officers. The mountains are aswarm with deer and small game; this is not a bad winter, hereabouts, it's a fine summer—a little dry, but no real drought. And even if there is little game on the plain, the Skohshuns are grazing a goodly-sized herd of beef cattle outside their camp, and, lacking any herd dogs, there's simply no way that they could keep a smart wolf from taking a steer or a heifer or two almost at his leisure. For that matter, there are ill-guarded or utterly unguarded pens and stables of animals within these very walls, so why does a starving wolf take the time to seek out humans for his meals, eh? Riddle me that, please."

"Duke Bili?" It was Freefighter Captain Fil Tyluh who now spoke. At Bili's nod, he went on, asking, "Does my lord recall the tales of those long-ago wars that wrenched the old Middle Kingdom into the present three? How it was said that wolves fed so well and so often on battlefields and in slighted towns that they took to following armies on the march, even cutting out and pulling down stragglers or wounded soldiers? I've heard that they would completely ignore a side of fresh, bloody beef and the mule that carried it to attack and kill and eat the peasant who led that mule.

"Now there've been a spate of battles hereabouts, last year, as well as this latest one where the old king died. Mayhap some corpse-fed wolf followed us back here?"

"It's possible, Fil," Bili nodded slowly, adding, "but if such were the case, why did he wait so long to strike us?"

"Perhaps," put in Rahksahnah, "this wolf followed not our army but the enemy army, these Skohshuns, my Bili."

He shook his shaven head. "No, love, that makes no sense, either. If he followed their march, fed off them the length of it, then why does he not now do so still? After all, it were far easier for a cunning animal, such as him or Whitetip, to enter their camp of nights than this city, to reach which he must negotiate cliffs and walls.

"And, speaking of Whitetip, he knows well the proper scents of wild creatures, men and Kleesahks, and he avers that this thing that has twice now killed and eaten New Kuhmbuhluhnburk townsfolk smells unlike any beast he ever before has encountered. We called it a wolf, at the first, from the very wolflike paw prints; now a sighting has assured us that the creature does indeed resemble a wolf, albeit a very monster of a wolf."

"But who ever before saw a roan wolf, Duke Bili?" asked Sir Yoo Folsom. "Every one I ever saw or hunted or killed was mouse-brown or some shade of gray."

"That may be true of the local race of wolves, Sir Yoo," replied Bili, "but off-color sports seem to abound among most wolf packs I've encountered in the Middle Kingdoms and the western marches of the Confederation. I've been in at the kills of at least two reddish wolves in Harzburk's royal wilds, and I saw the pelt of a fine black wolf killed in the Duchy of Vawn, whilst we were besieging Vawnpolis. No, I find it far easier to credit a wolf of a roan color than I do a wolf of a size of two hundred to three hundred pounds weight and near on to ten hands height at the shoulders.

"Nor can I really persuade myself to credit even the biggest wolf's being able to jump high enough to get onto our walls, even at their lowest points. Much less can I persuade myself to credit that this huge creature has been able to transverse those heavily guarded, torchlit walls four times in two nights unseen by any officer or sentry of the wall watches."

Sir Yoo Folsom's face had suddenly become as white as curds. "You mean . . . Duke Bili, you don't think that critter is denning up right here among us, do you?"

"Yes, that is just what I do mean, Sir Yoo," said Bili solemnly. "It makes more sense in my mind than does the thought of a four-legged predator—be it wolf, bear, cat or whatever—that can scale sheer rock cliffs and jump up onto thirty-foot walls without being seen by multitudes of alert, keen-eyed men."

"But, dammit, Duke Bili," Fil Tyluh burst out, "where, pray tell? With the influx of fighters and dependents, every single habitation in all the lower town is occupied. As for this palace and the citadel, there's at least one noble officer in every room, suite, nook or cranny and . . . Oho, your grace is thinking of the magazines, back in the core of the mountain, I take it?"

"Just so," Bili agreed. "We two think much alike, Fil. It's late in this day to do much, and this night I want large, well-armed patrols walking every street and alleyway of the lower town from dusk to dawn. Reinforce the usual wall watch—I want every running foot of those battlements within sight of someone throughout every hour of every watch.

"Whitetip will have to forgo his customary nightly meal of Skohshun beef. I want him to stay in the palace and sleep well, this night, for tomorrow morning, he and any available Kleesahks will accompany me and several strong search parties back into the unused parts of the tunnels and chambers within the mountain. I mean to not only find and slay that strange man-eating beast, I mean to find just how it got into King's Rest Mountain, lest it be followed and succeeded by another of its unsavory ilk.

"And strengthen the guards within the palace and the keep, too, Fil, except for the Kleesahks' section, for I doubt one of them would have any trouble barehandedly dispatching even a beast of this size. Which means that we need not waste men guarding the king, for those Kleesahks would never allow him to be harmed by anything or anyone."

The young commander turned to Sir Szidnee Gawn, the royal castellan. "Sir Szidnee, have your folk see to it that every single door that lets into the mountain passages from palace, keep or stables is closed and solidly secured before nightfall. Also, every door connecting the various wings and those letting onto the walls or the outer courtyards. Understood?"

Before Bili could issue further orders to those present, however, he was recipient of a far-beaming from one of the younger Kleesahks, Lehnduhn. "Lord Champion, I am just above the area that cannot easily be seen from the walls or the keep, just below the first stretch of the ascending roadway, and I think I know why the man with that strange, long-distance killing thing was sent to where he is."

With that, the Kleesahk opened his mind that Bili might see through his hominid eyes. Some fifty or sixty feet below the watcher, on the last level stretch of the plain before the precipitous cliff, scores of Skohshun artisans were hard at work at siege carpentry. Obviously, one or more buildings out somewhere upon the plain had been wholly or partially demolished and the long, thick, strong, well-seasoned beam timbers from that destruction were being worked and joined end to end—slotted, dovetailed, augered and tree-nailed. At regular intervals, shorter timbers were being used to connect each of the three pair of uprights, with wooden latticework meshes lashed across the spans and wetted green hides stretched atop all. One of the giant devices lay almost complete, and the two others were nearing completion.

Seated at table in the hall of the palace, Bili felt his nape hairs all a-prickle. Those Skohshun leaders were clearly no fools, tyros or incompetents. Faced with a fortress-city so cunningly designed and situated, so massively constructed and stubbornly defended as to render frontal attacks so hideously expensive in terms of casualties as to not bear repetition, a city so well supplied and watered as to be capable of outwaiting even the most determined armies, a city that could not even be undermined, they had rightly concluded that new and extreme tactics were required.

Every officer in the city was aware that the Skohshun army vastly outnumbered their own trained fighters, but secure in their stonewalled, well-supplied and elevated fortress, they still could have probably held the foe at bay with half their present numbers. Since the very inception of the siege, no single Skohshun foot had ever rested for even a moment upon any portion of the walls, and damned few had ever achieved so far as within spear cast of them.

But this advantage rested upon the sole fact that the city could be approached and, therefore, attacked by any numbers only from the front. Of the two sides, one was at the edge of a high, sheer cliff made even more treacherous by being almost constantly wet and slimy due to the fact that all the city drains exited

at the base of that stretch of wall; the opposite side overlooked
some hundred and fifty yards' expanse of a steep, shaly slope,
broken by another, lower cliff, then extending on for several
hundred more yards of loose, treacherous footing beyond. The
rear of the fortress-city was unwalled—there was no need for any
other defense than the mountain into which it had been built. So
the front wall and its gates, alone, were vulnerable to the attack
of enemies unable to fly.

"Those damned Skohshuns have a running mile of guts," Bili
thought, "I have to give them that!"

Early on, the besiegers had essayed not just one but two
full-scale frontal assaults, with their thousands running up the
inclined roadways and scrambling up the exposed slopes and
taking dreadful losses from the accurate loosings of engines,
bows, crossbows and, as the few survivors got closer, staff
slings and darts. Only the luckiest or the hardiest had gotten
close enough to die under the walls of the barbican, and Bili and
his officers had seriously doubted that the aliens would try such
suicidal bravery again.

But they had! Only a week later, the Skohshuns had marched
out of their camp, bearing short polearms and long scaling hooks
and clumsy, two-men-abreast ladders. The parties carrying the
heavy ladders had headed up the roadway and the rest had
poured up the flanking slopes to face the large and small stones,
the pitchballs and pots of flaming oil, the arrows and bolts and
engine spears which were capable of piercing through three or
four men in a row, steel breastplates and all.

Also, on that ill-fated day for Skohshuns, a stray splash of
burning oil from one of the pots flung by the wall engines had
ignited the pitch-soaked, oakum-stuffed wooden corduroy of the
roadway. It had not been intentional, for the garrison was holding the attackers off, executing terrible amounts of death and
maimings within their ranks, without it. But when the highly
flammable stretches once were fired, there had been no stopping
the ensuing fires, and all of the environs had stunk unto the very
skies of charred, overdone meat for long days, and then of the
sickly-sweet stench of rotting flesh until at last the carrion birds
and beasts and insects had accomplished their grisly but necessary purposes.

The Skohshuns had seemed to have learned their lesson, a
hard, very bloody lesson. After that second attack they had
limped, hobbled, crawled or been carried or dragged back within
their stockaded camp; there had been no more attempts on the
front wall and barbican. The third attack had come boiling up the

slippery, uneven and terribly exposed shale slopes to the east of the city-fortress. But such had been the losses on the lower slope that the assault had been wisely aborted before a single man had reached the upper slope.

In recent weeks, the Skohshuns had given every outward appearance of having settled in for a long, passive, interdictive siege. But Bili knew them for the stark fighters that they were and had been dead certain that they were but resting, licking their wounds and planning new and different means of striking again at the walls and the city within them.

Stealthy nighttime patrols by Whitetip and various of the Kleesahks had verified that the Skohshuns were hard at work in constructing stone- and spear-throwing engines of several varieties and sizes. But as both the prairiecat and the huge hirsute hominids had had, perforce, to take a roundabout way to and from the camp, they had never spotted the construction site at the very foot of the front slope or what was being built there . . . until today. That was why the Skohshuns had sent up the Ganiks with their Witchman weapons: fear that the watchers upon the front walls and towers might espy the work going on below.

Now the certain tactics of the coming assault—the third, against the front wall, it would be—were crystal-clear to Bili's quick, perceptive mind.

The Skohshuns would drag their engines into place on a dark night, setting them, their crews and the projectiles for them somewhere just out of easy bowshot, probably in preselected and prepared positions. A chosen group of shock troops would be massed just below the front bulge of the mountain—that up which the roadway snaked its way—and there they would wait, protected from any but high-arching, indirect loosings by that same, rocky bulge. Possibly they would also send all three of the Ganiks armed with the Witchman weapons, these "ryfuhls," up the slopes during the hours of the dark to, with the first light, aid the engines in making the walls and the tower-engine positions most unsalubrious places for humans or Kleesahks.

Then, when it seemed that the time was ripe, those long, long, immensely long lengths of timber would be somehow set up on end. Then, probably guided by ropes, their other ends would be lowered to span the roadway cuts and the difficult slopes to finally come to rest—if they were long enough, and the parapet of the front wall was actually less than a hundred feet above the level of the plain when measured in a straight line—on the very walls of the city.

The Skohshun engines would be able to continue their work

up to and until only bare moments before the first Skohshun was close enough to come onto the wall of New Kuhmbuhluhnburk. With a few score or more Skohshuns upon the front wall, the engines would probably either increase their range and begin dropping boulders and flammables within the city itself, or change direction to support the other attack, most likely one against the east wall. And, all things considered, the scenario Bili's mind conjured up might very well succeed where earlier, less well-planned ones had failed.

That was not a chance that Bili, feeling keenly the crushing weight of his undesired responsibilities, was willing to take. Several optional plans for the destruction of these oversize scaling ladders crowded the young *thoheeks'* mind. Whether or not the guards and craftsmen were slain, the devices and raw materials must be fired, burned to ashes. But how best to accomplish this aim?

He could have Lehnduhn the Kleesahk retrace his way back up the forward slope to the riflepit and there either slay or incapacitate Counter Tremain, the Ganik; then man the wall engines and the six larger ones positioned just inside the forward wall, load them with oil pots and pitchballs and loose at a high angle designed to drop them directly at the base of the slope, possibly accompanied by a few volleys of fire arrows for insurance that there would be fires *and* casualties, as well.

But careful as these Skohshuns seemed to be in most other matters, he reflected, they were certain-sure to have made some provisions against this kind of attack on their cliffside site. Moreover, there was a slight overhang of rock down there, and a seepage pool of water beneath it, as he recalled—ill-smelling water, true, unpalatable to either man or beast, but wet enough to help retard fires, nonetheless, were there men still about who had the time and ability to so use it.

Of course, he could send a number of the Kleesahks down by night—despite their height and size, they could move as silently as cats and, also like cats, they could see well in almost no light at all—to set the devices afire, but these Kleesahks, because of their size, strength and other talents, were too valuable a resource to encourage Bili to risk them on so chancy a venture. Now if all of them were capable of the mindcloudings that Pah-Elmuh, Oodehn and some few others of the strange hominids had mastered . . . but then, if warhorses had wings warfare would be fought significantly differently.

Dismissing most of the officers and nobles still at table, the *Thoheeks* and Chief of Morguhn began to plan the sortie that he would lead out of the mountain fortress in a few hours. He would need men and women upon whom he knew he could depend in a pinch, yet he also could not, dared not, take all of these, and for various reasons there were certain individuals who had to be stricken from the list, automatically.

The Freefighter officers, Captain Fil Tyluh and Acting Captain Frehd Brakit, could not be spared from the garrison under any but the most extreme circumstances, for they were the most experienced—indeed, the *only* truly and long experienced—siege engineers in the city. It was likewise out of the question to risk the loss of Pah-Elmuh and his Kleesahk surgical and medical assistants. And most of the members of Bili's staff were too important to the ongoing defense to chance losing them in the course of a risky and highly dangerous, though very necessary, midnight sally forth against opposition of unknown quality and quantity.

This would tend to strike Lieutenant Kahndoot, the very level-headed and most competent of the Moon Maidens, Vlahkos Kamruhn of Skaht, Mikos of Eeahnopolis, Hornman Gy Ynstyn, Sir Yoo Folsom and old Vahrtahn Panosyuhn, the Ahrmehnee, and of course Rahksahnah, who was giving suck to their twin infants.

"Hmmm," he pondered. "This is going to take more than a mere couple of hours of thought, so it might be better to plan it all for tomorrow night. It didn't appear that those Skohshuns had enough materials to finish those other two immediately, so we should have at least that little amount of time yet to go."

Shoving it all into a corner of his mind, he beamed a farcall to Kahndoot on the forward wall. "How many of our special troops has that tame Ganik of ours shot, so far, little sister?"

Her return mindspeak came: "So many that we're almost out of sawdust to stuff them afresh, Bili. Those projectiles his thing throws burst with enough force to near tear the heads off these dummies, or to rip huge, well-nigh unrepairable holes in the fabric if they chance to strike farther down.

"Moreover, one of the Maidens who was holding up a dummy, earlier this morning, had a tiny bit of what looks like lead driven completely through her left cheek and into her tongue. She was far from pleased by the happenstance, has been heard to say some rather uncomplimentary things about this plan of yours and about you, personally, big brother—mostly some speculations upon your ancestry, appearance, daily habits and preferences, general level of intelligence and suchlike."

Bili chuckled to himself and beamed, "And does my little sister agree with this aggrieved Maiden?"

"In some of her observations, oversized brother," Kahndoot replied, "but not in all, not in all. However, I would like to know how much longer we are going to play this game with that Ganik yonder."

"The remainder of this day and all of tomorrow, Kahndoot. After that, you have my permission to drop a few hundred-pound pebbles on him, quill him with arrows, pepper him with slingstones or whatever you wish. So send for some more sawdust and canvas, and tell those who support these dummies to either not stand so close or to borrow a helm with both visor and beaver. If there are none easily available, have a few fetched from the keep armory."

"*How* many rounds, Counter?" growled Erica Arenstein in a rage. "Twenty-seven, you say? Dammit, you fool, that's more than a quarter of our entire remaining stock of ammunition! And how many of those were clean misses? Hell, I knew I should have sent Horseface Charley back up, that or gone myself. At least he and I can hit what we aim at with consistency."

"Wal dang it, I hits 'em, too, Ehrkah!" Counter asserted heatedly. "I swan, I seen ever man jack of them Kuhmbluhnuhs go down, evun heerd one the bugguhs scream oncet, kinda real garglylike scream, too."

Erica reflected on that. She had never before known Counter to lie to her, so he should not be starting now. But if only three shots from Horseface had kept the Kuhmbuhluhner garrison down off the walls and towers all of the day before yesterday, why should Counter Tremain have to shoot more than a score of them yesterday? Unless . . . unless they had begun to suspect that something was going on below that bluff.

But when she broached her suspicions to Brigadier Maklarin, suggesting that the work be expedited, he just shook his snowy head. "Doctor, there is no way to do it faster. We own a limited number of artisans, for the one thing; for another, latticework of the strength and quantity we require is not quickly woven. This is Tuesday; the attack date chosen is this Friday. If they have not already found us out, I doubt that they will within the next two days.

"No, my dear doctor, just give each of your riflemen one more tour of duty up there, then you all will be free to go south or wherever you wish with my blessing and that of all the Skohshun nation."

\* \* \*

"I cannot truly attest that he is improving in any way, Lord Champion," said Pah-Elmuh, "for still I cannot contact any portion of his mind, I only can report of observations. For one thing, he no longer seems to be losing flesh as he did for so long. For another, I am certain that his body must move itself at times when I am not there or not awake to see it done, for his muscles now seem to have regained a bit of tone, and twice now I have returned from nighttime errands or calls to find him in different positions on his couch and with his coverlets all disarrayed or even thrown from off him. This all bends me to the belief that King Byruhn may yet recover of his injuries and reign on the throne of his fathers."

The Kleesahk had been mindspeaking, but Bili's grunted reply was spoken aloud. "The sooner the better, say I, Pah-Elmuh. It can't be soon enough for me. I like not this extra work piled upon me, willy-nilly. New Kuhmbuhluhn, New Kuhmbuhluhnburk and New Kuhmbuhluhners should all be ruled over by one of their own, and I give you fair warning, when once the siege is broken and these damned Skohshuns hied back to their northern glen, Chief Bili of Morguhn is gone, too, whether or no King Byruhn be recovered. Let the royal council elect a New Kuhmbuhluhn nobleman to be regent . . . or the new king. I, my wife, my children, my stallion and all my condotta who wish to do so will be headed first for Sandee's Cot, then east, toward our various homelands. I have seen me enough mountains to last a lifetime long, or more."

# CHAPTER XI

Undaunted, in the strength of his vastly superior weapons, by the two reserve regiments—actually, in practice, training commands—of pikemen and the half-troop of light cavalry, Jay Corbett finally set up his headquarters in the spacious, stone-built house of Earl Devernee, bringing in a couple of heavily armed squads to garrison it and leaving Gumpner in charge of the camp and their hostages.

In the absence of the hostage earl, Corbett quickly noted, Lady Pamela Grey—Earl Devernee's half sister—seemed to rule over the glen rather competently, in his stead. He was impressed with his less-than-willing hostess, mightily impressed. He found her to be intelligent, quick-witted and, when she wished to be so, charming. She also was very strong-willed, with a keen and deeply embedded sense of justice and morality—of what was right and what wrong, by her standards.

Her son, who served as Corbett's guide and companion as the officer searched the nooks and crannies of the glen for any sign of Erica and her Ganiks, shared her strict senses of justice and honor, of responsibility and duty. The grave, one-legged, fourteen-year-old combat veteran was, in Corbett's mind, a thoroughly admirable young man, a credit to his mother, his dead father and his people; but he could not but wonder if Ensign Thomas Grey would ever come to rue and regret so early a loss of childhood, so sudden a transition into the responsibilities of maturity. He sincerely hoped not.

A week of searching and of questioning Skohshuns of all stations and ages, civilian and military, of both sexes, at last convinced him that Earl Devernee had indeed spoken the full truth at their initial meeting—Dr. Erica Arenstein and the Ganiks she now led had departed the glen long weeks ago, bound for the field army. Now he must march fast in the wake of the wagon train that had borne them southeast, but he wanted to arrive unannounced, without the large and powerful Skohshun army being apprised that he was bound toward them.

This matter could have been simply enough handled by the shooting of every horse in the glen, but to do so he and his two squads would have been obliged to penetrate some of the narrow, twisting defiles quite deeply and would likely have had to fight their way back, killing or wounding a sizable number of the outraged Skohshuns in the process, so he chose an easier method of achieving the same end . . . or so he then thought.

During the night before the departure of him and his two squads from the house of which Lady Pamela Grey was the temporary chatelaine, he tried several times to mentally frame the words he would say to her in parting, telling her of just what he must do to protect his command, to provide security on the coming march; but each new speech rang lamer than the one preceding it in his mind, and when at last the morning came, he simply thanked her for her courtesies and bade her farewell.

When he released Earl Devernee, however, he laid it flat on the line to the nobleman. "Mr. Devernee, I'm now going after Dr. Arenstein and her party."

"Do you know the road, General Corbett?" the earl blandly asked. "If not, I can supply you with a few guides."

"Thank you, but no," Corbett grinned in reply. "You have already supplied me with a fine map from the office in your house. My compliments to your military cartographers—they do first-class work with primitive equipment."

The earl nodded once. "Thank you, sir. You are, of course, more than welcome to the map. I know well that you could easily have taken much more, had you so desired, slaying anyone, everyone who might have opposed you."

"I'm a soldier, Mr. Devernee, not a bandit," said Jay Corbett. "And while killing is often my job, it seldom if ever has been my pleasure. But I have my command to protect, too, Mr. Devernee, and so I am serving you fair warning that any messengers you try to send on ahead of me to give your Brigadier Maklarin word of my approach will be most harshly, most fatally, dealt with—not of my desire, for I admire you and your people, but of my necessity.

"Further, because I know that you will try to send gallopers, and my warning here be damned, I'm going to make it as difficult as I can for you and for them. I have seen every inch of the glen and the steeps that surround it, and while it might be just barely possible for a skilled rider on a very surefooted mount to get over those steeps in a very few places, it would take a drooling lunatic to try it to begin, and when he reached the outside, he would have lost a goodly bit of time, for I would be well on my way."

"You mean to leave a force, then, to hold this entryway to Skohshun Glen, general?" inquired the earl, with a worried frown.

"No, Mr. Devernee," replied Corbett. "I have already made

my preparations and I will shortly blow down the cliffs on either side of that narrowest section of the entryway. By the time you and your people have cleared it sufficiently to ride a horse through it, my business with your field army should be over and done and I should be marching back south with Dr. Arenstein.

"I reiterate, sir, I greatly admire you and your people and I wish you and them success in all endeavors—save those that bear upon me and mine—so please do not consider the thing I now must do as a hostile act, for it is not; rather, it is a military expedient, a necessary act of bloodless destruction. Do you understand me, Mr. Devernee?"

The earl sighed and smiled wanly. "Yes, General Corbett, I do; I truly do understand you, more, I think, than you understand me. I have learned much of you, you know, in conversations with your officers, notably Colonel Gumpner. I deeply regret that we two are not, cannot be, allies, for I think we were cut of the selfsame bolt of the cloth of honor.

"You have done and will do that which you feel you must for the welfare of those you rule. I have done and will assuredly do exactly the same, as God wills me the strength to do it. I am not and have never been a soldier, a fighter, and precious few of my forefathers have been, for we are the civil rulers of the Skohshun people. But I have lived with and among soldiers for all my days. I have seen the good and the bad, the brave and the cowardly, the competent and the incompetent, the careful plodders and the glory-hunters, and I have learned—I pray God—to winnow the grain from the chaff.

"I judge you to be a superlative officer, general, an officer who demands much from his subordinates, but even more from himself. You probably get everything you ask from your officers and other ranks, too, general, for one and all they love and worship you to a degree that is almost sacrilegious. They will allow you to drive them cruel hard, but only because they know that you drive yourself even harder, that you return their love and that their individual and collective welfare is paramount in your mind and your decisions.

"My late brother-in-law, Sir Edmund Grey—God keep his gallant soul!—was a man much like you, and his loss was a bitter cruel one to endure. But at least poor Ed left a fine son who has already, at the age of only a bit over fourteen years, brought added luster to his distinguished name and house."

"Yes," Corbett nodded, "Ensign Grey served as my guide in my search of the glen. He is indeed a fine young man, and any parent would be proud of him.

"But, now, Mr. Devernee, we must be on our way, shortly. You and your retainers please exercise due haste in getting back, well back, into the glen. Get those soldiers off the lines of cliffs, for I well know just how tricky rockslides can be, and the slide that my devices precipitate may well result in sympathetic slides all along those cliffs. Also, you'd be well advised to keep your people out of that entryway for at least a day, for rocks may continue to fall at odd intervals for some time."

As young *Thoheeks* Bili of Morguhn sat planning out his sally against the Skohshuns, great, dark-gray banks of rainclouds were blowing down from the north. There were severe downpours three or four times that night and misty sprinkles in between, and the beefed-up patrols on the city streets and the members of the enlarged wall watches all cursed the chilly, unpleasant weather and scoffed at the reasons for their being forced to bide out in it.

But, for whatever reason or reasons, the monster wolf was not seen, nor did it kill or feed within the burk of New Kuhmbuhluhn that night. Bright and early on the next morning, armed, armored search parties of men and Kleesahks led by Bili, Captain Fil Tyluh, Acting Captain Frehd Brakit, Vlahkos Kamruhn, the *Vahrohneeskos* Gneedos Kamruhn, Sir Yoo Folsom, Lieutenants Roopuht and Kahndoot—both gritty-eyed from lack of sleep but keen still to help put paid to the account of the bestial trespasser—Mikos of Eeahnopolis, Tsimbos of Ahnpolis and several Kuhmbuhluhn noble officers all fanned out through the multileveled galleries and chambers and winding corridors of the honeycombed mountain behind the palace and keep, lighting the way with torches and lamps and bull's-eye lanthorns.

But they found no wolf, nor any sign of one, old or recent. They found a few stoats, semidomesticated ones whose ancestors had been deliberately released there to retard the proliferation of rats, mice and similar vermin among the stores in the magazines. They chanced across a long-forgotten chamber packed with pipes and casks and kegs of very old and very potent wines. They found other antique artifacts, some of them as old as the kingdom, or so the Kleesahks attested. But they could not discover even so much as the bare scent of their quarry, so with the sally scheduled for the night of this day, Bili called off the search and the various parties made their respective ways back to the palace.

It was not until on their return they reached the spot where keep abutted palace that Whitetip mindspoke Bili. "The creature was here, cat brother, perhaps a day ago. He left his scent there, on the angle of the wall, as any dog or jackal or wolf would do.''

Bending close to the indicated section of stonework, even Bili's far less sensitive nose could detect the rank odor of animal urine . . . and he resisted the impulse to rub at his flesh to lay the goosebumps, for just here the narrow stairway led upward into the wing of the Kleesahks and the chamber wherin lay the helpless, comatose King Byruhn; downward, three flights of stairs would deliver the person or the thing which descended them only bare yards from the suite which now housed him, the infant twins and Rahksahnah.

"You are certain that this mark is that old, brother?" he beamed to his big, furry companion. "It was not done last night?"

The cat's beaming bore a touch of impatience. "You sniffed at it yourself—did that smell like a recent marking to you?"

Bili sighed. "Brother, you have again misremembered, we twolegs do not have such keen noses as do you and the Kleesahks. I can smell that the spot has been pissed upon, but that is all that my nose tells me of it.''

"I am sorry, cat brother," apologized the prairiecat, "but so well developed is your mind that I sometimes forget how retarded are others of your senses. Yes, I am indeed certain that this is not fresh scent. It is at least one day old, maybe even two.''

Bili nodded to himself. "Then it surely must be denning up back there in the caverns, whether we found traces of it or not.''

The cat wrinkled his nose, then suddenly dropped onto his haunches and began to scratch vigorously at his neck with one hind paw, mindspeaking all the while. "Unless it is denning here, in the keep or the palace, cat brother.''

"Then why have you not smelled it out long ago?" Bili beamed inquiringly.

Reversing paws, Whitetip went savagely at the other side of his thick, muscular neck, eyes closed to mere slits. "For a very good reason, cat brother: Before it began to kill in the town, I never before had sniffed a scent like this one, so if I had chanced across it here in the palace, I would most likely have dismissed it as just an unpleasant variant of the usual twoleg stench. For, as I have said before, there is a tone of twoleg stench to this scent although the cleanlier, animal scent predominates, Sacred Sun be thanked.''

"Well, after tonight's sally," decided Bili, "I mean to set you and some of the younger Kleesahks to prowl these corridors and stairways every night until the creature is apprehended, or tracked down and scotched for good and all.''

The cat's reply bore a tinge of sulkiness. ''But cat brother, Whitetip enjoys spying upon the camp of the men-of-the-long-long-spears. Besides, their cattle are most tasty. Why cannot he continue at that which he does best?''

Bili rubbed a hand across the top of the cat's big head, between his ears, and kneaded the neck muscles, eliciting a deep, deep purr in response. ''Brother, you will be continuing to keep track of what the Skohshuns are up to on most nights. Only on a couple of nights in each six-day will you be here.

''Understand, please, brother, there will be times when I must be absent from my suite for long periods and I need to know that a strong, fierce and dedicated brother will be about to competently protect my female and our cubs.''

''My brother-chief need not fear,'' replied the huge feline. ''His female and his cubs will be as safe as any cat could keep them.''

Bili kept his sally force small, for their principal aim was not to kill large numbers of Skohshuns, but to reach and destroy the assault devices and regain to the burk with as little wasted time and effort as would be possible. Pah-Elmuh and Oodehn were the two Kleesahks he finally had chosen, for their mighty thews would be necessary to silently remove the cyclopean stones blocking the particular hidden sallyport he had decided was best situated for this excursion. Immediately the stones were removed and the way cleared, Bili mindspoke Fil Tyluh and Frehd Brakit, each of whom was, for this night exercise, commanding two of the oversized engines constructed under the supervision of Brakit; too large to be mounted on the walls, they squatted in cleared areas just behind the front wall.

In receipt of Bili's telepathic command, the two officers issued their own orders and triggering devices were released, almost as one. There were four tooth-jarring, contrabasso thumps of massive beams against equally massive, thickly padded crossbars, and four fiercely blazing pitchballs—each bigger than a bushel basket—sailed up and out in a parabolic flight that came finally to ground in the highly flammable canvas-and-wood camp of the Skohshuns.

Assisted by teams of draft animals, as well as several of the preternaturally powerful Kleesahks, the crews of the engines quickly recocked and reloaded their throwers, this time with bushels of fist- to head-sized stones, of which a goodly supply was ready to hand, each load premeasured out in strong wicker containers.

When Bili, standing in the now-open mouth of the previously concealed tunnel, saw the first tongues of yellow-red flame spring up, high overtopping the wooden palisades of the Skohshun camp, he took a fresh grip on the steel haft of his axe and mindspoke his score and a half of fighters; "All right, let's go."

Instead of keeping watch into the darkness which was the west, Pikeman Edgar Makellahr was, naturally, watching the blazing camp and scurrying dark figures, thanking God that he was not over there this night and keeping a wary eye out for the sergeant of the guard or a wandering officer. Therefore, the sixteen-year-old junior pikeman's very first intimation that anything might be amiss closer to his post than the camp was when, all at once, a hard hand—big and stinking of garlic—clamped over his mouth, a rocklike knee slammed into the small of his back and something traced a line of agonizing fire across his throat. Abruptly the hand was removed and Edgar tried to scream, but he could not, nor could he draw in the air for which his lungs were clamoring. Then infinite blackness closed about him.

Vahk Soormehlyuhn carefully eased the still-twitching body of the big blond boy to the rocky ground, taking pains that no portion of his victim's equipment clang or rattle. The soot-blackened Ahrmehnee warrior briefly regretted that so fine a head would have to be left to go to waste, then he moved on in a cautious stalk of his next victim, this one also observing the ongoing fires rather than keeping the watch to which he had been assigned.

The sentry killer reflected that Dook Bili had again been proved correct. When old Vahrtahn, among others, had questioned the wisdom of alerting any portion of the Skohshuns by loosings of fire and boulders upon the sleeping camp, the young leader had said, "Look you, gentlemen, precious few humans possess really decent night vision under even the best of circumstances. But all of us twolegs—even the Kleesahks—are cursed with an abiding curiosity. Now if their main camp is all ablaze and the garrison is milling about and taking casualties and screaming shouts and curses, just how many of the sentries guarding that work area do you imagine are going to be able to resist the natural, normal human impulse to steal at least a glance or three in that direction, eh? And each time they look at the blazes, they are going to weaken what little night vision they may normally possess, lessening the likelihood of our small sally party's being apprehended until we are ready to be seen."

When the last sentry was down, his lifeblood pouring out to soak the ground beneath him, Sergeant Eethah led her eight Moon Maidens toward the spot beneath the overhang of rock where the carpenters and joiners lay rolled in their blankets, while Tsimbos of Ahnpolis and his largest contingent—all of them save him laden with huge, bulging, heavy skins of oil—raced to the long contraptions of wood, wicker and hides.

Most of the carpenters and relief sentries were dispatched while still asleep by the dripping dirks and shortswords of the grim Maidens. One only of them escaped, to run naked and shrieking in the direction of the distant, fiery camp; that is, he ran for the few steps he was able to take before Sir Yoo Folsom's spinning, hard-flung francisca took him betwixt his shoulderblades and split his spine, at the same moment that an Ahrmehnee knife sank hilt-deep between two ribs.

Satisfied that no noise that they might make, no matter how loud or sharp, could be heard above the furious pandemonium emanating from the Skohshun camp, Bili set most of his band to work with the enemy's own tools hewing and splitting and smashing what they could of the long, weighty devices before soaking them well with oil, throwing among them those tools and weapons they themselves were not taking back into the burk, then heaving the earthenware pot of live coals that Tsimbos of Ahnpolis had carried onto the site.

Bili held them until he was certain that the fire was well on the way to becoming an uncontrollable conflagration, then led them all back around the cliffline and into the tunnel. All helped the patiently waiting Kleesahks to replace the huge stones, the outer faces of which were so cunningly disguised as to make detection of their true purpose most unlikely.

Red-eyed and grouchy with lack of sleep, his hair, eyebrows and even his flaring mustaches fire-singed, Brigadier Sir Ahrthur Maklarin assessed the reports littering the top of the partially charred table before him. Occasionally, he squirmed in another attempt to find a really comfortable seat on the section of sawn log which now was the best that still existed in the near-ruined camp to serve him for a chair. At length, he summoned old Sir Djahn Makadahm, the herald.

"Sit down, Djahn," the brigadier growled, indicating another sawn section of treetrunk, the bark still on. "If you brought anything to drink, I'll have a bit of it."

Unbuttoning his tunic, the herald drew forth a flat silver flask and proffered it, not speaking until after the brigadier had uncorked, upended, then recorked the flask and passed it back.

"I know it was a very bad night, Ahrthur, but just how bad was it?"

Maklarin huffed once or twice, demanding, "What the hell is that stuff you're passing out, anyway? It's as rough as a frozen corncob, I trow!

"Bad enough, old friend, and worse than that. Every single regiment lost men last night, killed or wounded. The surgeons and Dr. Arenstein are clearly like to drop of exhaustion, so long and hard have they been at it. At least we still have the most of our supplies, and we can thank the Kuhmbuhluhner who cast the load of stones on the supply tents, early on, for that fact; the barrels at the tiptops of the stacks were holed, and with everything soaked with beer and vinegar and brine, the fires never had a chance to get at anything more substantial than the tents.

"Am I rambling? It seems that I am, old friend. Blame it on lack of sleep and overmuch care. Whilst the Kuhmbuhluhner engines were wreaking their worst—or should I say their best?—on us, here, it seems that a sally was made from somewhere—though not out of the main gate and down the slopes, for the Ganik rifleman still was in his hole and he swears that no single man came out from the city in the normal way. I've had the idea all along that there must be two or three other means of egress from New Kuhmbuhluhnburk, and if only we could find even one of them . . . But that's neither here nor there and I'm rambling again. The bastards slit the throats of all the pikemen on sentry duty, then went on to murder the poor carpenters and the others, before hacking the ladder-bridges apart, then soaking them with oil and setting them alight. This morning, there is nothing more left of them than there is of our new batteries of catapults and spearthrowers, alas.

"And there will be damnall fresh beef for a while, too, Djahn. The herd is scattered to hell and gone, and if I could blame that on the bloody Kuhmbuhluhners, I surely would; but eyewitnesses aver that that huge mountain cat that has been plaguing us periodically spooked them on last night of all possible nights. Moreover, four of our herders were killed trying to turn that stampede, too.

"As of about an hour agone, there were one thousand, one hundred and fifty-two other-ranks casualties, twenty-three officer casualties—of course, that figure includes the dead, the missing and all classes of wounded.

"In addition, three entire battalions lost *all* their polearms—

long pikes, short pikes, axes, hammers, everything. We are going to have to find a new way to stack our weapons, possibly stack them in company lots or smaller, for battalion stacks are simply too large and dense to allow for saving many if any once they are well afire. All the pike carts were lost, too, damn it, burned to the axles and beyond.

"And in the confusion of getting the draft stock out the rear gate last night, no less than four of our good lady doctor's wildmen disappeared, along with two mules and two good horses, one of them my riding horse, True. One of the bastards was that fellow Tremain.

"Let me have another taste of that foul rotgut, Djahn, then I'll touch on why I sent for you this morning."

The brigadier again upended the flask and took a long pull. A shudder shook his whole body. "Saints preserve us all, Djahn, that is truly devil's brew. Where did it come from, pray tell?"

Sir Djahn shrugged. "I'm sure I have no idea, Ahrthur. My batman bought a half gallon of it—at a whopping price, I might add!—from one of that fellow Potter's people. I usually have brandy, as you know, but my keg blew up when my tent burned last night, and all that was available this morning was this . . . this decoction. Sorry, old man. Can't say that I'm overfond of the stuff m'self, but it's better than water."

"All right, Djahn, back to business. It's thankful we should all be that there are no more of those New Kuhmbuhluhnburkers than there are up there, for had they had the force available to attack this camp last night on the heels of that hellish bombardment, the siege would've been broken then and there and no doubt the most of us would be dead this morning. We might not be so fortunate a second time around. In fact, if there weren't so many wounded to transport, I'd move the camp, now, this morning, lay out a new one out of range of those damned Kuhmbuhluhn engines . . . if that's possible. I never heard of engines that could throw such weights of missiles so far, ere this—why, that boulder that came down atop my own tent must weigh a good four hundred pounds or more."

"You intend to lift the siege, Ahrthur? It might not be a bad idea, considering all the losses, and it's purely your decision to make," said Sir Djahn.

The brigadier shook his singed head. "Oh, no, Djahn, not yet. Even with our losses of men and matériel, we still outnumber the enemy by a goodly edge. I mean to make good use of that fact, and that's where you and your good offices enter upon the matter.

"We'll give it a few days. I don't want them to have any inkling of just how badly they hurt us last night—such knowledge might give them ideas which could breed further unpleasantnesses for us. Maybe, the first of next week, I want you to ride back up there and shame that king and that duke to march out of that city and meet us in open battle here on this plain."

Sir Djahn shook his head slowly. "I cannot credit it that I heard you say what you said, Ahrthur. Those men are not fools, you know, none of them. They can count as well as can you or I, and you can be certain that they know their only edge is those unassailable walls."

"But you did it once before—shamed the late king into leaving this abomination of an invulnerable city to meet us in open battle at a place of our choosing," said the brigadier stubbornly. "You did it after the autumn battle, last year."

"That was then and this is now, Ahrthur," Sir Djahn replied, tiredly but patiently, to his old friend. "I was able to nose out the hidden weakness of an old monarch who was verging on senility and use it against him and the best interests of his people . . . and I can't say that I'm proud of what I then did, Ahrthur.

"But, be that as it may, this King Byruhn is purely a practical man. No old-fashioned ideals to trip him up with—he would most likely laugh in my face, if he even deigned to take me seriously, to commence. He strikes me as the kind of man who probably talks much of honor, but honors that honor more in the breach than in the observance . . . unless, of course, he can see possible advancement of his various schemes in such an observance."

"Well," the brigadier went on doggedly, "perhaps this condottiere, this Duke Bili, could influence his patron?"

Sir Djahn shook his head again. "Not bloody likely, Ahrthur, not bloody likely at all. As I said after my last visit to New Kuhmbuhluhnburk, Sir Bili, Duke Morguhn, is a vastly experienced mercenary officer and, although a thoroughgoing gentleman to his fingertips, as practical and hard-boiled a professional warrior as any I've ever come across."

The brigadier's shoulders sagged. "You refuse to go, then, old friend?"

"Oh, no, Ahrthur, I'll go." Sir Djahn grinned. "If for no other reason, to enjoy a few decent, well-cooked meals and an enjoyable tipple, though I think weedwine would likely be a distinct improvement on Potter's rattlesnake venom here."

"Thank you, sincerely, Djahn," said the brigadier humbly.

"This cast of the dice I am planning will be for all or for nothing. I am sending back to Skohshun Glen for the two reserve regiments and all of the light cavalry, along with every gentleman who can still sit a horse and swing steel. It will probably take them two weeks to get here, so take your time in talking the New Kuhmbuhluhners around and make that allowance in setting a date for the battle."

When he arrived at last back in his suite in the palace, half a dozen servants divested Bili of his arms, armor, pourpoint and outer clothing, while yet another bore away his huge axe to be cleaned, rehoned and oiled. He sent one of them down to the palace kitchens to fetch back hot water that he might lave off the soot from his face and the sweat from his body.

The man returned, white-faced, with an empty bucket and a stuttered story that set Bili to rearming far faster than he had disarmed, all the while mindcalling certain of his officers and Whitetip, the prairiecat.

The palace kitchens were at ground level and, because of the ever-present danger of fires, were not really a part of the palace structure, being connected to the serving rooms and the commodious pantry below the great hall by stone-built tunnels, all of which could be easily and completely closed off to prevent the spread of flames but were usually left wide open to facilitate the comings and goings of the various staffs of meat cooks, bread bakers, pastry cooks, confectioners and such.

There was work of some sort in progress in the kitchens from sunrise to sunrise, and Bili had often remarked, only half jokingly, to his own staff that the senior palace chef, Master Blakmuhn, could probably give them all needed lessons in proper divisions of labor and available resources, so smoothly and effortlessly did his kitchens seem to operate.

But the kitchens into which Bili and his trailing, half-armed and -clothed staff stalked that night were a very study in disorganization, rather, a howling chaos, with Master Blakmuhn howling as loud as or louder than any. It required most ungentle shakings and slappings of the howling staff to obtain some quiet and a report, and, at last, Master Blakmuhn led them to a space between an outer wall and one of the immense ovens, where lay what was left of a baker's apprentice.

Keeping his eyes averted from the incomplete body of the once-rotund young man, the chef told the horrifying tale to Bili and the rest. "Young Nehd had done been sent in here for to sweep up from the last bakin'. He be . . . he was almightily afeered of eny kinda snake, so when he screamed thet oncet, we all jest laughed, thinkin' he'd done seen one the big black rat snakes we keeps in the kitchens. But he dint come a-runnin' out, he jest stayed and stayed and stayed, so I sent one of my journeymen, Hwil Dukhwai, to hurry him up. Then Hwil, he yells and comes a-runnin' back to say it's a big critter has kilt Nehd and is eatin' him.

"Hwil has been knowed to joke and josh around a lot, but you could look at him and tell he was scairt plumb shitless of sumthin'. So I grabbed up a steel boar spit—there it lays, right there." The chef gestured at a six-foot shaft of sharp-pointed steel smeared with blood for a good third of its length.

"And told everbody elst to git them a knife or a hatchet or suthin, and we all went back here and . . . and, m'lord duke, it wuz plumb awful! I never seed any critter big as thet one. He jest layed there a-lookin' at us, and a-snarlin', even while he still was a-tearin' off chunks of pore young Nehd and a-swallerin' them. Them eyes was terrible, jest like fiery coals, they wuz.

"Then sumbody behint of me chucked a cleaver at the critter, hit it, too; the edge went deep and stuck in its neck. But the critter jest jumped up, shook the cleaver out and come dead straight at us . . . at me! Well, in my time I done dressed out a plentynuff beasts for to know where you spose to spear them, so I crouchted down and jammed my spit square betwixt the critter's front legs and he run right up on it. Well, I could tell he'd be right at me in a blinkin', so I let go of the spit and jumpted back and slammed the door and shot the bolt, then we all went a-runnin' like everythin. And that be all I knows, m'lord duke."

With Whitetip still not returned from his part of the evening exercise, Bili and his armed gentlemen took up the hunt, but the bloodtrail ended halfway through the stone corridorway leading into the palace. More men were summoned and the ground level searched thoroughly, but the seriously wounded beast had again vanished.

# CHAPTER XII

Whitetip did not return for three full days. When at last he did, he was not alone. With him was a female of his species, this cat some half his weight and less than two thirds his height; her coloring was that of the native treecats and her cuspids were not much larger than theirs, mere shadows of the huge, cursive dentition of the male prairiecat.

"Chief Bili," beamed Whitetip formally, "this retarded, deformed number-cat cannot remember simple orders for long, it would seem. She was told to remain with her cubs at the den of Count Sandee, yet I found her wandering the plain near to the mountains, trying to find a way to sneak past the Skohshuns."

"We'll get to Stealth in a minute," Bili replied sternly. "Chief Whitetip mentions the obeying of orders, yet he chose to be gone for three days in utter disobedience of his orders. I had feared him slain by the long-long-spear-men."

Leaving the big cat to squirm and stew for the nonce, Bili beamed to the newcomer, "Greet the Sacred Sun, Stealth. How is my cub, and your own?"

Her delight was obvious; she paced to Bili's side and laid her neat head against his knee, purring her joy while beaming, "Greet the Scared Sun, chief of cat brothers. Your cub is well, though not yet ready to join mine own in hunting lizards and voles. As for your orders, all the other fighters you left at the den of Count Sandee were marching north to join you, so I asked the advice of Count Sandee himself, and that of my wise twoleg cat sister, Zainehp, and they both assured me that you would assuredly welcome even one more proven fighter, beset as you were by enemies. Were they wrong in their counsel, cat brother? Should I have stayed behind and let them ride to aid you without me?"

Bili ruffled the cat's neck fur reassuringly. "No, my sister, they were not wrong; when the horn is winded, all charge as one. How many horsemen and Maidens ride with Count Sandee?"

"Almost as many hundreds as I have claws on all my paws, cat brother," she replied.

"Sun, Wind and Sacred Steel!" beamed Bili in consternation. "Where did old Sir Steev come up with almost two thousand men?"

"Those of Count Sandee and the others of Kuhmbuhluhn are

but half or less, cat brother. The others are strange Moon Maidens and strange Ahrmehnee, many, many of them, along with certain of your fighters I remember from the long march and the battle before the earth moved and the burning rocks set the forests all ablaze. They are led by a twoleg called Sir Geros.''

"Geros! Sir Geros Lahvoheetos? Here, in New Kuhmbuhluhn? But how? Why? No, no need for you to try to answer, Stealth. I think I know the answers to those questions, though what I ever did to deserve such a degree of loyalty . . . I wonder just how many long months that brave, faithful man has ridden these mountains in search of me.''

He beamed again to Whitetip. "This will teach you, I hope, brother chief, not to jump to erroneous conclusions . . . if that's what you did, this time. Nor shall I inquire further as to the reason for your lengthy absence from your assigned duties. For now, your assignment is to see Stealth here well fed and furnished a comfortable place to rest until I am ready to again meet with you two. A Skohshun herald is due this day, and I must welcome him and entertain him. When I am free to do so, I'll mindcall you. Dismiss.''

*Thoheeks* Bili's mindcall, however, came far sooner than either the sulking Whitetip or Bili himself had expected. It was issued hard on the heels of the young commander's initial meeting with the Skohshun herald, Sir Djahn Makadahm.

"Chief Whitetip," Bili beamed urgently, "immediately it is dark enough to hide you, hie you down to the Skohshun camp and bring me back a report on the following: how badly the camp was damaged, if there are significantly fewer twolegs, and how many of those twolegs seem to be seriously hurt—that is, unable to easily stand or walk about without help.

"When you return, I'll probably still bet at meat with Skohshun, the old one. Don't come into our presence. I still don't wish him to know that the bane of their herds is one of my valued warriors. Instead, beam the information to me. Then stand ready to cross the plain into the southern mountains. I need to be in communication with Sir Geros as soon as possible, and only my loyal cat brother's mind is powerful enough to allow for such distance.''

"Must Whitetip take that useless number-cat with him on his scouting tonight, cat brother?'' inquired the prairiecat.

"No," Bili replied, "Stealth lacks your endurance for long-distance travel. Tell her she is to go up to my suite and bide therein with my own female and our cubs until I return abovestairs. That strange killer still stalks, it seems—it killed and ate a man on two of the last three nights, despite a bad wound it suffered on the night you left to stampede the herd of the Skohshuns.''

The great furry brown beast slowly, softly approached the cradle wherein lay the two youngest Morguhns. Cruel, sparkling white fangs gleamed as the two infants were sniffed thoroughly from end to end. Olfactory investigation completed, Stealth gently licked those skin surfaces she could easily get her wide tongue at.

"They are good-sized cubs, cat sister," she mindspoke Rahksahnah. "But still are they both smaller than was your first cub, last year. It is not the usual for your kind to birth more than one at the time?"

Forgetting that she was mindspeaking, Rahksahnah shrugged, beaming, "That varies with strains and individuals, I think, my sister. My own mother, who was the *brahbehrnuh* before me, never bore more than one child at the time, but one of her blood sisters bore three, although two later died before reaching maturity. Another of their kin bore two sets of two; so I suppose that the possibility of bearing more than one is a part of my bloodline.

"But what of your own little cubs, sister? My Bili tells me that they are said to be well on the way to putting Count Sandee's stoats out of business."

With sharp knife and strong teeth, Sir Djahn Makadahm stripped the tender meat from off the bones of the young goat, repeatedly complimenting the consistency and delicate flavor of the whole-roasted kid.

"Meat of any fresh kind, not full of brine and pickling, is pleasing to me just now, Sir Bili, mightily pleasing. On the very night of your shrewd attempt to damage our camp, a huge mountain cat which has plagued us intermittently since first we went into camp stampeded our entire beef herd. The bawling bastards scattered to the four winds, and since then fresh meat has been rare and dear, leaving us usually with only salt pork and suchlike, that and the occasional stringy wild hare."

"We have our own animal problems, here, Sir Djahn," Bili remarked morosely, "but of a somewhat more serious nature than yours. Near every night for over a week now, a lean, reddish wolf has killed and eaten a man or woman in the burk."

Sir Djahn leaned closer, saying excitedly, "Perhaps, Sir Bili, it is the same creature? This cat hunts only by night, too, as I think I said."

"No." Bili shook his shaven head emphatically. "No, there was clear spoor at the first kill we discovered, and there has been more since, as well as sightings, and it is truly a wolf. But such a wolf—a wolf as big as a small bear, that leaves paw prints a hand and a half long and at least a hand broad.

"And tough! Why, Sir Djahn, the beast slew and was eating a baker's apprentice—a grown man, sizewise—one night last week when a party of cooks and bakers surprised him at it. One of them gashed the monster deep in the neck with a hard-flung cleaver and another ran a steel spit a good inch and a half in thickness some two *feet* into the creature's body, yet still he not only managed to get away, but killed and ate again on the very next night, seemingly none the worse for being hacked and pierced. What do you make of that?"

The herald laid down the bone and the knife, dipped his fingers in the bowl of warm water and floating rose petals, then carefully wiped them on the cloth provided to the purpose, before answering softly and in a most serious tone.

"Have you considered the possibility, Sir Bili, that you might be dealing not with a proper, natural beast, but with a werewolf?" At Bili's blank stare, he asked, "Does this wolf ever slay and eat other beasts?"

"No, Sir Djahn, and that has been an almighty puzzlement to us. The creature will pass directly in front of, leave spoor all around, a pen of helpless sheep or goats, then go into a house to kill and eat a grown man. Certain chambers back in the mountain, wherein we think he dens—for all that a thorough search failed to turn up trace of him—are all stacked high and hung with smoked flesh of all descriptions, yet he has never touched one flitch, that we could tell. He seems to crave only fresh-killed human flesh."

"Just so, Sir Bili," the elderly Skohshun nodded sagely. "When in his beast form, human flesh is all that a werewolf will ingest. And I find it understandable that you could not discover his lair, for he has none and needs none; in daylight hours, he passes freely and unsuspected among you, as one of you. Perhaps he even trod that dark warren beside you, or behind you, secretly laughing as he "aided" you in your search for that which he well knew did not exist."

Bili did not try to repress or hide his shudder. "Then, Sir Djahn, is there no way to recognize, to detect, such a murderous monster in daylight?"

"A few," answered Sir Djahn, "but they are not hard and fast or accurate in all cases, I have been informed; quite often, in fact, one or more of them will be possessed by men and women who are as normal as are you and I, so be most exceeding careful lest you make a hasty and erroneous judgment.

"When in their human guise, werewolves often are excessively hairy of body and limbs, with fast-sprouting beards and thick, coarse hair on their heads. More werewolves, it is said, have red or auburn hair than any other coloring. Their teeth are large and the upper cuspids are said to be noticeably longer than the other front teeth, and sometimes they are sharply pointed, as well. Often the two eyebrows of a werewolf will, when he is in his man form, grow thickly together above the nose, so that he appears to have but a single eyebrow. Men and women who are secret werewolves are exceeding strong and agile. The ears of these human monsters are said to be always small and laid flat against the skull, and sometimes they are pointed at the upper tip, as well. The third finger of their hands is right often as long or even longer than the middle one, whilst the nails of all the fingers are rounded rather than flat and very strong.

"Please understand, Sir Bili, I have never that I know of met or even seen a true werewolf. The knowledge that I pass on to you here is but a compendium of the ancient legends of my folk. The Skohshuns, long centuries agone, lived for a few years in a far northern land where real wolves were a constant menace and werewolves a hidden threat. But in my own life, I have known or at least met men and women bearing one or more of those supposed telltale traits who were no more werewolves than am I.

"I wish you luck, Sir Bili, whether you discover your manslayer to be natural or unnatural beast. But that discussion is not, you must know, the reason why my superior sent me back to enjoy your most generous hospitality."

When the Skohshun herald had stated his case, he sat back and waited for what he was certain would ensue—probably polite refusal, possibly a refusal verging upon insult. He had been steeling himself for this latter possibility since he had ridden across the booming timbers of the bridge, for what he was here proposing was, indeed, ludicrous, all things considered. And so he was shocked to the innermost core of his being when his host answered.

Rolling the stem of his gold-washed silver goblet between his broad fingers, Bili regarded Sir Djahn for a longish moment, then nodded brusquely. "That which you suggest is not out of all reason, sir. Certain of my garrison, especially so the noblemen of New Kuhmbuhluhn, are become quite bored with the dragging aspects of siege warfare, and our sally the other night seemed rather to increase their thirsts than to slake them. What would you say to planning this set battle for next week?"

Old Sir Djahn felt as if the flat of a poleaxe had crashed upon his balding pate. But as it had been years in the forging, his steely self-control immediately asserted itself and his voice and outward demeanor rang calm and assured in tone and appearance.

"I believe that Sir Ahrthur was thinking more in terms of *two* weeks hence, Sir Bili, or perhaps even three."

Bili shook his head. "Two weeks, Sir Djahn, no more. The autumn is short hereabouts, as well you should know, and the winter snows follow quickly upon autumn's heels. Are my noble New Kuhmbuhluhn officers who are landholders to get back to their fiefs and properly prepare the earth for next spring's planting, it must be done soon."

Sir Djahn's white eyebrows rose a careful half inch. "You assume that New Kuhmbuhluhn arms will triumph over somewhat superior numbers, then, Sir Bili?"

"Why not?" grinned Bili. "You obviously assume that your quantity will triumph over our superior quality. Expect you not a near rout of Kuhmbuhluhn arms such as you Skohshuns enjoyed when last we met at swords' points, either, Sir Djahn. The late King Mahrtuhn in his dotage and senility deliberately crippled that field force, denying us the use of what are the most effective means of dealing with schiltrons and similar formations. Neither his present majesty nor I will be so foolish and deluded in our own choices of strategy and tactics, you may believe that. We will meet you armed with every advantage we may possess, expecting no less from you and your army.

"So, where shall we fight, Sir Djahn? On the plain between the base of the mountain and your camp, perhaps? I think me that that would be the logical place."

Sir Djahn smiled fleetingly. "Logical, maybe, but not a safe place for Skohshun regiments to group, you must admit; not with the range of your engines to be considered or the weights they can throw for that range. No, let us meet on the other side of the camp."

"I march my men into the jaws of no traps," Bili stated flatly. "Nor do I commence a battle with foemen both before and behind, not if I have the ordering of it.

"But, too, I can empathize with you, so let us plan it in the following way. . . ."

"That was the very best that I could do, Ahrthur," Sir Djahn told the brigadier immediately he returned to the Skohshun camp. "It is not the three weeks I know you would have preferred, but it is not either the bare single week that Duke Bili originally suggested; we compromised on that as well as on other matters."

The brigadier just sat listening and fingering idly the small, blunt-ended dagger he used to ream out his pipes. When Sir

Djahn was done, he said, "You seemed so certain when you departed that those New Kuhmbuhluhnburkers would refuse at the very least, might even laugh you out of the city, yet this so canny war leader of theirs apparently accepted our outrageous—patently outrageous, all things and conditions considered, and I'll now be the first and the foremost to admit that fact—proposal. Now I want to know why, Djahn. Why did this man willingly toss away a brimful basket of real advantages and agree to meet our regiments openly, on the plain, where the clear advantages are ours?"

The herald shrugged. "It's a true gamble to take for gospel what any opposing war leader says, especially if he happens to be a known professional, a mercenary with damnall ties to the troops he commands. You are not wrong to suspect that this mysterious Duke Bili of Morguhn may well be dicing with a tapered cup or may well have a double bushel of aces up his sleeves, but I, who have met and talked with him, am a bit more inclined to believe the explanations he gave for wishing to get it all over and done with now.

"For one thing, he is saddled, afflicted, with a gaggle of noble fire-eaters of Kuhmbuhluhn who are growing bored and dissatisfied with the inactivity of a siege. For another, even the steadier vassals of King Byruhn are all a-itch to get back to their lands and prepare them for the planting season, next year. For the last, Duke Bili gave me the impression that he would like nothing so well as to leave New Kuhmbuhluhn with his condotta and go on to a new contract elsewhere, which is, one supposes, understandable in a professional.

"But the crowning reason, the one which leads me to believe all of the rest is truth, is the unpleasant fact that there appears to be a werewolf preying upon the burkers and the garrison of New Kuhmbuhluhnburk. The descriptions Duke Bili rendered of the habits of the creature, the various attacks, the fact that hounds become hysterical and refuse to trail the beast, not to mention the evidence that it survives what would be death wounds to a less uncanny animal, these all lead me to the belief that this bane of that unhappy burk can be nothing save a werewolf."

The brigadier shuddered. "No wonder he and they are more than willing to sacrifice advantages to get out of that city.

"All right, Djahn, I'll dispatch another galloper to our glen, and then you and I will go render your formal report to my staff and the regimental commanders. Did you bring back anything decent to drink, by chance?"

"Indeed, yes," smiled Sir Djahn. "Duke Bili gifted me a

small keg of an old and potent applejack.'' He produced his silver flask and proffered it.

The third night on the road from Skohshun Glen, Johnny Kilgore's big, bred-up pony ambled into camp with the old Ganik in the saddle and a hogtied captive jouncing uncomfortably belly-down, across the withers. ''Guess whut I founded back up the trail a ways, ginrul,'' he crowed good-naturedly. ''A pegleg Skohshun, thet's whut. Too bad I ain' still a bunch-Ganik—he's a young 'un and'd be raht tenduh and tasty, I 'low.''

General Jay Corbett set aside his tin plate of rabbit stew and stood up to regard the fine-boned, one-legged young man standing unsteadily before him. The pale face was drawn with strain and pain, but it still bore the stamp of firm resolution and the gaze of the eyes was steady, purposeful.

''Ensign Thomas Grey, I presume,'' he said wryly. ''Does your mother know where you are, Tom?''

''Of course she does, sir,'' the boy snapped. ''Not that it is needful for her to know, for I am no child, if that is what you meant to imply, General Corbett, sir.''

''How the hell did you get here so fast?'' Corbett demanded. ''Those charges blocked that defile solidly, of that I'm more than certain. And no man could have gotten a horse over any part of those mountains—of that I'm equally certain.''

A smile flitted briefly about young Grey's lips. ''No, sir, no horse, but a mountain pony; one of those ponies ridden into the glen from without, last spring, by one of Dr. Arenstein's wild men. Had I been able to be astride a decent horse, your rearguardsman there would never have caught me. But those little ponies have no endurance, no heart. The cursed beast foundered yesterday.''

Corbett nodded. ''So you came on afoot, despite all the odds. Knowing full well that your chances of getting through us and on to the field army ahead of us ranged from infinitesimal to nonexistent, still you hobbled along that deep-rutted trace for more than twenty-four hours. Unless you stopped long enough to sleep, which I doubt.'' Thought of the suffering the boy must have endured brought a lump into Corbett's throat. Gruffly, he demanded, ''So, now, what am I to do with you?''

The young man drew himself up to rigid attention. ''Sir, I was aware of what you told his lordship you would do to any Skohshun messengers, aware of my fate if caught. If I've a choice, I would prefer the sword or the axe to the rope. I have made my peace with God, sir. I am ready to . . . to die."

Corbett's throat contracted painfully around the still-present lump and he found it necessary to noisily clear it before he said, "Lord love you, lad, I have no intention of killing you. Give me your parole, and I'll set you on a mount and let you ride back to the glen, after breakfast, in the morning."

But Grey shook his head stubbornly. "I would that I could, sir, but I cannot. I have undertaken a grave responsibility and I shall not willingly rest or tarry until my obligations are discharged."

Jay Corbett sighed. He should have known better, he reflected. Of course such a young man as Thomas Grey would not give a parole unless he intended to abide by its conditions.

The officer shrugged. "All right, Gumpner, we now have a prisoner. Get him fed and bedded down for the night . . . under guard, of course. And please have the corpsman take a look at the stump of his leg, too. I'll give long odds it's rubbed raw and bleeding after all that walking on this abomination of a wagon track."

As the mindspeak abilities of Sir Geros Lahvoheetos were at best marginal, the initial contact with Bili of Morguhn and all subsequent ones needs must be of a roundabout nature. Bili farspoke the prairiecat Whitetip, who then mindspoke one of the Kindred warriors who had ridden out in search of Bili with Geros, Hari Danyuhlz, who then spoke to Geros and mindspoke that night's reply back to Whitetip for farspeak transmission to Bili. Even so, it was far and away faster and easier than would have been the only alternative—trying to get gallopers the full width of the plain through the Skohshun lines and back again the same distance.

"The battle is set," beamed Bili, "for the second hour after dawn, eleven days from today, and I want your force to stay just where you now are until the last possible moment, and give yourselves just enough time to reach the battlefield by the third hour after dawn of that day. It is imperative that no one of you come out of those mountains, for if these Skohshuns even suspect your existence so close, they will surely call off the battle; the only reason they are willing to fight it at all is that they think to win it, considering that they outnumber us.

"Now when you attack them, Geros, whatever you do, don't just charge in, hell for leather, and try to hack your ways through that pike hedge. That's just what they will want you to attempt, and it cannot be done. No, sit off at easy dart range and let your archers and Ahrmehnee dartmen and the Kuhmbuhluhn axe throwers whittle the formations down a bit, disorganize the bastards, take out their front ranks, their sergeants and any officers you can spot and range. *Then* you charge.

"These Skohshuns seem to basically scorn missilemen of any sort and they number no archers in their ranks. They do have a few crossbowmen, prodmen and slingers, but hardly enough of them to worry about, and they will probably be on camp guard, anyhow. They have also three highly unusual, very long-range missile weapons called ryfulz which are invariably fatal and very accurate, so if you lose a few men at seemingly impossible distances, don't be surprised.

"That's all for now, Geros.

"Now, Whitetip, please mindspeak Count Sandee."

Near noon of the day after the capture of Ensign Grey, the vanguard, hearing fast-approaching hoofbeats from up ahead, ambushed and captured another Skohshun. The man they hustled back to the head of the main column was about five years the senior of Thomas Grey, but looked and acted to be of the same breed and kidney.

Corbett questioned the galloper briefly. Again, he offered a parole that was courteously refused. So, then, he pushed on with two captive Skohshuns rather than one. Early the next morning, that number became three and the officer wondered if he might run out of men to guard the prisoners, if this pace continued. Like it or not, he might have to begin executing captured Skohshun messenger riders.

But the next stranger, brought in by Merle Bowley, would require no guard. He was another Ganik, he was armed with a Broomtown rifle and he was mounted upon a finely bred, most spirited riding horse. His name was Counter Tremain.

It had rained every nightlong for the best part of a week, and Bili hoped that the residents of the Skohshun camp—their tents and huts mostly burned up or holed by Kuhmbuhluhnburk engines—were thoroughly miserable. Although dry and well fed, he was none too happy himself, what with the endless rounds of inspections, supervisory duties, receipt of and evaluation of reports, arbitration of the seemingly endless disputes among members of the royal council and similar tedious minutiae of command. His days stretched from dawn until late into every night, so he sometimes slept in one of the side chambers of his huge suite rather than take the chance of awakening the twins and Rahksahnah at midnight or beyond.

For her own part, Rahksahnah was not overfond of her mate's lengthy absences, either. She had become accustomed to the warm, familiar nearness of his big body whether sharing with him a campaign pallet, a camp bunk or a palace great-bed, and the inability to reach out and touch his flesh, to listen for his steady breathing, to lie with her nostrils full of the dear, unmistakable scent of him caused her to be even more wakeful than she ordinarily would have been through constantly listening with at least half an ear for the twins, who slept in their cradle in one of the side chambers with their wet nurse, a strapping peasant girl whose own baby had been born dead. Pah-Elmuh had used his mental accomplishments to ease the girl's mind of that tragedy, so that she now was smiling and cheerful in addition to producing quantities of rich milk for the two ravenous young Morguhns.

The creature was again abroad, after an enforced four days of fasting. So weak was it become that it could barely place one huge paw ahead of the other, and the digestive organs within its shrunken belly were a gnawing, growling, ceaseless torment. They demanded food, instantly—hot, rich, red, still-quivering manflesh. But in its present sorry state, the creature knew without consciously thinking that it was no match for any adult man, armed or no. So it prowled the dark, benighted corridors and stairwells seeking prey less able to defend itself.

Finally, from far off, borne on air currents circulating in the drafty corridors and open stairwells, it caught the mouth-watering scent of blood, fresh-spilled blood, along with the scent of milk. The creature found previously unknown reserves of energy and, keen nose held high to keep the scents, it began to walk faster, following the odors back to their source, almost loping as they became stronger, only slowing its pace as the scent trail led it closer and closer to an area of corridors lit by chain-hung metal lamps and iron-sconced pine torches. Thereabouts, the blood-milk smells were almost overlaid with other smells, smells of danger to the enfeebled creature—adult men, several of them, along with the stinks of polished leather, oiled steel and, distantly or in very small amounts, a hint of something that bred a vague, ill-defined and uneasy dread in the furry breast of the hungry creature of the night.

But then that hunger drowned every other thought and emotion, saving only immediate caution in the stalk. This near, the creature could more closely identify the blood smell. It was moon-blood, and moon-blood meant a female twolegs, most of which were smaller and weaker than most males, thus more easily killed—a partial compensation for the lesser amount of edible flesh on such a carcass, such a compensation as the creature could appreciate in his present lack of full strength.

Moreover, the milk was twoleg milk, and that meant the availability of at least one young or infant twoleg, even easier, more vulnerable prey than a female. And its nose told it that all of this hot, tender flesh was just beyond the brightly lit place where stood the males with the long, sharp-pointed things of steel and wood. There were just too many of them to chance a rush at them.

But then, somewhere deep, deep down in a near-forgotten portion of its mind, there emerged the memory of another way, a secret way to safely pass those dangerous male twolegs and attain to the presence of its foreordained victims, its night's kill and its much-needed meal. Turning about, it slunk back up the corridor, head and tail lowered, bound for a certain dimly remembered spot. Its stomach gnawed and growled and gurgled on, but the creature now knew that soon the organ would be stilled while disgesting a full filling of tender, bloody flesh.

At the first sounds from the twins, the wet nurse had arisen, padded over to the hall door, lit a splinter from the wall torch outside that door, then closed it again, padded back over to light the lamp and taken up the infants. Sitting upon the sinfully soft bed that was hers so long as her milk lasted, she gave each little pale-pink mouth one of her brown, hair-fringed nipples and sat contentedly, rocking slightly on her ample rump and humming softly the strains of a folk dance of New Kuhmbuhluhn, while the babes filled their little bellies, sucking avidly at her engorged breasts.

A squeal of metal on long-unused metal startled her, and she looked in the direction of the sound in time to see a section of the old polished oaken paneling swing open and a huge, horrible, shaggy-furred beast stalk snarling from out the very wall of the chamber, the lamplight making hellish red coals of its eyes, deadly menace in its every movement.

In the brief moment before stark terror paralyzed her, she uttered a single, piercing scream, clutched her innocent charges close to her breast and stared helplessly at the slavering predator, now bare yards distant.

# CHAPTER XIII

Between mouthfuls of venison steak and baked wild sweet potatoes, Counter Tremain had been telling of all that had happened with Erica Arenstein and the rest of them since Merle Bowley had left Skohshun Glen in search of more ammunition for the rifles. He had progressed to near the present time.

"I nevuh thought I'd come to whar I'd cheer fer a damn Kuhmbuhluhner, but them bastids is flat beatin' the evuh-lovin' shit out'n them Skohshun pricks! And they doin' 'er 'thout evuh so much as comin' out'n the dang city, too. And thet thar tears the assholes of them damn Skohshuns up suthin fierce, 'count of they knows they got mo' mens then the Kuhmbuhluhners and they jest dyin' fer to get 'em to come out an' fight or to git in thet city after 'em, and the bugtits cain' do neethuh one.

"Merle, you recolleck them thangs the fuckin' Kuhmbuhluhners had whut would throw great big ole rocks awn to the main bunch camp fum three ridges away? Well, looks like them bastids is done dragged them friggin' thangs clear up here, 'cause they got 'em a-hint the wall of New Kuhmbuhluhnburk and, night I lefted, they'd throwed fireballs big as a warhoss's ass inta the Skohshun camp, set purt' near the whole thang to fahr, then cuminceted a-throwin' bunches of rocks awl ovuh the fuckin' place so it looked like it wuz flat rainin' rocks! So miny of the hosses and awl wuz eethuh gettin' hurtid by them rocks or a-frahted by the fires, some Skohshun ossifuh, he grabbed him ever swinging dick he could find and set us to a-leadin' the critters out'n the back gate. Well, I had mah ryfuhl crost of my back, 'cause we'd awl grabbed 'em and awl the othuh stuff of ours we could whin owuh tent cominceted to burn, so soon's me and thet nice hoss was out'n thet friggin' camp good, I jest jumped in thet saddle sumbody'd done not took awf'n him yet and then I made tracks 'crost thet plain, you bettuh b'lieve.

"It'uz two, three othuh bullies lawng of me to start out, but mah hoss wuz a lot faster'n they mules and I cain' say whut happund to 'em.

"Well, I rid souf fer near a week, a-ridin' by nahts and a-layin' up in the days, but I had to move slow, 'count of the bugtit Skohshuns out lookin' fer they cows whut awl stampeded the same naht I skeedaddled, but I fin'ly got to the dang mountins.

157

But them mountins is plumb full of mo' damn sojuhs—Kuhm-buhluhners, Ahrm'nees, eevuhn Moon Maiduhns. Aftuh the secun' tahm they damn near caught me, this ole boy, he come back down awn the fuckin' plain. Counter Tremain don' wawnt no dang Ahrm'nee a-drankin' beeuh out'n whu useta be his haid bones, thank you kin'ly.''

The riddle of the three missing Ganik bullies was solved a couple of days later, when Johnny Kilgore and Counter chanced across them camped in the woods and trying to decide what to do with their new-won freedom, where to go now that all of the Ganik outlaw bunches had been dispersed or driven out of New Kuhmbuhluhn.

Corbett simply added them to his command as scouts, under the command of Skinhead Johnny Kilgore and Merle Bowley.

Ravenous as he was, the creature was distracted by the excited voices of men, the poundings of fists and pike butts on the door—which the wet nurse had, as instructed, carefully bolted after lighting her splint from the wall sconce. Then there was another shriek of a twoleg female from close behind him, where-upon the attacks on the door redoubled, intensified.

Rahksahnah had been awakened from a light sleep by the single scream of the wet nurse. Scrambling across the width of the great-bed, she padded over the thick carpets to the door between the chambers. She opened it and took but a single step into the smaller room.

The wet nurse, nude to the waist, her brown hair disordered, was crouched far back in the bed alcove, her dimpled arms pressing the nursing twins tightly against her body, her brown eyes wide and bulging in an excess of terror, her mouth wide, too, but only a rasping whine emanating from it.

Rahksahnah screamed, even while her mind beamed out a frantic message, *"Bili, it is here, the killer wolf is here, in our suite, stalking the nurse and our children!"*

Bili had been meditating yet another of those increasingly common, increasingly petty disputes in the royal council, when the telepathic summons reached him. His face suddenly went as white as curds. Springing to his feet so violently that he sent the heavy canopied armchair crashing over backward, his big hand grasped the only available weapon—the heavy, ancient, Royal Kuhmbuhluhn sword of state, which always lay before the king's chair on the council table during any meeting, whether or not the monarch himself was present.

The sword had once, long, long ago, been the battle brand of a king, but now the blade was devoid of any edges and had, moreover, been inletted for the most of the blade length with designs and lettering inset in gold and silver. But to Bili it was simply a weapon there in a time of need, and it did at least have a good point.

As he half-ran toward the door, he shouted to the councilors, "Gentleman, the killer wolf has somehow got into my suite and is threatening my wife and children. Those of you with arms and the guts, follow me."

Unlike the peasant wet nurse, Rahksahnah was not the sort of woman to scream once and freeze, shuddering and staring in the face of impending doom. Scioness of a warrior race, a stark, veteran warrior, herself, she backed into the larger chamber. There she found by memory and feel the rack whereon hung her panoply and drew her oiled and gleaming saber from its scabbard with the one hand, while shaking a long, wide-bladed dirk out of its case with the other. Then the still-naked but now well-armed young mother raced back to the defense of her young and the helpless peasant girl.

The creature had been distracted but momentarily—his stomach brought his attention back to his waiting meal—but then there was sudden movement on his right rear and something sharp and hurtful sank deep into his chest, between his jutting ribs, just behind his right shoulder. Snarling his pain and rage, he turned his huge head, snapping toothy jaws at the source of his agony. By happenstance, his second snap closed on something solid, and he furiously wrenched at it. It came free with more pain and a wet, sucking sound, whereupon he let it drop from his jaws and turned back purposefully toward his victims, only to find that now another twoleg female stood between him and them, a long, shiny, curved thing of steel clenched in one of her forepaws.

Bili of Morguhn, bearing the bared sword of state in one big hand, trailed by some two thirds of the Royal Council, armed haphazardly with everything from dress hangers to ancient, rusty, dusty weapons wrenched from wall displays, pounded down corridors and up flights of stairs.

As the party approached the wing that housed the sprawling suite, the noises of the guardsmen furiously attacking the stout door became audible—shouts, grunts, poundings, all so far unavailing. Arrived upon the scene, Bili motioned the men all away and threw his own powerful young body against the unyielding portal; it groaned protestingly, but held firm. Again he hurled himself at the old iron-bound door, but still it stood solid. He wasted no more time or effort so fruitlessly.

"Sergeant," he snapped to the leader of the guards, "that oaken bench down the corridor there—fetch it back up here at the double. With three of you on each side of it, only a few swings should have that door down or at least open."

Rahksahnah was horrified when the massive wolf not only did not seem hurt unto death as it should have been by the accurately cast dirk that must surely have pierced its heart but, with seeming sentience, took the hilt of the weapon between its slavering jaws and pulled it out of its chest. Nonetheless, she had gotten to where she knew she must be, where she would make her life-or-death stand, between the hellish beast and her babes.

Snatching a thick, heavy woolen shawl from the nearby crib, she flung it over the head of the charging wolf, then sidestepped and chopped down with all her might, feeling in her very marrow the solid impact of her saber against the dense bone of the beast's skull . . . but still he came on, shaking his head to try to rid it of the blinding, heavy cloth.

Again she struck, but with no more apparent effect. She could feel the edge of the bedstead against the backs of her legs; there could be no more retreat.

She was, in her deadly concentration, unaware of the fact that the thick door had at last been battered in until Bili suddenly was looming there before her, with the lamplight glittering along the length of an old-fashioned longsword, and the room behind him seemingly crowded from wall to wall with armed men.

". . . dirk through his heart, Bili," she gasped, forgetting her mindspeak, ". . . didn't stop him, he . . . jaws, pulled it out! Full arm swing across head, should've cracked his skull . . . I think . . . be demon, witch-beast . . . can't be killed! Beware!"

Huge and unnaturally powerful as the wolf assuredly was, Bili's mighty two-handed swing of the heavy old sword still drove him belly-down onto the floor, though it failed to crack his spine, as it would have that of any more mundane beast. His head now free of the woolen shawl, his fiery eyes fixed upon this new antagonist, the wolf furiously scrabbled his clawed paws for purchase, making to rise. That was when Bili drove the ancient blade completely through the furry body, pinning it to the floor.

The howl that the beast then voiced was unearthly, ghastly, sounding far less like the death howl of an animal than the dying scream of a man. A terrible shudder rippled the length of the massive beast's body, it let go its dung and its urine, vomited a great gush of blood, then it's fearsome head fell into the blood, the eyes lost their fire and began to glaze over.

Bili bore the mercifully unconscious wet nurse into the main bedchamber, while Rahksahnah followed with the fed and now-sleeping twins. He was just striking flint on steel to light the lamps when shouts and cries of depthless horror smote his ears.

"The . . . the wolf, Bili. It must be, I told you, can't be killed!" stuttered Rahksahnah.

"Now, damn it, the beast is *dead*!" snapped Bili. "You saw it die, we all did." Nonetheless, he lifted his great double axe down from the wall hooks before hurrying back into the smaller chamber.

In the wavery light of the dim and flaring, flickering lamp, Bili did not at first recognize what the men all were staring upon with such fascinated horror. The great sword still stood up from the hairy body it pinioned, lamplight setting the golden hilt and crossguard, the jewels of the pommel and the gold and silver insets of the exposed portions of the wide blade to flashing like bits of fire.

But then Bili moved to where he could better see the focus of the others' attention . . . and the mighty axe dropped from a suddenly nerveless hand, while his bemused mind whirled with a chaos of half-formed thoughts.

That body pierced through with the royal sword of state of the Kingdom of New Kuhmbuhluhn, that huge, big-boned body, covered almost entirely with thick, curly, dark-red hair, that body lying dead in its own dung and blood, pinned to the floor by Bili of Morguhn's single, powerful thrust, that body was not the body of the monstrous wolf Bili had slain. That body was the dead body of Byruhn, King of New Kuhmbuhluhn!

Two hours later, the sword of state had been cleaned and once more lay in its accustomed place, but now serving as the surrogate for a monarchy permanently extinct in the original line of succession, representing a dead dynasty. *Thoheeks* Sir Bili of Morguhn sat once more in the tall, canopied armchair, and the still-shaken councilors, white-faced and dumb, for this once, ranged both sides of the long walnut table. At the opposite end of the table, occupying a specially crafted, outsized seat, towered the hairy bulk of Pah-Elmuh, the Kleesahk.

"The . . . the body," Bili informed the council members,

"is back on its couch in the chamber above. None saw what was borne from my suite, and as the guardsmen who did it are all Freefighters of my own squadron, none will ever know.

"Up in that chamber, the guardsmen and I found the corpse of poor Oodehn, the Kleesahk whose turn it was this night to bide with the late king. Oodehn still lay upon his pallet—his throat had been torn out, apparently, whilst he slept, for there was no slightest sign of any struggle or combat.

"New Kuhmbuhluhn is not my land and people, New Kuhmbuhluhnburk not my city, yet I feel strongly that those outside this chamber be told only that King Byruhn, after lying long near to death, finally succumbed of his fearsome head injury, on this night. Then let us get the body encrypted as soon as is decently possible.

"Insofar as the war and the siege and the impending set battle are concerned, since both of the monarchs to whom I swore my oaths now are deceased, I could—both legally and morally— march out with my squadron. But I shall not. I shall continue in my present capacities, if that is agreeable to all of you gentlemen, until the battle be won by our combined arms, the siege be broken and the Skohshuns put to flight.

"Meanwhile, I strongly urge that you all forget, forgo your rivalries and senseless grievances long enough to choose a successor to King Byruhn. Well, have not one of you a suitable candidate in mind?"

Archcount Sir Daifid Howuh cleared his stringy throat. "Actually . . . no, your grace. With the . . . the, ahhh, demise this eve of our lamented King Byruhn, the House of Mahrloh, the ancient, royal house of New Kuhmbuhluhn, be extinct."

"Well, dammit, man, this is no time to quibble in regard to legal niceties," snapped Bili peevishly. "If the main line be done, surely there are cousins, cousins-german, bastards—any degree of kinship will do at this point in time. You are going to need a single, strong authority in the wake of this Skohshun business and in getting the kingdom reorganized, are you to escape rebellions and civil war."

"There be no way we'll get that or eke anything approaching it," remarked young Count Mak Kahnuh, "not out of the remaining kin of the House of Mahrloh, lord duke. With the sole exceptions of you and Pah-Elmuh, everyone in this room is of some distant blood kinship to the former royal house, but we're none of us of close enough kin to lodge the claim of one above that of the others. That would be the surest road to unrest within the kingdom, to the very real possibility of a full-scale rebellion right here in this still-beleaguered city, Skohshuns or no Skohshuns. As regards bastards, there are none, in fact.''

"Oh, come, come, now, Count Mak," said Bili, "Prince—rather, King—Byruhn was a very lusty man. He had at least one mistress he kept at Sandee's Cot—that was common knowledge, there. Surely, he had many more over the years, here, there and elsewhere throughout the kingdom.''

Archcount Sir Daifid sighed. "At least a score and a half that come to my mind immediately, both of common and of noble antecedents; young Prince Byruhn was intensely masculine and he remained so throughout his life. But, your grace, he never, ever sired offspring; no single one of his many and legion bedmates was ever known to conceive of his seed, and that is fact.''

"Well, then," Bili pressed on, "what about his nephew, Prince Mahrtuhn Gilbuht? Surely the old king, King Mahrtuhn, had seen to it that his chosen heir had wed and bred.''

The old archcount sighed once again, even more deeply. "Oh, yes, the young prince had been wed, twice, in fact. His first wife—my own little granddaughter, Mahrsha—died of a broken neck when her horse fell on a hunt, only six months a bride. His second wife—a younger sister of Sir Yoo Folsom—lived for nine years without ever conceiving of him.''

"She still lives, then?" inquired Bili hopefully.

"No," replied the archcount in a low, embarrassed tone. "Her majesty died by her own hand some years agone.''

"And as well for everyone that she did, too," snapped the eldest of the councilors, Duke Klyv Wahrtuhn. "That would've been a sticky, stinking business, helpful to none and exceeding hurtful to full many, had she not belatedly recalled the constraints of honor and duty to her house and her class.''

"Now just a minute, your grace!" a red-faced and obviously riled Count Djohsehf Brahk, Sir Yoo Folsom's overlord, stood and almost shouted. "Adultery was never proven, and you know it! Both poor little Dahna and your ne'er-do-well nephew were dead before any of us knew anything had occurred. But I'm more than inclined to believe the letter she penned before she used the dagger. She was always an honorable woman—I'd known her from very infancy.''

Archcount Sir Daifid, virtually radiating hostility and bloodlust, shoved back his own chair to stand leaning across the broad table and shaking a bony fist at the younger man. "Son of a shit-eating bitch," he snarled, "you've accused my late, lamented nephew of the foul crime of rape over and over again. I'd have long since had your wormy guts for garters, had I thought for one minute that any sane nobleman of this kingdom would believe, could believe you or your false and utterly baseless calumnies of the dead. But everyone who is anyone in New Kuhmbuhluhn knows the truth—your poor little Dahna was precious little less than an arrant whore!"

Three other councilors had arisen and were adding their shouted threats and insults to the cacophony when Bili grasped the hilt of the sword of state and brought the flat of the blade crashing down upon the tabletop—once, twice, thrice. *"Sit down, and shut up,"* he barked, when he had gained their attention, adding, in a tone that dripped sarcasm, "Gentlemen!

"Please understand me and do not think for one minute that I am but voicing a false threat. There are deadly-serious matters to be here considered, now, this day, this hour, this minute, and it is we—all of us—who must consider and decide. For long weeks now I've sat in on your so-called meetings and I've seen far too many of them devolve into name-calling, insults of the basest orders and threats of maimings, death and blood feuds, as you all dredged up—for little cause or none at all—disagreements dating back years or generations. In the current crisis, I'll no longer tolerate such childish, selfish conduct from you, be clear on that point!

"Now, I am not your ruler, thanks be to Sun, Wind and Sacred Steel; were I, I much fear me that I would be inclined to clap you all in irons and incarcerate you somewhere back in that warren carved out of King's Rest Mountain, then choose me a set of royal councilors who were more serious about their responsibilities toward me and the good of the kingdom.

"I have said that I will remain here with my squadron until the Skohshuns be put to flight, but if there is only one more outbreak of the disgraceful sort I've just witnessed here, I shall mount my people and ride out under a flag of truce. The Skohshuns are aware that me and mine are mercenaries, not Kuhmbuhluhners, and I have the word of their herald, Sir Djahn Makadahm, that our passage out of the city, the burk and the kingdom will not be in any degree disputed or hindered by their army.

"Now, whilst you gentlemen calmly and politely discuss the available options and alternatives of this matter of a new king, I shall be mindspeaking with Pah-Elmuh, and if you all lapse into yet another spate of threats and name-calling, you can figure upon working out your surrender to the Skohshuns alone."

Abashed, never doubting for a single minute that the young commander meant every word he had spoken, that he and his squadron could and would ride out and leave the city and the kingdom to the will of fickle fate, all of the councilors resumed their seats and began to converse in low tones, one with the other.

"Now, Pah-Elmuh," Bili mindspoke, "I will have the truth of this matter. From what you said upstairs, when we found your son, Oodehn, dead, I would imagine that you knew more of the probable identity of our night killer than you chose to tell me. I was obviously wrong—I had thought that I had your trust and your loyalty."

"You had and you have, both, Lord Champion," the Kleesahk beamed forcefully. "But . . ."

"Then why, Pah-Elmuh? Why did you not even so much as suggest to me the possibility of what we now know was fact?" Bili demanded, the gaze of his blue eyes boring relentlessly into the ovoid-pupiled, unhuman eyes of the hominid.

Pah-Elmuh sighed resignedly. "Because of loyalties that far antedated any other, newer ones, Lord Champion. Loyalties to the House of Mahrloh, the first true-men who treated my forebears as men, as equals, and did not hunt us or consider us to be just another variety of beast. Now that revered house is extinct and I much fear that ere too many more years go by, we Kleesahks will be extinct, as well.

"Know you now, Lord Champion, that poor King Byruhn was not the first of his house to be so grievously afflicted; it was a blight which surfaced in almost every generation at least once, but in the last two generations it seemed almost a universal plague of the blood of Mahrloh. King Mahrtuhn himself had it, but it was in far milder form, and with the help of my instructions to his brain he was able to successfully fight it to a life-long standstill quite early in his young manhood, it being an affliction that does not manifest itself until the victim becomes pubescent.

"Prince Gilbuht, King Byruhn's younger brother and the sire of Prince Mahrtuhn Gilbuht, also had this milder form, as too did his only son, and we Kleesahks had long since given the same help to them.

"But the more serious form of the affliction was the legacy of the unfortunate King Byruhn, though the severity was not at first apparent. When it did become evident—in the form of a couple of full-scale seizures, complete transformations into the beast shape along with its terrible appetite—I at once devoted long years to slowly helping him erect a mental control over that regrettable tendency. By the time he had attained his twenty-fifth year, he had the ability not only to recognize the incipient onset of an attack of the affliction but that of competently coping with it, staving it off, with mental powers alone.

"Of course, although I doubt seriously that either of them ever told of it abroad, this hereditary affliction is also the real reason why neither of the last two princes—young Mahrtuhn Gilbuht and King Byruhn—ever sired offspring on any of their wives or women. Byruhn wished to take no slightest chance of passing so heavy and loathsome a burden on to any son he might sire—for some reason, females do not seem to be afflicted—and so he years ago prevailed upon me to perform a certain surgical procedure that rendered him completely sterile, but without affecting in any manner or means his performance as a whole man.

"Prince Mahrtuhn Gilbuht, although he bore but the milder variety of the affliction, also sought me out for this same procedure and I accommodated him, for it did much to ease his gentle nature and troubled mind. Upon his accession to the throne of New Kuhmbuhluhn, or right soon thereafter, it had been his intent to formally adopt an heir who might not be of so close a relationship as to carry the same intensity of the beastly affliction of his house. But as you know, Lord Champion, poor young Mahrtuhn Gilbuht died most gallantly before he ever had the chance to carry out aught of his plans.

"What King Byruhn would have done, I know not, but there on the road from that dreadful battle, when I told him that his royal father's spark of life had winked out, he remarked to me that he and I both knew that he must be the very last king of the House of Mahrloh and why. Perhaps he too intended to adopt a distant cousin as his heir—I know not."

"But, Pah-Elmuh," probed Bili, "you say that you had long ago taught Byruhn how to suppress these changes into wolf form. Then why did he suddenly lose his control and begin to stalk by night, killing and rending and devouring innocent folk? Why would he have slain Oodehn, yet not even try to eat him?"

"As to the sad death of my Oodehn, Lord Champion, I know not why he was slain—perhaps mere bloodlusting ferocity of the shameful thing King Byruhn had, through no fault of his own, become. As to why he did not then eat of my son, because none of these men who become beasts in this affliction ever will eat, in the beast shape, of any save human flesh.

"Why King Byruhn lost his carefully nurtured control, well, I can but speculate that perhaps the injury to his head had a detrimental effect on that part of his brain that housed his control. It also could be that as his man body lay slowly dying of lack of proper nourishment, the basic survival instinct awakened the beast in him and sent it out in 'search of the food needed to sustain them both. But now we never will know the real truth.''

# CHAPTER XIV

The morning of the set battle dawned with a bright glare of sunlight, presaging a hot day to come. Cottony islands of white cloud floated here and there in the pale-blue skies, peacefully sailing the high, airy oceans far above the bloody affairs of men.

But on this particular area of the earth, below that serene, celestial calm and stillness, drums had begun to roll even before the dawning, bugles to peal their imperative notes, men to shout orders, while horses stamped and neighed and snorted, metal rattled and clanked, leather creaked. There was neither quiet nor calm anywhere in the camp below or the city above, as two groups of warriors prepared to do again that which they did best—fight and maim and kill other warriors.

As prearranged, Sir Djahn Makadahm was the first man to ride out from the stockaded camp onto the space between camp and mountain that had been agreed upon as the site of the coming passage-at-arms. Almost immediately, he was joined there by the chosen herald of New Kuhmbuhluhnburk, Freefighter Captain Sir Fil Tyluh.

They two had met before, whilst Sir Djahn was being entertained in the city. Now both shucked gauntlets and clasped hands. "When will his grace of Morguhn arrive?" asked the Skohshun.

"Shortly, Sir Djahn," Fil Tyluh replied. "What of your own command party?"

"As soon as they see enough of your officers and nobles down here to reassure them that none of your long-range engines are likely to cast a wainload of rock upon them."

Silently, Tyluh beamed the reply to Bili, who sat his big stallion at the head of his already formed-up column within the passageway of the barbican, and Bili, in his turn, mindspoke the black horse he bestrode, "Now, my dear brother. At a slow walk, proudly, impressively."

Down the full length of the curving and recurving roadway, Mahvros progressed, his steel-shod neck arched proudly, prancing and capering, lifting his hooves high in a practiced parade walk. In all the cavalcade of New Kuhmbuhluhn noblemen and their mounts, Mahvros knew that he was the biggest, most beautiful, strongest and most dangerous warhorse, and his pride was plain to any man or horse watching his performance along the route of the column.

Bili had flatly refused the strong suggestion of councilors and certain others that he allow the palace smith to alter a harness of the late Prince Mahrtuhn Gilbuht to fit him, instead wearing that same three-quarter suit of plate he had worn when first he met the Kuhmbuhluhners nearly three long years agone. The only concession to their desires he had made was to allow a golden circlet, such as their own dukes displayed, to be affixed around the brows of his helm and a bunch of gold-tipped red plumes to be fastened atop the bowl of the helm.

He carried his own big double axe cased at the off side of his saddle pommel, a selection of Ahrmehnee darts in an open quiver on the near side. The sword he had taken from his downed opponent on the last occasion he had fought Skohshuns hung at his left side, a target hung from his cantle, and a long, broad dirk from his waist belt; a slender dagger was tucked into the top of one boot and a thick-bladed knife into the other. A two-quart skin of brandy-water hung from the off side of the cantle, balancing the target, and between them was lashed a head-sized ball of netting.

Once upon the surer footing provided by the soil of the plain, Mahvros curvetted twice, then settled back into his proud, graceful, strutting walk.

Immediately the column of riders had been seen to be proceeding down the mountainside, the main gate of the camp of the Skohshuns had been gapped and, as Bili led his followers out onto the open ground toward the spot whereon the two heralds awaited them, a similar column of mounted officers and standard-bearers had issued from that open gate.

Even before Sir Djahn introduced them, Bili had recognized Brigadier Sir Ahrthur Maklarin as the armored officer who had attacked him at the last battle.

"So this is the famous Sir Bili, Duke of Morguhn and most accomplished war captain, eh?" remarked Sir Ahrthur, smiling. "You've cost us dearly, young sir, dearly indeed, and we hope to reciprocate in greater or lesser measure, this day."

Bili grinned. "You have an exceeding hard head, apparently, Sir Ahrthur. I'd have thought that I cracked it wide with the toe of my boot, back at that battle in the spring."

Sir Ahrthur flushed dark red, his eyes narrowed and his lips thinned beneath his mustaches. "Yes, you're big enough to have been that bast . . . ahhh, to have been that man. What do you know of the sword I was using that day?"

Grasping the weapon carefully by the scabbard so as to give no slightest appearance of drawing steel, Bili showed the hilt to the brigadier, whose lividity deepened in hue.

"That was my father's sword, sir duke. You stole it from me!" There was clear fury in the old man's tone and demeanor.

But Bili just continued to grin, further infuriating the Skohshun commander. He shrugged, saying, "I'd not call it so, Sir Ahrthur, not at all. I was, shall we say, in dire need of a sword just then, because you had broken mine. I took yours because, as I now recall, you were in no present need of one. Or do I misremember, Sir Ahrthur?"

"Now, damn you, you mercenary bastard," snarled Sir Ahrthur, "I'll have my sword back!" He extended his right hand.

Bili just laughed. "If you win, today, you'll get it back . . . one way or the other."

Led by southern Kuhmbuhluhners who knew the northern plain well, with Whitetip ranged far out ahead to detect any parties or patrols of Skohshuns, Sir Geros' force had been moving at a slow, cautious, horse-saving pace for two days and nights and now were nearing the chosen battleground. King's Rest Mountain now loomed close enough to differentiate certain larger details of the city built into its flank.

When the young knight was assured by men who well knew whereof they spoke that his command was within a half hour's easy, ambling ride of the projected battle site, he ordered a halt and had his command dismount, loosen girths and rest, cautiously throwing out a staggered perimeter guard of keen-eyed Ahrmehnee dartmen and Freefighter archers with orders to loose or cast first and check identities afterward.

Raikuh smiled to Guhntuh, Bohluh and himself at the completely unprompted string of orders, remarking, "Our young war leader is fast learning his trade. Those months in the field against the Ganiks were at least good for that. I think that our dear lord Duke Bili will be pleasantly surprised at how well our Sir Geros has turned out."

Some miles to the left of Sir Geros' halted command, yet another warband was on the march, this one completely unbeknownst to Bili, the Kuhmbuhluhners, the Skohshuns or Sir Geros. But there were a few within the Skohshun camp who knew . . . and said nothing.

Late on the preceding afternoon, a lone rider had come from

the west, reined up at the rear gate of the stockade and, upon being recognized—him and his mount, both—had been admitted.

Disarmed and marched before the grim old brigadier, Counter Tremain had firmly, flatly denied having purposely stolen that officer's favorite horse or deserted, swearing over and over again that he had mounted the near-hysterical animal in an attempt to calm him down, that the gelding then had bolted and run so far in the darkness of the night that the dawn had found the Ganik with a spent horse in an area with which he had been completely unfamiliar and from which it had taken him this long to find his way back to the camp.

The mere fact that the man had returned with a valuable animal was, to the brigadier, reason enough to believe his story, so he formally thanked Counter, had his arms and effects returned to him and sent him to rejoin Erica Arenstein and her other followers. There, as soon as he was certain that they would not be overheard, Counter took the woman and Horseface Charley aside and told them the exciting truth of the matter.

The transceiver hung to the near side of the saddle pommel of General Jay Corbett's mount buzzed, signaling an incoming transmission on its wavelength. Lifting it to his mouth and activating it, he answered, "Corbett, here. Over."

"Oh, Jay, Jay," came Erica's well-remembered voice, "you can't believe how good it is to hear your voice again, to hear the voice of any civilized human being again. Christ, I've been afraid I'd live out this body and die in this stinking wilderness, with only gibbering barbarian apes for company."

"So, Tremain made it back safely, eh? And managed to snocker those Skohshuns, too? Over."

"Yes, Jay, that old fool of a brigadier is convinced he has a monopoly on brains. Hah! Just because Counter brought his pet horse back, he's convinced that Counter never even tried to desert, but rather did something almost heroic.

"Not only that, but this tinpot Napoleon thinks he has all but won his asinine little war because he has persuaded a numerically inferior enemy to come down out of a damned near impregnable fortified city and fight him on the plain. He thinks—hell, I don't think the old fart knows how to think.

"You know and I know that those New Kuhmbuhluhners—who have cost these Skohshuns hundreds of casualties and almost burned down their whole fucking camp some weeks back with catapults throwing fireballs and boulders—wouldn't just file down out of that city and bare their necks for the sword. They're bound to have a few dirty tricks in store for Sir Ahrthur and his damned pikemen, you can bet on it.''

"Did you tell your suspicions to this brigadier, Erica? Over," asked Corbett, thinking that if the senior Skohshun officer happened to feel himself in Erica's debt, he might let her and the others go without a fight.

"Oh, yes, I tried to," she answered wryly. "The arrogant old pig, he let me know that he considers war to be an exercise in machismo and that the only function of women is to bear sons to fight wars and, just possibly, nurse wounded soldiers. I hope he gets the ferrule end of a pike jammed up his arse today!''

One good look at the "porcupine" formations in which the Skohshuns were formed this day warned Bili of the folly of once more essaying the dismounted attack with the nets. Not only did the pikes now project in all four directions, the ranks were formed around a spine of men better armored and armed with an assortment of shorter, handier weapons—poleaxes, beef-tongues, partizans, greatswords and various types of flails and war hammers. Such troops would make bloody mincemeat of such an attack as Bili and his squadron had so successfully undertaken at the previous battle.

So he adopted the favored tactic of the late King Byruhn —leading his horsemen at a fast ambling gait along the front of the four schiltrons, while the Kuhmbuhluhn mountaineers cast their deadly little hatchets and the Ahrmehnee of his own squadron cast their equally deadly darts. On those occasions when the Skohshuns armed with the shorter weapons ventured out to close, Bili refused them combat, galloping his force off beyond their range at a pace too fast for them to follow afoot.

When the axes and javelins were expended, he mindspoke Captain Frehd Brakit and the archers commenced their deadly rain on the scantily armored pikemen—Freefighters with their short, powerful hornbows, Kuhmbuhluhners with hardwood selfbows as long as the archers were tall, loosing arrows three feet in length and tipped with tempered steel.

Twice during this phase of the battle, units of mounted and armored Skohshun lancers made to charge the lines of dismounted bowmen who were wreaking such deadly havoc on the helpless schiltrons. But each time these Skohshuns were met and bloodily stopped in their tracks by Bili and a portion of his heavy-armed squadron, reinforced by the Kuhmbuhluhn nobles.

As the archers expended their initial stocks of arrows and slacked off their death-dealing sleet of shafts, an armored man bearing an unpointed lanceshaft from which fluttered a white banner paced his horse slowly forward into the empty, hoof-churned space between the two forces. A brace of other armored horsemen followed him.

Recognizing the horses if not the riders at the distance, Bili sent Captain Sir Fil Tyluh out ahead with a white banner of his own and followed behind him with Lieutenant Kahndoot, who had happened to be the closest officer to hand.

Vainly hoping to stave off another confrontation between the seething brigadier and Duke Bili of Morguhn, Sir Djahn spoke first and fast. "Your grace, Sir Ahrthur is of the opinion that you are in violation of the agreements as regards this set battle. Not only are you deliberately avoiding any contact with our main force, but you are employing most dishonorable means to whittle away at men who have no chance to defend themselves or to strike back at those who are killing them. Do you intend to close, to press a charge through to the pikes? If so, when?"

Bili could scarce credit his ears, could hardly believe that any sane warrior would speak such arrant nonsense to another. "When will I charge, Sir Djahn? When it suits me to do so, that's when, and not until I can see that it will be to *my* advantage to press home a charge. Do you seriously believe that I led these men out here to let your pikemen butcher them? Spear them like so many fish? You yourself have admitted that your troops outnumber mine own, I'm simply evening those odds a bit. If that upsets your delicate sensibilities, why, then, I suggest that you form up your men in column and march them all back behind yonder stockade, whilst I and mine return behind the walls of New Kuhmbuhluhnburk. Perhaps you will feel better after you've wasted a few more hundreds of men against those walls, in a couple of days . . . if I haven't pounded and burned your camp, meanwhile.

"Now, do you want to fight a battle or sit here talking for the rest of this day?"

The brigadier could abide no more silently; he kneed his gelding forward and stared hard at Bili as he addressed Sir Djahn. "Fagh! I told you it would be an exercise in utter futility to speak of honor to this puling thief; I doubt me he ever knew the meaning of the word, and I cannot but wonder if this King Byruhn knows just what sort of scoundrel he has hired and placed in command of his army. Perhaps we should declare a truce, Sir Djahn, while you ride up there and try to determine if this cowardly kind of warfare be the will of the true ruler of New Kuhmbuhluhn."

Fil Tyluh spoke before Bili could. "Sir Ahrthur, poor King Byruhn died of his injuries last night. Until a new king is chosen, since he was the last of his house, New Kuhmbuhluhn's regent is Sir Bili, Duke of Morguhn. So the royal council has declared this morning."

Hurriedly, still trying to prevent the inevitable, Sir Djahn said, "Your grace, I never met your late king but the once; nonetheless, I grieve with you and all of New Kuhmbuhluhn."

"Well, I don't!" snapped the brigadier hotly. "I hope he's roasting in hell with the rest of the heathen! And I demand to know why this treacherous, backbiting mercenary bastard never mentioned to Sir Djahn during the negotiations for this so-called battle his intentions to not come to grips and fight breast to breast as honorable warriors should, as the late king's predecessor did, but to avoid real fighting in a most craven manner, while using the weapons of dishonor—bows, darts, slings and throwing axes—against his betters."

Bili looked speculatively at the snarling, red-faced old man. At last, he said, "Sir Ahrthur, either you are a complete ass and a fool or you think that I am such. To answer your first question: I told Sir Djahn that I would use every arm, every advantage in my possession or power to command, saving only that I would not employ my engines during the course of this battle, either against your formations or your camp.

"Now, if he or you chose to interpret that answer to mean that I would leave my missilemen—my archers, my dartmen, my axe throwers and my slingers—behind, as did poor, bemused old King Mahrtuhn, such was *your* choice of possible meaning.

"You carry on and on about fighting breast to breast, yet both King Mahrtuhn and Prince Mahrtuhn Gilbuht died without getting any closer to any of you Skohshuns that the length of an eighteen-foot pikeshaft. What honor in such a death, say I? You were able to delude an aging and nearly senile man and lead him on to his death with such hypocritic claptrap, but not Bili, *Thoheeks* and Chief of Morguhn and Knight of the Blue Bear of Harzburk.

"*If* all you spout out is to be taken at face value, then you are at the best a fool and should be locked away with the rest of the madmen, not left to command anyone's army. War is not a game, to be played by strict rules or not played at all. War is something to be avoided at all costs, except when it becomes a necessity. When it does become necessary, it is something akin to lancing a boil—you do it hard and quick and with all available force, so that it is the sooner done and men can return to the pursuits of peace.

"If, on the other hand, you are the cynical hypocrite I suspect you are—and if you are an average representative of your race—one who mouths the usages of honor in a self-serving attempt to rob war leaders of their natural advantages, warriors of their lives and folk of their lands, then I feel you all to be even more despicable than the Ganiks, the men who eat men, or than certain Ehleen rebels who butchered little children and drank their blood!

"If you truly want to close with my force so badly, Sir Ahrthur, let your schiltrons reform and charge us. Or do you Skohshuns lack the stomach to fight save in close formations and against men whose weapons are shorter than are yours?"

With a roar of inarticulate rage, Sir Ahrthur drew his sword and lashed out at Bili's face, exposed by the open visor. But quick as the old man drew and struck, Bili brought the huge, heavy axe up faster. Catching the edge of the blurring blade in one of the gaps between axehead and steel shaft, he gave his thick wrist a practiced twist which tore the sword from Sir Ahrthur's hand so forcefully as to snap the leather sword knot and send the blade clattering to the rocky ground.

The other three men and Lieutenant Kahndoot all held their breath, hands seeking out hilts, awaiting the general melee they all expected and feared would come when Bili axed down the truce-breaker.

Sir Ahrthur's red face had gone pale, as he sat panting with exertion. His only other weapon was a slim dagger—a mere joke against that monstrous double axe. "Well," he finally gasped, "kill me, you butcher! Or would you rather send for an archer to do your execution for you?"

But Bili was even as the old man spoke lowering his axe to rest again across the bow of his saddle. "If I meet you in battle, Sir Ahrthur, I'll kill you if I must, but needless killing or maiming is not a part of my nature. I think that we may consider this in-saddle truce to be done?"

Bili had just reached his own lines when a farspeak from Sir Geros by way of Count Steev Sandee by way of Whitetip beamed into his mind. "We are some quarter mile from the camp of these Skohshuns, Lord Bili. What are your orders for our advance?"

"Pass wide of the camp," beamed Bili. "There are crossbowmen at the corners of it, and I'll be unsurprised if they have a few engines, as well, for all that we burned up the last batch they had

built. Bypass the pike formations, too. Once past them, ride
directly into my lines. I'm hopeful that the mere sight of you and
your reinforcements will overawe them enough to allow for a
peaceable settlement and their withdrawal, after all; but if not,
I'll let your archers and dartmen and my own nibble at them a bit
more; then we'll all charge and roll over the buggers. With you
and yours, we'll finally have the numbers and the weight to do it
up brown.''

Erica's transceiver buzzed insistently. She picked it up, held it
in position and activated it. "Yes, Jay?"

"Erica, I thought you said that that battle was going on
somewhere just north of your camp—rather, the camp of the
Skohshuns? Over.''

"That's right, Jay, though it looked damned little like a battle
when I was up on the gate platform a little while ago. The
Kuhmbuhluhners were riding up and down in front of the
Skohshuns throwing darts and small axes, and the damned stupid
Skohshuns were standing so close together that I doubt if any of
those things thrown had a chance to miss. Anyway, at every
circuit those riders made, those poor damn pikemen dropped like
flies. Now they're raining them with arrows; I can see the sun
glinting on the shafts from here. What was that battle where the
British wiped out a whole German army with bows and arrows?
Apparently these Skohshuns never heard that particular story.''

"It was the English, Erica, not the British, fighting the French,
not the Germans, and it was two battles—Crécy and Agincourt.
But the reason I radioed you again was that my scouts and I have
spotted a very large force of cavalry riding in your direction from
the southwest. Scads of them, maybe as many as fifteen hundred,
and about half look suspiciously like Ahrmehnee warriors, to
me. Over.''

Erica chortled gleefully. "That pompous, presumptuous old
goat! Sir Ahrthur has gotten his hairy balls in a crack for good
and all. He refused to listen to the advice of a mere woman, and
he will, no doubt, shortly be in the shit up to his silly mustache.
It serves the chauvinist pig right!''

"Well, Erica, in light of these new developments, what do
you want us to do about getting you all out of there? Over.''

"Just blow out the back gate, Jay, and come on in. All of the
fighters are either out there getting their asses beaten off or
standing up at the front corners or above the front gate. The only
people left in the camp are cooks, servants of the officers,
medical personnel and quite a number of wounded men.''

"I don't like the thought of getting trapped in there, Erica. Look, I'll set my mortars up a couple or three hundred meters off and blow that gate, then drop a few mortar bombs in and around the front gate just to put the fear of God into them all, maybe throw in a rocket or two for luck. You and your men hotfoot it out to me. Bring along mounts if you can easily come by them, but don't waste a lot of time trying to if you can't. Over."

"Oh, all right, Jay. Your plan is probably best—after all, you're the professional soldier, not me. I'll send half my men up to the picket lines and get them to saddling mules. All of the horses are out there getting their asses peppered as thickly with arrows as their riders are, I'd imagine."

"Okay, Erica. Just tell your types to stay clear of both of those gates. My Broomtowners are good, but hand-held mortars have been known to be somewhat inaccurate on occasion. Over."

"I will, Jay. Immediately you blow out that back gate, we'll be on our way to you, to Broomtown Base and a long, hot, luxurious *shower* with real *soap*! Out."

Brigadier Sir Ahrthur Maklarin and his staff could but sit their horses, gaping in goggle-eyed astonishment, as the hundreds of armored horsemen swung wide around both their camp and their schiltrons to cross the space separating them from their elusive foes and rein about, forming common front with the bare thousand or so New Kuhmbuhluhners.

When the last of the seemingly endless files of riders had joined the Kuhmbuhluhn army, so that the wings of the reinforced host now greatly overlapped both of the Skohshun wings, three riders—one clearly Duke Bili, recognizable by his black warhorse and plumed helm—were seen to ride forward at a slow walk, following the Kuhmbuhluhn herald on his big white stallion.

"All right, Sir Djahn," the brigadier barked, "get out there. Let's see what the forsworn by-blow wants this time! Well, Senior Colonel Sir Djaimz, must I issue you an engraved invitation? You and one more, let's go."

Bili the Axe wasted no time with polite formalities through the two heralds, but addressed himself directly to Sir Ahrthur. "Old man, you first tried to lure me, then to shame or hector me into a battle to be fought on your terms against your more numerous forces. When I refused to lay my brains on the shelf and accede to your wiles and shameful practices, you attacked me with bared steel in violation of a sworn truce, which goes only to show that no matter how much you prate of a lack of honor in others, you yourself own no shred of it.

"Well now, old, honorless man, the boot is on the other foot, and I lead enough force to make blood pudding of you and your pikemen. But I'll do that only if you force me to it.

"I hereby extend you three options, more than ever you gave to me. You may agree to immediately lift the siege of New Kuhmbuhluhnburk and the occupation of those lands and the glen you earlier seized from the Kingdom of New Kuhmbuhluhn, and depart with your army and your folk from the kingdom; I would suggest that you lead them due west or southwest.

"Your second option is to let a single combat decide the outcome of this stupid exercise in wholesale bloodletting. I will fight for New Kuhmbuhluhn and you, considering your lack of stature and your advanced years, may choose a champion to ride against me for the Skohshun army and people; I will be armed with axe and sword, your champion may ride with those weapons he prefers or favors.

"Your third option is a full-scale battle, which I now consider futile and pointless, as too should you. But let me warn you well in advance, if this last is the option you choose, there will be no immediate attack on your schiltrons. Rather will I do just as I did before—bleed you, further eat away at your strength from a safe distance with missiles. Then, when I feel your formations to be sufficiently disorganized and shrunken, I will lead my horsemen against you with a cry of *'Havoc,' 'No quarter.'*

"I'll have your choice, old man, *now!*"

Senior Colonel Sir Djaimz kneed his mount close beside that of Sir Ahrthur and, leaning closer, whispered, "It might be better to withdraw, Sir Ahrthur. We can hold the glen, fight again at a time and a place of our choosing."

"Never!" snapped the brigadier. "Do you want to kill him? You're damned close of a size, the two of you. I'd give my eyeteeth to do it myself, but the bastard is right, I'm too old."

Sir Djaimz eyed Bili critically, then nodded. "Yes, Sir Ahrthur, I'll fight him. But please understand, it's not to salve your foolish pride, but rather to save the army that our people need. But I want your sworn oath, sir, that if I die, if that young man kills me, you'll march the army out of here and straight back to the glen, then turn over your command to whoever the colonels decide should replace you."

The brigadier looked his hurt puzzlement. "But . . . but why, Sir Djaimz? Simply because we lost this battle?"

"No, Sir Ahrthur, because you enjoy the respect of every Skohshun—officers and nobles, other ranks, and civilians—and I want to know that you will retire and, eventually, die with that respect intact, unsullied. While in most ways, at most times, you still are the same brigadier, more and more of late you have been lapsing for varying times into childish rages for little cause or none. You've done it twice today already.

"The Sir Ahrthur who received me into the army as a pink-cheeked ensign, who nurtured me and trained me for years, that Sir Ahrthur would never have reacted with such unseemly violence to the good-natured twitting of a man who had fought you, knocked you down and taken merely your sword when he could have had your life as well. Nor would that Sir Ahrthur ever have even thought of baring steel during a sworn truce, much less of attacking another member of the truce party.

"Will you swear as I ask, Sir Ahrthur?"

Bili had never really liked the lance or the common practice of one-on-one tilting—lance dueling—but he had long ago, perforce, mastered that and all of the other martial arts during his years of training at the court of the Iron King, Gilbuht of Harzburk. He had announced his intention of fighting this duel to settle the Kuhmbuhluhn-Skohshun conflict with axe and sword, ahorse or afoot. However, when the Skohshun champion had chosen to run the initial contact of the engagement with lances, Bili, the Kuhmbuhluhn champion, had had no option but to comply.

A party had ridden up to the city and returned laden with necessary weapons and gear from the well-stocked armories of the palace—a selection of battle lances, horse armor, several tilting shields of differing shapes and sizes, additional bits and pieces of plate for strengthening Bili's own panoply to withstand the tremendous shock of the impact of a steel-tipped lance with the combined weights and strengths of a horse and a strong warrior behind it.

A swarm of men fitted the black stallion, Mahvros, with a combination of plate, mail and boiled-leather armor—a heavier chamfron, a segmented plate crinet to cover the lighter one of mail, peytral to protect chest and shoulders, flanchards on the flanks and the leather-and-plate crupper behind the high and flaring tilting kak to shield the hams and back—all covered with a thick, heavy, quilted bard of red-dyed doeskin. The warhorse was a good bit less than pleased by the additions, constituting as they did a confining and rather uncomfortable additional weight of upward of a hundred more pounds for him to bear even before his rider mounted him.

"Brother," he mindspoke Bili ominously, "if these twolegs try to burden Mahvros with one more piece of metal or leather,

Mahvros will show them how well his teeth tear manflesh, how easily manbones shatter under his hooves. Let them be warned!''

Bili, standing bathed in sweat while extra pieces were fitted to his own harness, beamed as soothingly as he could, ''Mahvros, my dear brother, do not harm those men. What they are doing is for *your* protection, just as the extra armor they are buckling to me is to protect me. It is a hot day, yes, and this extra gear is stifling, but it gives us both a better chance to still be alive in the cool of the coming evening.

''Husband your strength and your proven ferocity for the fight which will shortly commence, dear brother. The man and your brother are about evenly matched, but Mahvros should have little to fear from the mount; for all that he is as big as are you, he is merely a gelding.''

With flaring nostrils, the black destrier snorted and stamped one big forehoof to indicate disgust, beaming, ''Never has Mahvros been able to fathom why twolegs all call a sexless creature like that 'he,' as if it still had its stallion parts. Why not call it 'she,' instead?''

After carefully weighing the offerings, Bili chose a lance, then one of the long, narrow, tapering shields. But when his fitters made to buckle the shield firmly to his armor, he shook his head. ''No, I'll bear this thing only as long as I have to. Once the spear-running be done, I'll need both hands for my axe, so I'll need to quickly and easily shed the shield.''

He also refused to trade his battle helm for one of the huge, thick-walled, ornate tilting helms. ''I've seen men swoon with lack of breathable air whilst wearing those things on far cooler days than is this scorcher. Too, I prefer to see what I'm axing, thank you.''

But he did allow them to cover a good part of his harness with a surcoat of white samite stitched thickly with red and gold traceries, thinking that it weighed little enough, was not at all confining and would at least keep the sun from beating directly upon some of the steel plates.

However, when the Skohshun officers inspected, the barding was ordered stripped from off Mahvros, for there was not one available for Sir Djaimz's gelding, Jess, and the two champions were more or less expected to possess parity in defensive attire. For this same reason, Sir Djaimz was constrained to shed his oversize helm and redon his own battle helm.

Mahvros both beamed and exhibited great pleasure in being relieved of the weighty, stifling bard, which pleased Bili, especially since loss of the thing was no lessening of real protection for the great horse. Moreover, unaccustomed as the stallion had been to such a thing, there had existed the very real chance that Mahvros might step on the leading edge of the bard and lose his balance or even fall at a critical moment.

The shouting match and near cancellation of the duel came when the Skohshun officers, after all trying the weight and balance of Bili's great double axe, announced that the champion of Kuhmbuhluhn either must forgo the use of any axe or make do with one of more average proportions and heft.

At length, Bili mindcalled the Moon Maiden, Lieutenant Kahndoot. "Little sister, these Skohshun bastards are determined to weight this contest firmly in the favor of their champion and have, therefore, refused flatly to allow me to use my own axe, obliquely endeavoring to limit the fight to only lance and sword. But I mean to outfox the sharp-eared creatures. Ride over here and trade axes with me for the length of time it takes me to put paid to the account of this Sir Djaimz."

While the various armings and inspections and disarmings had been occurring, members of both armies had been engaged in the removals of corpses of man and of horse, dropped weapons and equipment and other battle debris from the narrowed space now separating the two armies, that space whereon the duel to decide the outcome of this affair of New Kuhmbuhluhners versus invading Skohshuns would shortly take place. A course of one hundred and fifty yards was decided upon for the tilt, and marker stakes were driven. Then all was declared to be in readiness.

Sir Djaimz, mounted on his big, battle-trained dark-chestnut gelding, took his place at the far western end of the course. Bili, on Mahvros, took the eastern end. Then both men waited for the bugle flourish that would announce the beginning of the bloodletting.

# CHAPTER XV

As they awaited the signal, Sir Djaimz seemed to be experiencing difficulty in controlling his gelding, to the point that finally a brother officer took a firm grip on the section of rein near the bit and lent his weight and strength to prevent the nervous beast from sidling.

Mahvros, on the other hand, stood stockstill, as Bili had telepathically instructed him to do, ready to charge at the first brazen notes of the trumpet.

Both riders had fully extended their stirrup leathers to the point where they actually stood in their stirrups, thighs tight-gripping the barrels of their respective mounts, their buttocks bunched up hard against the high cantles of the tilting saddles, bodies angled forward and shield held high so that it protected all of the torso, nearly the entire length of the left leg and the neck and head right up to the bars of the visors.

The mounted hornman, Gy Ynstyn, raised polished bugle to the lips hidden in his beard. Despite the deadly danger of the impending duel to his young lord, Duke Bili, still Gy could barely contain his joy. Though there had as yet been no chance to seek her out and exchange words, he had recognized among the Moon Maidens following the banner of Sir Geros his lover and battlemate, Meeree.

As his peripheral vision detected the flash of the sun on the brass horn, Bili lowered his lance, couching its butt end between right biceps and body and angling the steel-pointed and slightly tapering longer portion of the twelve-foot ash-wood shaft to the left over Mahvros' thick, steel-sheathed neck.

Bili did enjoy one distinct and most valuable advantage over his opponent that the Skohshun inspectors could not have suspected. The young *thoheeks* could devote the full use of his left arm to his shield, disregarding the reins and exerting what little control of his stallion was necessary through means of mindspeak or, occasionally, knee pressure. He and the massive black equine had traveled and drilled and fought as one for long years. A very real love bond existed between them, and in matters of combat the one knew the mind of the other as well as only true telepaths can.

Then, at long last, the trumpet pealed! Jess, the gelding of Sir Djaimz, was startled by the noise and reared, almost trampling the volunteer horse holder before that worthy could loose his grip and scurry clear of the flailing hooves. But Mahvros started smoothly forward, gradually increasing speed and momentum, his rolling muscles bunching and relaxing beneath the horse armor, his gait across the length of the course providing a firm platform from which his rider could fight.

Despite his concentration in aiming his lance and in keeping as much as possible of himself behind the body shield, Bili's experienced eyes told him a great deal about his onrushing opponent—some good, some possibly bad, but all of it useful.

The chestnut gelding was not so well coordinated as was the black. His gait was choppy and, probably, jarring to the rider, which circumstance most likely meant that Sir Djaimz would aim his point for the larger, surer target of the shield face, rather than essaying the potentially more deadly but smaller and trickier target of Bili's helm-clad head. This arrangement suited Bili of Morguhn fine, for otherwise, lacking as he did one of the stronger and heavier tilting helms, he just might end with the best part of the lancepoint in his skull.

But another characteristic of that chestnut gelding might make for severe difficulties, injuries, even death. The choppy gait meant that the equine did not always lead with the right forehoof, as did Mahvros and all others of the best-trained destriers. This meant that under certain combat circumstances, an actual collision of the two mounts was a distinct and unnerving possibility. Bili mindspoke this observation to his horse, but Mahvros had, he replied, already noticed and noted the sinister quirk.

But with both big beasts at a flat-out gallop, there was little real time for observing. Suddenly, Sir Djaimz's point was become a steel flicker just below Bili's line of vision and the dark-blue-and-silver face of the shield seemed to encompass all of the world.

Bili unconsciously gripped Mahvros' barrel the tighter, tensed his arm muscles for the coming, powerful thrust and braced his body for the inevitable shock.

Neither man heard the mighty shout that rose up from both sides at the impact. Bili had judged aright, and a shrewdly timed alteration of the angle of his shield sent the Skohshun knight's lancepoint sliding off the face of the *thoheeks'* shield into the empty air beyond, unbalancing Sir Djaimz even as Bili's hard-driven point took him clean in the helm and bore him far back over his cantle and onto the crupper of the chestnut gelding, his lance clattering from his hand and the man almost following it onto the rocky ground.

Mahvros' momentum kept him going on westward for several rods before Bili finally could slow and turn him, and by that time Sir Djaimz had more or less regained his seat and his horse control and was hurriedly unslinging a saddle axe only slightly shorter than the Moon Maiden crescent axe that Bili now bore at his own pommel.

Although the Kuhmbuhluhn lines were a tumult of gleeful or bloodthirsty noise and commotion, there was only silence from the Skohshun lines, for matters now looked exceedingly ill for their champion. Bili of Morguhn still remained fully armed, and, did he so wish, there was nothing to prevent him using that long, deadly lance to unhorse, injure, even kill Sir Djaimz well before that worthy was or could be close enough to swing the axe to any effect; and the cheers and shouted bits of advice from his own forces indicated that they all clearly expected him to do just that.

But he did not. Thrusting downward powerfully, he sank the ferrule of the lance into the pebbly ground, then unslung Kahndoot's balanced, well-kept axe. At sight of this selfless generosity, the Skohshun ranks, one and all, cheered their foemen's champion, while Sir Djaimz brought up his own axe in a complicated flourish of salute, reflecting that he would not be gladdened by this man's death. Not that that emotion would keep him from killing when the time came—after all, duty was duty and was not always pleasantly performed.

Neither horse was put to the gallop this time, rather to a fast amble. They met and, for long minutes, circled and feinted. Then Bili's powerful backhanded buffet came within bare inches of slamming into the section of Sir Djaimz's helm already weakened by the lance thrust. Barely in the nick of time the officer got his shield into place to block the blow. But the Skohshun returned as good as he got, and for a heartbeat of time, the two strained to wrench loose their axe blades, each sunk deeply in the dense hardwood laminate of the other's shield.

As the two warily began to circle and feint once more, with a sound louder than a thunderclap, fiery lightning first struck the distant back wall of the Skohshun stockade. Then, with no perceptible pause, equally ear-splitting explosions of sound heralded the virtual disintegration of the front gate of that stout stockade, both of the front-corner platforms and sizable sections of the front wall as well.

From out of a now-cloudless, blue sky, the deadly lightning struck again—among the tightly formed ranks of the Skohshun pikemen and even among the lines of Kuhmbuhluhners. The cheers and shouts suddenly were become screams of pain and terror. Kuhmbuhluhners and Skohshuns, Freefighters, Ahrmehnee, Ehleenee, Kindred, Moon Maidens, men, women, Kleesahks and horses, all surged in one mob this way and the other, seeking an escape, a haven of safety from this mysterious and terrifying new form of death and injury. The duel, the battle, even the war clean forgotten, the resultant thoroughly mixed mob, both mounted and afoot, surged first back to the base of King's Rest Mountain, then up the winding roadway, through the barbican and across the bridge and into the streets of New Kuhmbuhluhnburk itself, all of the long pikes and the more unwieldy items of weapons and equipment dropped heedlessly along the way in that flight of unthinking terror.

"Cease firing!" ordered General Jay Corbett into his transceiver mouthpiece. "All sections cease firing. Cease firing and dismantle weapons. Horse handlers forward. Out."

Turning to Gumpner, he said, "All right, Gump, you take over from here. Get the mortars and everything else repacked and get ready to march."

"There're a few rockets and some mortar bombs left, sir," replied the colonel. "It might be interesting to see what the effect of them would be on a stone-walled city . . . ?"

"No," responded Corbett, shaking his head. "I've no desire to kill or hurt any more of those poor buggers. The barrage was simply to keep them occupied, off our necks until Dr. Arenstein could get away and join us. We've accomplished that and, so far as I'm concerned, the action is over and done."

He turned to his waiting chief-of-scouts. "Johnny, you and Merle find me the shortest, easiest route back to the site of the landslide. My fondest desire, at this moment, is to get my original mission completed and get us all back to Broomtown in one piece."

As the scouts conferred one with the other, Corbett strode over to where the three Skohshun prisoners sat and dismissed the armed guards, ordering them to fetch back the prisoners' mounts and arms.

"Gentlemen, I'm releasing you, as I promised I would do once my mission was accomplished. Where you go now is up to you, but I would imagine they could use your help over in that camp, what's left of it. There are certain to be wounded men in there."

Then he turned to the youngest of the Skohshuns, a peglegged boy whose face looked somewhat older than his chronological age. "Ensign Thomas Grey, please convey upon your next meeting with your mother, the Lady Pamela Grey, my sincerest regards and my best wishes for her future happiness. She is a splendid woman, sir, a true lady in every conceivable way. Had I met a woman like her long, long, long ago . . . well, never mind. God speed you safely home, gentlemen, all of you.''

In the early evening of the day of that duel interrupted by fiery, deadly thunders, Duke Bili the Axe again occupied his accustomed place at the head of the table of the royal councilors of the Kingdom of New Kuhmbuhluhn, but that table and the chamber itself were both far more crowded than was usual. Extra chairs and stools had been lugged in from hither and yon, space made at the table sides to seat twice as many men, with others ranged against the walls on stools and a brace of benches.

They had all just heard what had really happened to drive them and their followers, willy-nilly, up here into New Kuhmbuhluhnburk that afternoon. Those who had recounted the fantastical tale—a one-legged boy-warrior a few years Bili's junior and a brace of Skohshun officer-gallopers, all of whom had been prisoners of the strange, alien force which had wrought such havoc—had been sincerely thanked and dismissed from the chamber. The first to speak, then, was Bili.

''Well, gentlemen, at least we now know the truth of that scary business down there today. The Eastern Confederation, of which my Duchy of Morguhn is a vassal state, has suffered much in recent years from the sinister plottings and incursions of those damned Witchmen, and I'm right sorry to see them this far west. But they seem to thrive best where there is warfare and dissension, nor are they at all loath to foment chaotic conditions where none formerly existed. They cannot seem to exist in a land of peace and order, and so, if you Kuhmbuhluhn and Skohshun folk don't want them back in your laps again, it is imperative that you settle your differences and begin to live amicably, one with the other.''

Noting the dark, sullen glances at each other of the two, previously warring races, the young commander went on to say, ''Understand, gentlemen, I don't give a real damn whether or not you all chop each other into gobbets, once I am gone. It's none of my affair, to speak true. My contracts all are discharged and as soon as I can gather all my followers and set them on the march, I mean to recross the mountains, collect the cubs—human and feline—that we left in Sandee's Cot last spring, and return back whence we came.

''You men all are my elders, and, it is bruited about at least, age imparts wisdom. Surely you men are wise enough to see that you must reconcile your differences and merge your two races into one, else you will soon be easy prey to the Witchmen or to any other united and disciplined force that comes your way. Such a race are your eastern neighbors, the Ahrmehnee *stahn,* nor can I truly believe that you have seen the last of the outlaw-Ganiks, the cannibals.

"I have talked with Sir Ahrthur, Sir Djahn, Sir Djaimz and Captain Baron Deveree, this day, and all agree that this war has been an ill-starred business from start to date. They admit to being as much at fault for the inception of hostilities as were you Kuhmbuhluhners, which is, I trow, a good place to commence the ending of it.

"They have no desire to extirpate the folk of New Kuhmbuhluhn. They are only seeking land to farm and live upon and raise their families on, having been driven from off their own lands by a hostile invader. Now, in the wake of the departures of the Ganiks, there are huge tracts of empty, tenantless, but potentially rich land south of the mountains, and there are nowhere near to approaching enough New Kuhmbuhluhn folk to adequately settle and work them. You know that and I know that, no matter how much you may protest the contrary.

"Now, the House of Mahrloh is extinct, so there is presently no king in New Kuhmbuhluhn, and, barring a miracle, I cannot imagine you councilors soon agreeing upon one of your number for that office."

Archcount Sir Daifid Howuh sneeringly asked, "And I suppose that your grace expects us to choose and try to live under one of these damned savage brutes of Skohshuns? Methinks your grace today took some stray buffet that addled your grace's brains. A Skohshun king of New Kuhmbuhluhn, indeed!"

Bili shook his shaven head. "No, Archcount Howuh, a king of any sort—Kuhmbuhluhner or Skohshun—was not really that of which I was thinking."

"Well, what the hell else is there, sir duke," demanded Duke Klyv Wahrtuhn, exasperatedly, "save anarchy?"

Bili steepled his thick, calused fingers and gazed over their tips at the men ranged along the two sides of the table. "There is the path that the Republic of Eeree took long ago when faced with similar difficulties; now that republic is every bit as strong and as prosperous as the kingdoms of Harzburk or Pitzburk."

"Ah, yes," responded Archcount Howuh, "I think I recall hearing tales from Old Kuhmbuhluhn regarding that strangely governed state. Please, your grace of Morguhn, say on."

Naturally, it was not as easy as all that. Sectarian differences ran too deep and wide in both New Kuhmbuhluhn and Skohshun, not to even mention the basic hostility of the one race for the other in the wake of the recent unpleasantnesses. It all required the best part of two weeks of almost ceaseless, day- and night-long discussions, arguments, name-callings, shouting matches, table poundings, wall poundings and other clear evidences of strong wills and adult temper tantrums. And it all devolved into no worse only because Bili wisely barred even the smallest, least innocuous edge weapons from the chamber and tried to see to it that the various factions were lodged as far from one another as was possible in the overcrowded palace and city.

To help in relieving some of this overcrowding, while at one and the same time keeping the former combatants—Skohshun and Kuhmbuhluhner—living cheek by jowl, Bili quartered the larger part of his own squadron and the reinforcements led by Sir Geros and Sir Djim in the much-battered camp of the former besiegers. He justified his actions with the excuse that there simply was insufficient space for so many horses and ponies in the keep stables and that the animals would, in any case, be happier and healthier grazing on the plain.

He retained his staff and that of Sir Geros in the city, along with enough of his veteran cavalry—mostly Moon Maidens and Freefighters of the old Morguhn Company—to provide him a loyal nucleus did the negotiations get out of hand and overt warfare between the Kuhmbuhluhn nobility and the Skohshun officers recommence.

Sight of a Kleesahk in the city confines was a rarity for a week and more after the "battle," Pah-Elmuh having led the huge hominids down to the battle site and the ruined camp as soon as he had heard that there were hundreds of sick and hurt and wounded men and horses in and about the area, all in crying need of care and healing.

Hard beset as he found himself, Bili saw it imperative to delegate authority and duties. All of the operational and logistical planning of the return march—first to Sandee's Cot, then through the southern tribal lands of the Ahrmehnee *stahn* and so on east through the *Thoheekahtohn* of Vawn into his own *Thoheekahtohn* of Morguhn—he piled onto the combined staffs. Governance of the fortress city of New Kuhmbuhluhnburk he placed in the capable hands of Sir Yoo Folsom. The overlord of Sir Yoo, Count Djohsehf Brahk, had had the misfortune to have one of the missiles thrown by the weapons of the Witchmen land squarely upon him (had the occurrence not been witnessed, no one would ever have known exactly what had happened to him, so little of him and his horse had remained of an identifiable nature), and, before all was done, Bili intended to see the royal council about the now-vacant peerage.

But even so, the young commander had no free time to devote to his wife and his children. His infrequent visits to his suite could only be for the purposes of snatching a few minutes of sleep, bathing, being shaved, changing his clothing, then returning to the council chamber and the disputatious men it contained.

But Rahksahnah sympathized and empathized with her harried, usually exhausted husband. A sometime war leader herself, she managed the suite and their personal entourage well, saw to it that he was properly served and provided for, that he ate and drank at least once each day and that his short snatches of rest were undisturbed until the time he had designated. Nor did she allow him to be troubled by such petty bothers and ills as her new spate of harassments by her once lover, the Moon Maiden Meeree.

All the way up from Sandee's Cot, Meeree had done her utter damnedest to poison against the *brahbehrnuh* the minds of the Moon Maidens who had ridden from the east with Sir Geros and Sir Djim. But her lies, accusations and exaggerations had held them only until they had had words with Rahksahnah herself, and Lieutenant Kahndoot, and had seen just how happy the other Maidens were become with their men and, some, with their children.

But obsessed as she was become, Meeree could not accept the loss of power over the newly arrived Maidens any more than she ever had been able to accept the Goddess-ordained loss of her sworn lover, the *brahbehrnuh*, Rahksahnah, to Bili of Morguhn and the new order. She continued to agitate, haunting any place where the Moon Maidens congregated.

Then, of a day, as she walked down a palace corridor, a powerful hand grasped the elbow of her good arm and dragged her into a dimly lit and smallish chamber. The door slammed behind her and, before her eyes had as yet adjusted to the gloom, her ears were recipients of the grating of a cold, familiar voice. She turned to behold the strong, stocky figure of Kahndoot.

"You stupid, ever-whining bitch," snapped the Maiden officer, "did a year of suffering and ostracism teach you no one thing? It is not simply against the *brahbehrnuh* you speak, but against Her, the Silver Lady, the Will of the Goddess, and that is blasphemy. If any woman—or man, for that matter—doubts that She will not tolerate or forgive such as your cesspit mouth churns out, they only need think of what you once were and look upon that which you are now become. No, keep silent; open that foul mouth before I give you leave to do so and you'll need to seek out a Kleesahk to see if he can help you grow a new set of front teeth!

"Look at yourself, Meeree. Once you were the second or, at least, the third best warrior of all the Maidens, but you in your foolish pride incurred Her wrath, Her terrible wrath, and what are you now become? You—"

But Meeree jerked her arm from Kahndoot's grip and put as much distance as the confines of the small chamber allowed between them, then her good right hand produced from the folds of her clothing a long, slim, double-edged dagger. "Get away from that door, damn you!" she snarled. "What I am now is nothing to do with the so-called Goddess, but the fault of Rahksahnah's parts itching unnaturally for that lumbering, hairless thing, Dook Bili. He it was smashed and ruined my shield and bridle arm, first took my own lover, then spoiled me for war; but he will pay. Soon or late, Meeree will see him pay with his own misbegotten life. Just as you, you sow, now pay!"

With the last, half-screamed words, the crippled woman lunged, all of her weight a strength behind the dagger she thrust at Kahndoot's thick body. But, with an audible snap, the slender blade broke off short and tinkled on the stone floor. Off balance, Meeree stumbled against her intended victim, whose strong hands grabbed her and hurled her lighter body into a corner. Then Khandoot paced to stand over her. She opened her gashed shirt, and the lamplight imparted a rippling sheen to the short hauberk of fine Ahrmehnee mail which had underlain the shirt.

Smiling coldly, she said, "Has hate and envy driven all reason from your mind, woman? Did you think I'd immure myself alone with such a creature as you now are without some sort of protection against such infamy as you just displayed? I'd be thoroughly justified to slay you, here and now, and no doubt I would save much suffering for other people if I did just that. But I say again what I said on the night of that duel at Sandee's Cot—there are few enough of us Maidens of the Moon Goddess left as it is, and I do not want any of that now-rare blood on these hands of mine."

Bili had Pah-Elmuh summoned back up to the palace for the penultimate meeting of the new council, which henceforth would not style itself "royal," but rather the Council of the Aristocratic Republic of Kleesahkyuhn—named after those who had preceded all of the present twoleg disputants to the area. The initial council that Bili would leave behind him when he marched would consist of three Kuhmbuhluhn noblemen, three of the Skohshuns and one Kleesahk, but eventually there would be a total of fourteen men and three Kleesahks to constitute the council, though most of the day-to-day affairs would be conducted by the smaller, seven-chair assemblage.

After seeing them all seated and a surprisingly peaceful meeting commence, Bili departed to his suite and slept for the best part of two full days and nights. He then arose long enough to dine, bathe, make long, unhurried, gentle love to and with Rahksahnah, then sleep for another day. Then he once more arose and threw himself into the preparations for the return to Sandee's Cot and then, eventually, Morguhn, into which he had not set foot for almost three years.

Things had been far less complicated, he thought, before he had been burdened with a household for which to arrange transport and supplies for the trip. In addition to himself, Rahksahnah, the twins—and, when they arrived in Sandee's Cot, young Djef Morguhn, now some year old—there were his hornman, Gy Ynstyn, and his woman, Meeree, his bannerman, his three orderlies, his secretary, his cook and that worthy's two helpers, his three horse tenders, Rahksahnah's three servants, the wet nurse and her young husband, six Freefighter bodyguards and four muleskinners to handle the household pack train on the march and in camp. Moreover, the prairiecat Stealth—now, once again, pregnant by Chief Whitetip—would be accompanying his personal entourage.

In the usual manner of all of fallible humanity, Hornman Gy Ynstyn had conveniently forgotten the sullen behavior of Meeree when he had departed with the squadron bound for the north and the Skohshun War, near six months agone. Because of her maimed left arm, she had been left behind along with some score of sick, injured or pregnant and near-to-term warriors. Poor Gy, who had come to love the woman, had deluded himself with the unfounded belief that when once more they two were together, they would commence a life of unmitigated bliss.

But from the very first day they were reunited, all his hopes and dreams were utterly dashed. No sooner were the woman and her gear installed in Gy's small chamber, which adjoined Duke Bili's rambling suite, than did Meeree seek out Rahksahnah and spend two hours alternately arguing with and screaming at the young mother. Gy could understand none of the words, since they were couched in the cryptic language of the Moon Maidens, but the tones left no doubt as to the general content of the heated exchanges.

Very soon thereafter, Meeree took to locking Gy out of his chamber for hours, sometimes, whilst she closeted herself with certain ones of the Moon Maidens who had marched north with the forces of Sir Geros and Sir Djim Bohluh. And when these meetings abruptly ceased, when the Maidens would none of them submit to private converse with Meeree, indeed, avoided her if at all possible, still did Meeree deny his access to his room and bed, right often, so that she might sit alone and brood.

And on those occasions when he was allowed use of his bed, Meeree either ignored him completely or hectored him for long, sleepless hours with all that she swore would be done to him and all the other men when the Moon Maidens at last realized the errors into which the forsworn Rahksahnah had led them, cleaved to her—Meeree—and took over the city of New Kuhmbuhluhnburk as a new Hold of the Maidens of the Moon.

Then, of a night, something awakened him from exhausted slumber in time to see Meeree advancing toward him, her good right hand gripping the worn hilt of her razor-edged shortsword, her lips curled back from off her teeth, her eyes as wild and savage as those of any predatory beast. Only his startled, sudden movement saved his genitals from the point and edges of her steel, and she still managed to thrust the broad blade so deeply into his inner thigh that the point grated agonizingly against bone.

Fortunately for Gy, Bili and Rahksahnah were but just closing the main doors of their suite for the night, having bid a good-night to Pah-Elmuh, when the hornman staggered naked out into the hallway, his wound gushing blood at every beat of his heart.

When once the Kleesahk had stopped the arterial blood flow, cleaned and closed the gaping wound, then instructed Gy Ynstyn's brain to pump natural anesthetics into the affected areas and to commence the healing processes, he and Bili entered the swooning hornman's mind and had the entire tale.

When questioned, Rahksahnah just shrugged. "It began while you were trying to persuade the Kuhmbuhluhners and Skohshuns to join together, Bili. You had a full load of cares, and I could see no reason to burden you with more. I'm of the opinion that poor Meeree's mind is become as twisted and deformed as her arm. Back during the first week after the battle, she tried to put a dagger into Kahndoot's heart, but with long months of bad blood between those two, it was perhaps understandable. But now this night's work, to attack and almost kill her own, sworn battle companion . . . ? Bili, she is not any longer the Meeree I once loved, and it's too bad, for that Meeree was an altogether admirable woman.''

"Pah-Elmuh," Bili asked, "lunacy such as this—is it at all responsive to your talents?''

"Yes, Lord Champion," beamed the Kleesahk in reply. "I have, over the years, brought reason back to more than a few unfortunates through first wakening them to their problems, then showing their brains how to correct them. But it is a long process, Lord Champion—months are required to do it properly.''

Bili thought for a moment, then nodded and mindspoke, "If I leave behind a sum to provide proper maintenance for this woman, Meeree, would you undertake to cure her, old friend?''

Pah-Elmuh smiled and beamed, "Speak not of gold or silver, Lord Champion. You have wrought here in New Kuhmbuhluhn more than a score of our generations could ever repay. Besides, you know that healing is my art and my joy. She will be well maintained, never you fear. Perhaps when once her mind is clear and rational, I can even show it how to restore that arm.''

And so, of a bright morning in early autumn, Sir Bili, *Thoheeks* and Chief of Morguhn, Lord Champion of the Kleesahks, and last legal ruler of the former Kingdom of New Kuhmbuhluhn, set the steel-shod hooves of his mighty warhorse to the boards of the drawbridge and rode out of that fortress-city he had defended so well. The throngs he left behind in the streets of the mountain city cheered him and his cavalcade, even while bitterly weeping over his departure. One and all, they had come to truly love the brave, astute, just and always courteous young commander and, agreements in council be damned, would have acclaimed him the new King of Kuhmbuhluhn, in a bare eyeblink, had they had but a suspicion that he might have accepted the crown.

Arrived down upon the plain, Bili, Rahksahnah, Hornman Gy, the bannerman bearing the Red Eagle of Morguhn, and Bili's six bodyguards took their places at the head of the long column and the march toward the central mountain chain commenced.

Excepting some of the servants and muleskinners, all were veterans, so the steady pace of the march did not fatigue them, and when finally Bili called a halt and an encampment was emplaced near to a purling brookside, they were only a day's additional march from the mouth of the pass that would take them through to the southern counties.

They were moving through a land that was at last enjoying peace, so Bili saw no reason to post guards or establish a perimeter for the camp. Consequently, it sprawled unevenly along both sides of the winding brook and soon became a place of joyous merriment for the homeward-bound men and women. With dinners consumed, barrels of Skohshun beer and Kuhmbuhluhn ale were broached, and wineskins circulated freely. The ever-present Ahrmehnee musicians drew out their instruments, and, to their wailing, drum-thumping rhythms, the other Ahrmehnee first raised a deep-voiced chorus, then began a sword dance.

The drinking and general jollity went on about the leaping fires until well after moonrise, when Bili, reluctantly, ordered all to seek their beds, as he intended to recommence the march at dawn. He and Rahksahnah stripped and washed in the icy water of the brook, then raced breathlessly up the bank to seek the anticipated warmth of their camp bed and blankets.

In his huge great-bed, where he lay dying with the stink of his own suppurating flesh cloying his nostrils, the old, old man that the years had made of young Bili of Morguhn once more castigated himself as he had nearly every lonely day for almost eighty years.

"*Why?*" he demanded of himself. "Why did I do it? Surely I knew better. I had been a-soldiering for more than half my life, even then. Had I set up a perimeter, posted sentries, had I even placed a brace of my personal guards at the entry of my pavilion . . ."

A protracted sigh rattled out of the throat of the dying old man, bringing the attending physician hurrying to his side to assure himself that the spark of life yet remained. But Bili did not see or hear this old friend. He once more was reliving the saddest moments of his ninety-nine years of existence.

Laughing through chattering teeth, young Bili and his dark, lovely and much-loved wife and battlemate, Rahksahnah, ran gaily into their pavilion, dimly lit by a single small metal lamp slung by chains from the ridgepole. After hurriedly stripping off their damp clothing, they tumbled into the camp bed to lie locked in close embrace until their bodies' heat reasserted normal temperature and they ceased to shiver.

That same closeness, however, aroused passions that had never been long quiescent in them. Then, after they both were sated, fulfilled one by the other, they lay long in silent, telepathic oneness before sleep finally claimed them.

Bili was never certain just how long they lay in slumber, but suddenly his danger-prescience, which rare talent had so many times before saved his life on the march or in situations of imminent combat, brought him completely awake and wary. He cautiously slitted his eyes and saw, through the scrimlike curtain of Rahksahnah's disordered black hair, a cloaked and hooded figure moving soundlessly across the thick carpets. The dim lamplight glittered on the watered-steel blade that the intruder held reversed, in the classic down-stabbing position.

Making as little movement as possible, Bili felt for the familiar hilt of his pillow sword . . . unavailingly. It was not in its accustomed place! So he mindspoke Rahksahnah.

"Do not move, my dear, not yet, not until you feel me do so. There is an intruder here, in this very chamber, creeping with naked steel toward us. Moreover, the servants forgot again to place my pillow sword in position when they set up the bed. But there's but the one and that one not very big. Wait."

Hornman Gy Ynstyn was sitting with a group of old Freefighter cronies around the fire before the tent of Sir Geros Lahvoheetos when oncoming hoofbeats were felt by them all long before they could hear them above the noise of the camp. Then there were shouts across on the northern bank of the brook, followed closely by splashings, and a dusty rider on a foam-flecked horse guided that stumbling beast close to the group of Freefighters.

Despite the mask of mud that copious sweat and trail dust had placed over his features, Gy still could recognize the drawn face of one of the squires of Count Yoo Folsom, so the hornman arose from his place and bore the wineskin they had been circulating over to the newcomer.

"Welcome, Master Pahrkuh. Here, take you a pull at this—you look like a wornout boot."

Without a word, the horseman accepted the skin and poured a good pint down his working throat before stoppering it and gasping out, "Please, Hornman Ynstyn, I must speak with Duke Bili . . . *quickly*! After your column was well on the march, a patient of Pah-Elmuh's, a Moon Maiden gone mad, escaped from his care, slew two hostlers, stole a horse and lied her way past the gate guards. Pah-Elmuh fears she means to harm his grace."

All in a single movement, Bili rose to his knees, threw back the blankets and heaved a pillow at the assassin, shouting, *"Hold, now!"*

The trespasser ducked barely in time, but so close came the

hard-flung cushion that it tore back the hood of the cloak to reveal the dusty-dirty face, dulled hair and wild eyes of Meeree, her lips twisted into a feral snarl. Even as Bili made to quit the bed, the lunatic hurled herself at him, her blade raised high for the stab.

Gy Ynstyn, running toward Bili's pavilion, with the New Kuhmbuhluhn messenger at a fast walk behind him, heard Bili's shout and increased his pace, at the same time drawing his long dirk and cursing himself for leaving his saber off this night. Bursting through the flaps of the ducal pavilion and then through the inner flaps that led into the bedchamber, he was unwilling witness to the climax of the tragedy.

Meeree, in her haste to flesh her blade, failed to watch her footing and tripped on an uneven spot in the carpet, and before she could regain her balance enough to strike at the naked, unarmed man on the bed, Rahksahnah had arisen to block her way, pity on her face and one hand extended toward the murderous madwoman.

"Meeree, my Meeree!" Rahksahnah forced her voice to calmness and low, soothing tones. "Meeree, give me the knife, please."

"No!" snapped Meeree. "He must be killed. He has taken you from me, led you into dark, evil practices. He would prevent us from a new beginning, a proper, natural beginning, a new hold, so I must kill him!"

"Then you must kill me first, Meeree," said Rahksahnah, softly and simply.

"Then die, you faithless, perverted bitch!" shrieked Meeree, plunging her blade to the very hilt into the full breast of her once lover. "You—*gaaarrrgghh!*" She shrieked once more and flinched forward across the body of her victim, as her battlemate, Hornman Gy Ynstyn—his face bathed with his rueful tears—buried his sharp dirk in her back.

Furiously, Bili pushed and shoved the cloaked figure from off Rahksahnah and the bed, but Meeree was not yet dead, and she held the hilt of her weapon tight-clenched, so the blade came out from her victim with an ugly, sucking sound, followed by a gush of blood, almost black in the dim lamplight.

Gy Ynstyn held Meeree's body in his arms, weeping, sobbing unashamedly. "Oh, my poor, dear Meeree, I'm sorry, my love, but . . . but I *had* to. Can't you see that? I truly love you, but I am Duke Bili's sworn man."

"Man-Gy . . . *Gy?*" The voice was little better than a whisper, and a trickle of blood began to trace through the dust from one corner of Meeree's mouth. She made as if to snuggle against his body, murmuring almost imperceptibly, "Good man . . . Man-Gy. You please . . . Meeree, much please Meeree. But tired . . . sleep now."

Meeree's body became limp, heavy, the knife slipped from her hand, the last breath left her body along with her life. Gy crouched there, still hugging her body to his chest, still sobbing out his explanations for killing her.

The pavilion was fast filling up with men and women, but neither Bili nor Gy noticed any of them. Rahksahnah had spoken but briefly before she died. "My Bili, my poor Bili. Be good I would tell you to our little ones, but no need is, you could not be other . . . always good, kind, patient, loving. Send me to Home of Wind, your chosen god . . . will wait for you there . . ." And she was gone.

# EPILOGUE

The eastern Karaleenos sky was a bright, deep red with dawn—Sacred Sun-birth—bare minutes away. Old Prince Bili Morguhn of Karaleenos opened his eyes to see the also elderly Zahrtohgahn physician, Master Ahkmehd, seated on the edge of the great-bed, his back curved and his chin with its wispy, white beard sunk onto his bony chest.

"Ahkmehd . . . old friend?" Bili's voice croaked, sounding strange and unreal to his ears.

With a start, the dark-brown-skinned man raised his head. "My lord Bili . . . you are in pain?"

Bili chuckled humorlessly. "When have I not been in pain, of one sort or another? But I mean to be shortly shut of all of it. Where is the Undying High Lord Milo?"

"I am here, Bili." The deep voice came from a dark corner of the large chamber, then a chair squeaked and Bili's overlord moved into the light.

"My lord, tell me true," croaked Bili. "How long until sunrise?"

The dark-haired man paced to the window and twitched aside one edge of the heavy draperies, then said, "Two, maybe three minutes, Bili. Why?"

"I was born with the birth of Sacred Sun, my lord. I would die then, too. Please, open the drapes. And where . . . where is my axe? Please, my lord, put it in my hands."

With his blotched and sinewy old right hand once more gripping— but most feebly, now—the worn, familiar haft of the ancient, dusty axe, Bili closed his eyes briefly, then opened them again and fixed his gaze upon the High Lord, this man whose appearance had never changed in the eighty years that Bili Morguhn had known him and served him.

"I . . . I have always striven to serve you . . . Confederation . . . well, my lord . . . best of my abilities . . ." The waves of agony from his terribly infected wounds now were breaking through the narcotic dikes and racking his dying body.

"None, no one, man or woman or horse or prairiecat or Ork, ever has served me and our Confederation so long and well and faithfully as did you, Bili of Morguhn," stated Milo. "I know not when or where or how I ever can find your like. You often have been the very salvation of all for which I have worked over the long centuries.''

"When you and Con . . . federation need . . . look for Bili . . . Bili the Axe . . . be there.''

"Now, please, my . . . lord,'' Bili gasped as the rising of Sacred Sun bathed his pain-twisted face in its holy, golden rays, "Pain too . . . too much, now. Your . . . dirk. Use it!''

Milo turned to the physician, who stood by weeping in his helpless frustration, and the other man who had come out of the shadowed corner of the room, "You both heard?''

At their nods, Milo drew his centuries-old Horseclans dirk, leaned over Bili's body and placed the point carefully, then, with a single, powerful thrust, drove it through the old man's heart.

Bili hardly noticed the pain of the stab, so great was the other, older pain. He was aware, briefly, of a dim mutter of voices, growing ever dimmer. The bright sunlight, too, was growing dimmer, darkening, darkening. Dark.

A sound wakened him, a sound much like the snort of a horse. He did not open his eyes, fearing lest any movement no matter how slight bring back the nauseating waves of agony, but when something, some force, strongly nudged at his right side, almost rolling him over onto the infected arm and leg, his eyes snapped open. Then his mouth gaped.

Standing almost atop his recumbent body was a huge black stallion. The glossy horse was the very spit and image of good old long-years-with-Wind Mahvros. There was a bridle buckled to the head of the horse; its reins dropped loosely over the pommel-knob of an old-fashioned warkak.

The horse lowered his head and nudged Bili once more, this time mindspeaking, "Will my brother then sleep all the day through? They are waiting for us, for you were overlong in coming and we have far to gallop.''

The mindspeak was unmistakable; there had never been another like it. *"Mahvros . . . ?"* Bili beamed incredulously. "But . . . but you are long ago gone to Wind!''

"Of course I am, my brother,'' Mahvros easily agreed. "And now my dear brother has joined me. Come, rise up and mount me. The others are waiting for us.''

"But . . . but I cannot rise, my brother. A bear clawed and bit me badly, and . . .''

"I'd have done worse than that, brother or no brother,'' beamed Mahvros, stamping, "had your men shot me full of arrows and then you made to run a spear through me. And all because of a few silly sheep. Yes, I spoke with that poor bear a short time back.

"But come, brother, get up, they're waiting."

"Who's waiting?" asked Bili dazedly, wondering when this strange dream would end and death would come.

Then a wide, rough, damp something scraped up his face, from chin to pate, while another, so-familiar mindspeak, said, "Me, for one, brother chief. Brainless twolegs right often slander us cats as being lazy. What then should be said of you?"

Slowly, gingerly, taking extreme care, Bili pushed down with his right hand, braced his right heel against the rather solid surface on which he lay and gradually came partially erect. A prairiecat sat on his left, tail curled about his big forepaws, tongue protruding slightly from between his fearsome fangs. The last three inches of that tail were white.

"Whitetip? Cat brother? Brother chief? Is it truly you?" Bili beamed hesitantly.

"No," came a sarcastic answer, "I'm really only four gray foxes inside an old prairiecat hide. Of course it is me."

Then Bili chanced to look down at his own limbs and body and could not believe his eyes. Although clad in shirt, trousers and boots, the body, the limbs, the hands, were not those of any old man of near a century in age. They were the strong, muscular body and limbs of a man in his prime. And when he experimentally flexed legs and arms, there was no slightest hint of pain. Still wondering, his mind whirling madly, he stood up . . . easily, and looked at his surroundings.

He seemed to have been lying on the grassy sward of a near-circular depression, in the center of which burbled a tiny spring. Striding over to it, he sank onto a knee and scooped up a handful of the cold water, drank deeply, splashed a copious amount of the bracing liquid onto his face, then turned back to find the horse and the huge cat still there. . . . But not alone, now!

A slender, dark-haired and dark-eyed human female stood beside Mahvros. She was clad, like Bili, in low boots, tucked-in trousers and an embroidered shirt, the proud swell of her breasts pushing hard against the fabric. Close by her side stood a well-bred red-bay mare, saddled, like the black stallion.

"*Rahksahnah* . . . ?" he croaked as he had on his deathbed. "No. It's all . . . none of this is possible! You all are dead, gone to Wind. You died in my arms, Rahksahnah. I lit your pyre with my own hand! I *know* you are dead."

She smiled, that so-dear, never-forgotten smile, then said softly, "Yes, I am no longer alive on earth, but then neither are you, my Bili, my love. I, we, have been waiting for you. Now you are here.

"But come, love, let us mount and ride. It is far and we can talk on the journey."

"Journey? What journey? Where must I ride?" asked Bili.

"Why, to the palace of the Silver Lady, of course, my Bili. She is desirous of knowing you. So come."

When once Bili had swung up into the saddle of the tall horse, he could see beyond the limits of the depression. He could see a limitless expanse of billowing, silver-white grasses in every direction, yet so soft-appearing were they that they might have been clouds, tiny clouds scudding at ground level.

The red mare's haunches tensed, and then she was on her way up the sloping side of the dip, Mahvros moving easily at her side, with the huge, tawny prairiecat racing out ahead of the two horses. Then suddenly there were two prairiecats, one but half the size of the other.

"Come," beamed Stealth. "Come—She awaits you."

# ABOUT THE AUTHOR

ROBERT ADAMS lives in Seminole County, Florida. Like the characters in his books, he is partial to fencing and fancy swordplay, hunting and riding, good food and drink. And when he is not hard at work on his next science-fiction novel, Robert may be found slaving over a hot forge to make a new sword or busily reconstructing a historically accurate military costume.